# Tails California

## Heads and Tails: Book 2

### Grea Warner

Tails California
Heads and Tails: Book 2
Copyright © 2021 Grea Warner
All rights reserved.

ISBN: (ebook): 978-1-953335-59-3
(print) 978-1-953335-60-9

Inkspell Publishing
207 Moonglow Circle #101
Murrells Inlet, SC 29576

Edited By Yezanira Venecia
Cover art By Najla Qamber

# OTHER BOOKS BY GREA WARNER

## COUNTRY ROADS SERIES:

Country Roads

Almost Heaven

Take Me Home

Teardrop in My Eye

The Place I Belong

All My Memories: A Prequel

## STANDALONE:

Every Mile a Memory

## HEADS AND TAILS DUET:

Heads Carolina

Tails California

## COMING SOON:

Whiskey Girl

GREA WARNER

# DEDICATION

The dedication I never wanted to write … this one is for my dad, who passed away shortly before the release of this book. He was and will continue to be my model of what a true hero is, embodying everything a father and man should be. Although my grief is deep, so is the love.

Hope your ride into the sunset was in a gorgeous classic car, Dad. I will always watch for the warm summer rain whispering on my windows.

And for my mom, whose love for my dad and her family is an unparalleled story all of its own.

GREA WARNER

# CHAPTER ONE

Nearly every woman enthusiastically added a point to their bridal shower scorecard. Aside from how Ryan and I met, how he proposed was the easiest question. After all, it had been shared in numerous media outlets. There had been four roses—three had thorns, but the final one did not. Instead, it hosted a spectacular, sparkling ring with the words "for real" inscribed inside. The proposal definitely personified all we were to each other and all that our future held.

"But tell them what he said right before that." My younger sister, Ella, was far from being a romantic, but she did love my engagement story from three months prior.

My internal smile was probably even greater than my external one. I couldn't help it. When it came to Ryan and our life together, I couldn't be happier. "We were playing a game we sometimes play with one another—naming a song about what we are feeling at that moment. He went first, which is never the case."

During my retell, the church's wooden basement door opened and the man himself appeared. But no one else noticed, since their attention was solely on me. I brought my hand up to my face and smiled the teensiest but happiest of bits.

"He said his song was Train's 'Marry Me.' And, at first, I didn't get it. But then I made the connection to the video's coffee shop girl, and the lyrics, and the title. And I … it was …" I met his eyes. "He is … everything."

A collective "awww" hummed from the group of women as my mother, looking every bit the part of a matron in her black skirt and red floral top, pronounced, "Speaking of …"

Next to me, Ella quietly growled. "He had one job to do—bring flowers. Geez, men!"

Both my sister and mother had been relentless about my groom-to-be bringing me flowers when he arrived at the end of the bridal shower. Ryan and I had even laughed about it. He'd said he would stop by the florist on the way from my parents' house, where he and the kids were visiting with my dad and Garrett. But where was the bouquet? In fact, where were the kids? He was supposed to bring them, too. And why was he so early?

Since he hadn't moved from the entry of the door, I walked to him, ignoring the soft murmurs and looks as I did so. He could broker major talent deals and appear live on national television, but it seemed he was intimidated by a room full of my female Carolina friends and family. It was only after I said hi and wrapped my arms around his burgundy button-down covered chest, that I realized something was wrong … very wrong.

"Ry?" I whispered, feeling the constriction of his muscles and witnessing up close the almost blank, yet weary, look in his eyes.

"Bethany, are you … Is this almost over?"

"Yeah. Dinner and gifts are done. Just having dessert and a last game," I replied. "What? What's going on?" All the happiness in my body was draining, and fear was rapidly taking its place.

As if to confirm the feeling, he pulled me away from him. "Is there somewhere we can talk?"

"Uh …"

"I thought you were with the men," my mother questioned her future son-in-law as she approached with my sister at her side. "My husband didn't scare you off, did he? He's harmless."

"It's a passive-aggressive, I'm-a-man-of-God kind of scare," Ella added.

"Ella …" Our mother practically *tsked* out her middle child's name.

"There is some truth to what she said," I admitted, and wondered if my father *did* have something to do with Ryan's disposition.

"No," he denied. "No. I'm sorry. Bethany?" He was never so short with his words … even in his role as a "mean" TV talent show judge on *Singer Spotlight*.

Was that it? Was it business-related? Did Ryan find out some kind of bad news he had to tell me as my manager? I had sold a couple of songs to country artist Finn Murphy that weren't released yet, but the process had been beautifully smooth. So, I doubted Ryan's demeanor had to do with that, but whatever it was, he was scaring the daylights out of me.

"I need to talk with Ryan." I looked to my mom, and for the first time I think she saw there was something tilting our happy world in an unbalanced way.

She glanced at Ryan and then back at me. "Use your daddy's office," she suggested.

"Okay?" I questioned the handsome, dark-haired man next to me, trying to somehow, by just looking in his eyes, figure out what was troubling him.

"Yeah … yeah," he agreed.

He let me take him by the hand and guide us through the women gathered at the tables and serving window of the adjacent kitchen. Some came up to us, wanting introductions. And while Ryan was polite, it was obvious he was also distracted. Luckily, my loudmouthed sister saved the day by saying she was going to announce the final raffle winner.

We made our way past the bathrooms, through the old narrow hallway, and started up the stairs. The crowd noise began to fade at the landing with the stained-glass window. It was there, when I had lived in Carolina, where I had liked to sit and think. Glancing again at an introspective Ryan, I continued to lead him up the remaining steps, surrounded by walls decorated with spiritual quotes.

Finally, we turned left to find the door that led into my dad's office. It was only steps from the serene, empty sanctuary where Ryan and I were set to wed in a few days' time. The silence in the room and the nearby chapel was a sharp contrast to the boisterous women a floor below. And I hoped it would provide the right setting to help explain whatever was going on.

When I shut the door behind us and looked at him once again, he immediately pulled me to him. Admittedly, a wash of relief flooded my body. He wanted us close. Good. But the fierce hold he had on me, combined with the fact his body was actually trembling a little, brought back my initial concern. I tried to meet his eyes, but he wouldn't let me right away. He kept me too secure to his torso.

After another moment, he allowed my release, tried a half-hearted smile—that nowhere near met his usual full-teeth grin—and said, "Any toasters? We could—"

"Ryan!" I quickly admonished.

"I love you," he said plainly but with an earnest heart— a positive sign in an ocean full of scary uncertainty.

"I love you, too. What's wrong? What's going on?"

"Bethany?" His voice cracked on my name. The vocal delivery and the fact he actually called me it instead of his usual loving "Lenay"—my middle name—worried me further.

"Yeah?" I tentatively replied.

"Kari is ... she's dead."

And then my world spun one-eighty, three-sixty ... ten

thousand. I had heard him. But I couldn't quite comprehend.

"Wh ... what?"

Ryan rapidly blinked a few times and seemed to be a step away from hyperventilating. And I wasn't sure I was much better. But I knew I needed to be. I needed to at least do or say something.

"What? What happened? What ... Oh, man. I ... she's ..." I wasn't helping. "Oh, geez. Here, let's sit down," I finally managed.

Somehow our two bodies managed to meet the old, weathered, brown sofa in my dad's office. We gave ourselves a collective moment to catch our breaths. And then I covered and caressed my hand on his.

The tender touch must have allowed him to unleash a little more. "OD'd," he announced the cause of death. "The cleaning service found her at her condo. Not sure if it was accidental or her choice."

"What?" Because everything was still so new ... so fresh ... so shocking, my question was still mostly to reiterate that his ex-wife was dead.

Kari had been clean since the prescription drug issue ... since rehab. It had been a year. She ...

I stopped my internal thoughts and outwardly tried to clarify. "Suicide?"

"They're not sure," he repeated blandly.

"Who? Who is 'they'? How did you find out?"

"Maks called me." Ryan gave Kari's younger brother's name in the same monotone of his previous answer.

"Oh." I was starting to realize the truth of our conversation ... of the situation. "Did you talk with her parents?"

"Not returning my calls." His eyes, which had been partially withdrawn from mine since sitting on the sofa, lifted, and I could understand, just with his look, the contempt he felt when dealing with his ex-in-laws.

"Hmmm."

There wasn't much else to say regarding the Hynes family. Besides, they weren't whom I was concerned about. Of course, it was Ryan. But also … also …

"Ryan, what about the kids?"

His eyes became misty and almost spooked at the same time. Along with needing to feel successful and having to prove himself, his children were definitely Ryan's weak spot. "I … I don't know. How am I … Oh, man, how am I supposed to tell them?" On top of absorbing the shock and sorrow of her death, the responsibility of telling their kids had to be overwhelming.

I leaned onto him, hoping my touch and bond would bring him some comfort. "Where are they now?"

"With your dad."

"Does he know?"

"Yeah. I needed him to keep the kids away from it, and I wanted to be here. I wanted to be here with you. To … tell you." After I kissed his cheek, he kissed the top of my head. "Your dad's a pretty good listener."

"It's a big part of a pastor's job." I looked across the room at my father's simple wood desk. The desktop calendar was cluttered with ink markings indicating such jobs—hospital visits, counseling sessions, and more.

"Yeah, I guess." Ryan sounded as though he was only half in our conversation.

"What do you want me to do? What can I do for you?"

He pulled me a little away from him. "Will you be there when I tell the kids?"

"Yeah, yeah, of course," I immediately agreed. "Yeah."

Looking into his normally sparkling deep blue set, which housed such sadness at the moment, made my own eyes fill with tears. That, along with anticipating the grief of a seven-year-old little girl and a five-year-old little boy. They had already dealt with too much in their young lives and, somehow, had remained innocent. How would the latest shocking news affect them at such a young age? Geez, I couldn't even process it myself at the age of twenty-four.

"Bethany?"

"Yeah?"

"There's something else."

Something else? Oh, my stars. What else could there be?

"We have to talk about the wedding." His voice reached a whole new low, sad tone, and my heart felt as if it had exploded and left my body. "It's ..." he continued when I didn't—or couldn't—speak. "I don't think we can."

"Huh." I had somehow said a sound, trying to still process everything that was coming down in the matter of minutes. Had it really only been less than fifteen when I had been beaming so brightly, surrounded by friends and family and knowing my heart couldn't possibly be filled with more love?

"Maks said they want the service to be as quick as possible." Ryan was still talking, and I needed to focus on him. "I'm guessing by the end of the week." The end of the week ... He meant our wedding day. "And the kids ... they need me, and they ... they need to be there and home in LA."

"Closure."

That word was more solid coming out of my mouth and also so fitting. Closure meant an end. And I was beginning to understand it might be in more ways than one.

"Mmmm-hmmm. Lenay?"

A tear actually rippled down my cheek when he used my favorite version of my name. "But if the funeral's not on Saturday, could we still ...?"

He breathed through his nose before answering. "Do you really want our wedding to be at all associated with this? The press is already trying to contact me as it is."

Of course they were. Kari wasn't only Ryan's ex-wife. She was an international singing superstar. And she somehow, despite an extramarital affair and rehab, had remained a sweetheart in the eyes of her fans.

"I want our day to be our day." He said the last two words slowly and poignantly. "I don't want it marred by—"

"I know."

I knew all along. I had just been holding on to a glimmer of hope that our special day was still going to happen. That was selfish. And for all the places for me to be self-centered—in the holy setting of a church. I internally berated myself.

"And the kids. They need support."

"I know," I repeated.

"I'm sorry. I'm so sorry." He touched my hand.

He didn't need to apologize, and I told him so. "You didn't do anything."

"Hmmm." He looked down.

"Ryan." I touched his smooth, chiseled face that I loved so much and waited until he looked back up at me. "We'll figure it out. The first priority is the kids." I gathered my strength and became the woman I knew my parents had raised me to be. "My mom and sister ... they can contact whoever we need to about canceling the wedding."

"Postponing," he amended, which, admittedly, made me smile.

"Yeah, postponing." I hesitated for the slightest of moments and then went for it—because, along with thornless roses, our witty banter was a cornerstone of our relationship. "Good thing because I'm not returning the toaster." I was glad I said what I did since it produced the smallest of smiles on Ryan's face. "I'll tell my mom we're leaving."

"You okay doing it yourself? I don't—"

"I understand." It was going to be hard enough for me to repeat the words Ryan had divulged to me, never mind him having to do it again ... especially in near a bunch of strangers who couldn't help but gawk a little at his own celebrity status. "I'll tell her to be discrete." I had plenty of practice with that, I thought.

"It's all right. It's already out." He joined me as I stood.

"But she can tell them not to gossip."

"Is there such a thing?" he mocked. "At least they'll know I wasn't the runaway groom."

I half-smiled at his attempt to bring his own lightheartedness back to our extremely depressing conversation. "Stay here. I'll be back in a minute."

I clasped my fiancé's hand, gave a reassuring squeeze, and left the still room. On my way down the stairs, I took a moment to pause on the landing with the stained glass. An extreme gust of air left my lungs as I thought about what had just taken place. I had imagined all kinds of wedding horror stories over those past couple of days—someone spilling red wine on my dress, there being a huge tear in it right before I was to walk down the aisle, or a snowstorm hitting Carolina … in the beginning of June! But not … not … I breathed in a few more times.

After pulling myself together, I found my mom, grandma, and sister and drew them into the privacy of the back hallway. My mother instantly gasped at the news and started praying for Kari and the kids. Ella took out her phone in an obvious attempt to find additional information online. And Maw-Maw—my mom's mom—gave me a hug.

"We'll take care of it." My mom nodded reassuringly.

"I guess I'll forgive him the flower gaffe." Ella tried her own jab of humor.

"He'll appreciate that." My lips rose in a partial smile. "I love you guys."

"We love you, too." And then it was my mom's turn to give me a hug before I made my way back to Ryan.

But when I returned, he wasn't in my dad's office. Thankfully, though, I didn't have to wonder long or search far. I found him in the chapel, about halfway up the center aisle, facing the altar. The way he leaned against the wooden pew and how his shoulders were raised closer to his ears than relaxed down spoke of his sadness and stress.

I started toward him, trying hard not to think about how in only a few days I was supposed to be walking up that aisle in a much longer white dress than the one I was wearing. It wasn't going to happen ... then. But I also realized it didn't splinter or fracture our love even in the slightest.

When I got to where he was standing, I took his hand in mine and, appreciating the silence the room seemed to demand, stared straight ahead without saying a word. After a beat, he forced his head to one side to crack his neck and relieve at least the physical pressure. And then he gave my hand a squeeze.

"For better or worse," I whispered, looking at him. "I do."

"I love you."

He breathed out and, with watery eyes, brought our foreheads together. And that is all that mattered. Because, in reality, we really didn't need anything more.

# CHAPTER TWO

It didn't take long to drive back to my parents' home. In fact, most of the time I would have walked to the church from their house rather than drive. Sure, it took a little longer but was very manageable. Despite growing up in Iowa, Ryan was used to the Los Angeles lifestyle for many years and drove everywhere, though. And … it wasn't the time for a leisurely stroll.

When we entered the family room, my dad had Sallie and Joel's full attention. He had four oranges and was showing the kids how to juggle—a skill he had humored his own three children with growing up. Garrett spotted us first. And, as a freshly minted seventeen-year-old, he couldn't mask his feelings well. The awkward look of sorry-your-whole-world-just-went-to-crap was written all over his face, but he didn't know how to say it.

"I can do it!" Joel exclaimed.

And Ryan, by my side, interjected immediately. "Uh, no. I don't think Bethany's dad wants orange juice all over the floor."

Both Joel and Sallie swung their gaze to Ryan and me, as my dad stopped the circling rotation of fruit. "Daddy, I am not going to drop them. I am a great baseball player,"

11

Joel said with the cutest of scrunched-up pouts.

"Uh-huh," Ryan agreed, surely just to agree.

A big part of me—despite knowing Joel would instantly drop the oranges—wanted to stay there and have him try. I wanted him to have a fun moment ... and to savor it. It was because I knew his next so many days, weeks, months, and probably lifetime would be haunted by the words he and his sister were soon to hear.

"We have to be going, Joel. There's something ..." Ryan paused and looked at my father, who nodded. "There's something Bethany and I need to talk with you two about. Could you please tell Mr. Opala and Garrett thank you for—"

"I was already going to say that, Daddy," Sallie interjected Ryan, who, even in all his grief and worry, had somehow remembered to remind his kids to use good manners.

"Thank you, Garrett and Mr. Opala."

"You are welcome," my dad replied, and Garrett looked away. "You can call me Barry if it is okay with your dad." He offered his first name, which he did to most everyone he knew. He found it to be a more friendly, open way of connecting with people.

"Sure, yeah, sure," Ryan responded, almost absentmindedly. Although, I knew his mind was anything but void. He was doing a decent job not showing that to the kids, but the adults and one teen in the room understood.

"Like strawberry," Joel chimed in. "Mr. Straw-berry."

Garrett laughed, and I couldn't help but smile, too. Without saying it, I'm pretty sure we were both thinking of how we could use the new nickname to our advantage. Despite the age and other differences between Garrett and me, we had a true sibling bond.

Ryan looked at Joel with a slight shake of his head and roll of his eyes. He then turned to my dad. "Thanks for helping. I—"

"Son, I'm here. We all are. We'll do whatever we can."

My father's genuine offer, although I expected nothing less, made my heart joyful. Sure, he meant it as a disciple of God but also personally to the man who held his eldest child's heart. I knew the latter wasn't necessarily the easiest. Not only because I was his daughter and the first of his children to truly fall in love, but also because when my parents had first found out about my relationship with Ryan, it had been surrounded by secrecy. That and the fact Ryan was divorced cast a bit of a shadow. Thankfully, though, once they met him and saw us together, there was no denying what Ryan and I had known almost immediately after meeting … or at least writing music together.

I buried myself in my dad's arms—Sallie wasn't the only girl in the room who needed her father. "Thanks, Daddy," I said. "I'll see you later tonight."

"No, Bethie." He called me by the family name I had learned to accept but nearly made me cringe every time. "Your place is with them tonight."

I pulled away from my father as he nodded toward Sallie holding Ryan's hand, and Joel, despite being told otherwise, examining the oranges. My father's words both shocked and warmed me. My parents were both traditionists for the most part and expected me to stay with them as an unmarried woman. They were not thrilled with the fact that I lived with Ryan in California and, therefore, it was never really discussed, besides the current mailing address information. So, when we had blocked off a group of rooms for family and friends at the hotel, it included one for Ryan and an adjoining one for Sallie and Joel.

"They need you," my dad continued. "Give them comfort."

I looked at Ryan, who seemed possibly even more thankful for my dad's offer than me. I smiled softly, hugged my dad again, and told Joel to bring the oranges. I had a feeling our life was going to involve a lot of juggling for a while. When life gives you oranges …

\*\*\*

The drive from my parents' house to the hotel was a longer commute than from the church, but it was still less than twenty minutes. With each passing mile, I could see Ryan, sitting in the passenger seat, growing grimmer. The fact that Kari died was horrific, but the task in front of him—telling their beautiful, sweet children—was possibly even more daunting.

The sun had yet to set when we pulled into the lot, but I knew it would within the half-hour or so. It had already been a long day with flying in early from California and going directly to my dinner bridal shower. And the night I feared would be just as long.

Ryan held me tight in his hotel room while the kids got dressed in their pajamas. When they yelled from their adjoining room that they were ready, my strong man thanked me for being there. I reassured him there was no place I would rather be, and watched as he walked toward the partially open door. As much as I was a part of their life, telling them the devastating news was something we both knew Ryan should do on his own.

I spent my time responding to some of the multitude of messages on my phone—all related in one way or another to Kari's passing. I texted my friend Willow and confirmed with my sister that she was getting a hold of the people on the guest list. That included my dad's out-of-state older brother and widowed mother, who was in a nursing home. Ryan had talked with his parents on the way to the church, but I called his sister, Megan, who had reached out to see if there was anything they could do. His whole family had been set to fly in the next day since there had already been a separate small bridal shower in Iowa when we had visited for Easter. So besides telling Megan to cancel their flights, I asked her to keep Sallie and Joel in their prayers. What else was there, really?

After hanging up, I walked over to the adjoining open doorway to see Joel looking at Ryan and asking, "We don't have a mommy, anymore?"

"Joel, buddy, Mommy will always be your mommy. She just can't be with us." Ryan was stretched alongside both of the kids in one of the two beds. "We can't see her anymore. She will be looking after you, though."

"From Heaven." Sallie's words were part question, part statement.

"Right, sweetie. She loves both of you more than anything in the world." At first, I didn't even realize he said it in present tense.

"Then why did she go?" Sallie was always logical and inquisitive.

Before Ryan could answer, his son pouted out what was pretty much a fact. "She goes all the time."

I could see Ryan's face. His cheeks, eyes, and mouth all seemed to drop. I knew his dilemma of trying not to scare the kids but wanting them to understand. It was by far not an easy task.

"Joel, you understand this is different, right? Mommy's not on tour. She's not ... she's not coming back." His voice broke a little before he returned his attention back to his daughter. "She didn't want to go, Sals."

He said it convincingly, but I couldn't help but wonder about the doubt that it was simply an overdose and not intentional. I couldn't imagine Kari actually doing that to herself. She had a phenomenal career and the kids. She and Ryan were amicable. And even though I had little interaction with her, we managed. So, what had made her take the drugs again? She wasn't physically hurt and hooked on prescriptions like the last time. As far as we knew, she had been clean and healthy.

I rezoned into Ryan's explanation. "She got sick. She was tired."

"The angels wanted her."

"Uh, yeah." Ryan seemed a little perplexed by Sallie's response.

"The angels wanted Yasmine's grandma," she explained.

"Yeah. Okay." We both had talked to Sallie after her friend's grandmother had passed away.

"Is Mommy with Yasmine's grandma?"

Ryan smoothed his son's hair, so blond like his mother's and sister's. "Yeah."

"I wanna see her." Joel's request came out part hope, part whine.

And I could tell by the quick shutting of Ryan's eyes that he was about to break. But, instead, he remained calm and steady with his answer. "Can't. I'm sorry. We can look at her photos and videos if you want, and you can talk to her in your heart."

I liked his explanation until Joel added, "And video chat."

"No. Oh … no. She passed away." Ryan sighed, and I wondered if I should help him. But, in reality, I didn't know what else I could offer.

"She's dead, Joel," Sallie said in the corrective tone she often used with her younger brother when he didn't understand something.

Usually, it necessitated Ryan warning his daughter, but that time he let it go. Even though the word "dead" sounded harsh, it was the truth and maybe the only way a five-year-old boy could start to understand. Kari wasn't lost. She was gone. She died … dead.

"I know this is a lot for you two to understand. We're going back to California. We're going to see GiGi and Grandpa, Uncle Maks, and some of Mommy's friends, and they'll help us. What you need to remember is, we all love you guys so, so very much. We love you and are here to help you and talk with you."

"What about Bethany?"

"Of course Bethany," Ryan answered his son. "She loves you, too."

"She's our family," he said, and I instantly felt my eyes water.

"Even before the wedding," Sallie added, as if to outdo her brother by one, I'm sure.

"Yeah, that's something else we have to talk about. But right now ... anything more? Anything about how you're feeling?"

"I love Mommy."

"I know, Joe-Joe. She knew, too." And there it was—past tense ... geez. He pulled them both a little tighter onto his sides. "What do you say we just lay here and try to sleep?"

\*\*\*

When I heard the door click softly shut, I turned from the window, which was darkened by the overcast, nighttime sky. Ryan didn't move from the doorway. He stood there—feet away from where his kids were hopefully able to find some peaceful sleep. He looked stunned ... shell-shocked. Seeing him so distraught made my heart ache and eyes instantly tear up.

"I blew apart their world. I changed their lives forever."

I couldn't deny that, as I swiped at my eyes. "Yeah."

"I didn't know what to say. I mean, I don't know that they get it."

"Probably not completely." Again, it wasn't necessarily what he wanted me to say, but it was the truth.

He took a deep breath and managed a few steps toward me and I him. "I think they need to actually see her."

"I know. That's a toughie." I felt like we were speaking in spurts. And it seemed so quiet—like the aftermath of a destructive bomb where everything is powered down unexpectedly and we were the only two left standing, stunned in miles of silence and rubble. "You're doing good, Ry," I finally offered. "No matter what, they know they have you. You will get them through this."

"We both will. You were listening, right? Did you hear them include you?"

"I did," I admitted with a soft smile. I touched his face with the back of my hand before I continued. "What you said ... how you answered them ... I don't know how you found the words."

"Your dad gave me pointers."

"Like I said, he would know. You can call and talk with him any time. He'll help."

Ryan's royal blue eyes were not leaving my brown-hued ones. "Right now, I need his daughter."

I melded onto him, holding on fiercely, as if I could squeeze out the pain encompassing every part of his being. His chest rose and fell beneath my cheek a few times before he used his hand to tilt my chin and head so my eyes could meet his once more. His lips gently touched mine three times.

"I love you." It was all I could think to say, and I hoped those words soothed and warmed him just as they did whenever he said them to me.

"Be with me," he whispered, using the same words as the first time we were ever together.

I kissed him and tried a touch of humor. "I don't think that is what my dad had in mind when he said to stay and give you comfort."

Ryan let out a short chuckle before saying, "I love you, Lenay. For real."

"For real," I repeated our personalized words of love.

I started with soft kisses on his mouth and then slowly began to undress him. Still in our wedding shower outfits, I knew we would have taken gorgeous photos together had the day turned out differently. In a way, it felt good to shed ourselves of those reminders, though. There was no denying we weren't the same couple we were that morning, but our love was not scathed. Ryan, reciprocating my kisses, stopped momentarily as I removed my dress. Normally, we helped each other and were in much more of a hurry to connect. But the mood and circumstances warranted me taking the lead ... slowly and with great care. In the same manner, I played with his dark brown hair and watched as he stretched out on the bed. There were still no words, besides his appreciative moan, when I positioned my body on top of his, and we rocked together as if we were a lost boat trying to find a safe shore.

# CHAPTER THREE

Leaving Carolina the next day was excruciating. Everything was sinking in … even more so. We had woken and realized it hadn't just been a horrific nightmare. All of it was true.

The kids seemed, more than anything, tired—and the time change didn't help. It was going to be a process for them to come to terms with what happened to their mother. Ryan looked as though he had been through twelve rounds of boxing, only to be knocked out. And I'm sure I did, too. After all, neither of us had slept well … tossing and turning throughout the entire night.

We stopped by my parents' home on our way to the airport. For one thing, I wanted to drop off Sallie's white dress, which was a simpler mini version of the gown I had been set to wear that Saturday—a sleeveless V-neck, both front and back, beading only on the sides, and a full bottom encircled with ribbons. There was no need to transfer either of our dresses back to California because, as Ryan had said, there would be a wedding … eventually. When it would actually be … we would have to discuss later. The kids had to be our number one concern.

But more than that, we went to see my family because I

21

needed to. I needed the extra hug and in-person support before leaving. I had been expecting to be celebrating with them for four days. What I got instead was an overnight filled with mostly tears.

Right before we boarded the plane, Ryan handed me his tablet, wanting me to read his press release before sending it out. *Thanks to everyone for your kind words and condolences. Although I am shocked and saddened over Kari's sudden passing, I will forever be grateful for the time we had together, as it gave us the precious gifts of Sallie and Joel. Please allow my children, fiancée, and myself some privacy during this difficult time.*

When I did a one-shoulder shrug and handed it back to Ryan, he immediately picked up on my uncertainty. "What?"

I hesitated to say anything because I knew he was already a bit ticked off about writing one in the first place. But, with the onslaught of messages and notifications he had been getting both personally and via his office, he knew he should put something out. Walking the line of exactly what to say was the difficult part. And I thought he handled it well, except for one minor thing.

"I think you should take out the last part."

"The part about not bothering us?" He scrunched his face and burrowed his eyebrows. "That's the main point."

"They still will." We both knew a polite request wouldn't hinder the efforts of the media. "But I don't think you need to include me in the statement." When his creased face jolted back, I explained. "Mentioning me will agitate all the—" I stopped myself and attempted to find the right words, trying to be the compassionate woman I was raised to be, especially when talking about someone who had passed away. "Kari-lovers … fans," I decided on. "I'm still persona non grata where they are concerned."

He denied it with an immediate punctuation of his words. "You didn't do anything. Kari and I were divorced before you and I even met."

"You know it doesn't matter to some people. They'll

feel like it's a stab and not needed." I tried using a calm voice to contrast his. And it wasn't like I was completely hated—most *Singer Spotlight* fans adored our love story, from my audition to our tweets to the live show where we revealed our relationship.

He shook his head ever so slightly and his words came out just as defined as his previous ones. "I had to pretend—deny—you weren't a part of my life before. I will never do it again."

"Ry …" I partially sighed at the sentimentality of his words. But that was the end of my rebuttal as an announcement soared through the airport's speakers, letting us know it was our turn to board.

"All right, kiddos." He looked at Sallie and Joel, innocently playing a traveling tic-tac-toe game my parents had given them. "We're heading home." Surely submitting the release, he pressed a button on his tablet, powered the device down, and took my hand.

***

We had tried to keep the exact details of our nuptials private so there wouldn't be any interference from press on our sacred day. They knew of the date but not the location nor when we would be traveling. It had worked for the most part. Until, of course, the news of Kari's death brought an even more powerful star-studded spotlight on everything. So, unfortunately, the clowns and the circus grew intense once we touched down in LA. There was press at the airport, people at the entrance of Ryan's neighborhood, and phone calls galore.

For the remainder of Thursday and all of Friday, we stayed holed up in our home while protecting and sheltering the kids as best we could. We steered them away from all forms of media and occupied them with games and such. And while we kept the dialogue open for talking about Kari and their feelings, neither child seemed to say much. Reality hadn't quite set in, I was afraid.

In a weird way, keeping busy helped Ryan. He was in constant contact with someone—his family, his staff, and Maks, who kept him in the loop of the funeral arrangements. As first presented, the Hyneses were doing things quickly and with as little hoopla as possible, considering Kari's celebrity status. Ryan and I both knew it was an attempt to sweep the cause of death under the rug. They didn't want their shining-star daughter's reputation tainted, even in death. There would be no public viewing. The immediate family would see Kari privately on Saturday morning at the church, followed directly after by a friends and family service.

But, once again, it didn't really work. The press had their eyes and ears on everything. And the more private the family wanted things, the more the media persisted. Speculation ran ramped over the cause of Kari's death. The combination of her being a healthy thirty-two-year-old and the coincidence of the timing of her death definitely led the guesses in the right direction. Headlines read: *Did Kari never get over Ryan? Was the wedding the final nail? How could this have happened to America's sweetheart?*

Because of that, as well as Ryan being the connection to Kari's most precious family—the kids—he was hounded nearly nonstop for some kind of comment. By Friday evening, when he couldn't take the persistent pressure of the celebrity world anymore, he, uncharacteristically, threw his phone across the room. Luckily, it was the family room and the plush carpet allowed the device to land softly. And ... the kids had just gone to sleep.

"Sorry," he said as I closed my eyes and nodded slowly. "I don't even want Joel and Sallie to be a part of this anymore."

I took a soothing breath, hoping he would mimic it. "They have to be. You know that."

"I—" His low grunt stopped his words. "Uhhh!" After

calming down a little bit, he asked me, "What do *you* want to do?'

I did my own internal "uhhh" to his question. I was so torn about attending the funeral. I wanted to go so I could support Ryan and the kids, but I also wondered if it was my place or even if I was going to be a distraction. We had talked about it throughout the day, and I knew I needed to make up my mind.

I turned his question around. "What do you want me to do?" I started to say "honestly," but he interrupted me.

"Bethany, shit, I can't think. I can't make one more decision. Can't you—"

Wow. I knew for sure then that he was worked up. For one thing, he very rarely swore and, for another, he was getting testy with me … an even bigger rarity.

"Ryan …" I managed a reassuring voice. When he tilted his head as if he wanted to crack his neck, I walked up to him. His body was tense as I put my hands tentatively up to his cheeks and kissed him. "I want to be there with the three of you … *for* the three of you." The words came out of my mouth and, admittedly, they scared me a little. "I want the kids to know I respected their mom." I had, especially as a vocalist. "And if there is any trouble with the press or whoever else …" I paused—Ryan knew my relationship with Kari's mother was just as tumultuous as his. "If there's any problem, I'll leave."

"No, you won't," he replied decisively. "And thanks."

"Because you want me there?"

"Yeah," he admitted, although I knew up to that point, he was purposefully trying not to steer me in a particular direction. "And thanks for not flipping a dang coin to make up your mind." He tapped me on my nose with his index finger.

"Ha!" I exclaimed. "I didn't even think of it. Do you have our—"

"No."

I managed a full smile. He had our coin. He always

carried it. It had become another one of "our things." But the heads/tails game had always only been used in jest when I couldn't make a simple decision like what to have for dinner or what movie to watch … not for something so serious.

"Good thing I didn't need it when you proposed," I teased.

"Lenay …" He sighed. "I'm sure the past couple of days have had you tossing that quarter around and around in your mind."

"Of course not," I said legitimately, and then added with a sweet sarcasm, "But the dartboard with your picture on it …"

He managed the slightest of laughs. "I still don't doubt you made one after our first meeting." His phone vibrating across the room halted our at-ease conversation.

"Leave it," I insisted.

"I should probably get it." He closed his eyes and took a step.

But I denied him getting the phone with a cute distraction. "Lyric! Lyric, baby. Come." I patted my leg. "Come here."

After returning to Los Angeles, we had retrieved the family goldendoodle from the overnight pet boarder. The one-year-old pup was supposed to have stayed through the wedding and honeymoon. And we could have housed him there, regardless of our return. But getting him back seemed like a positive idea for everyone, and, at that moment, particularly for Ryan.

I heard the little puppy feet right before I saw the dog himself. "Go get Ryan. Get Ryan, baby. Give him kisses."

Ryan shook his head at me but picked up the dog at his feet and accepted the loving licks. I melded onto Ryan's side, getting in on some of the puppy action myself. The buzzing coming from the phone stopped and, for a moment, we were actually at peace.

\*\*\*

Geez, the knots in my stomach would not unravel even in the slightest. I didn't regret going to the church and the service. In my heart, I knew it was the right thing to do. But it didn't make me feel any more comfortable or secure.

My father's job as a minister had him consoling and attending plenty of funeral services throughout his career, but I had not. Both sides of my family were relatively healthy and hearty. The only deaths I had been around were my dad's dad—but I was pretty young when he passed—and a fellow student during my high school senior year who was killed in a car accident. And there hadn't been a viewing.

After getting past the security guard hired to wean out the press who were beginning to gather outside, Ryan, the kids, and I walked into the somber setting of the church. The clergyman greeted us in the narthex. He told us what to expect from the service and offered some supposed comforting words. But he seemed stiff, and it made me appreciate my dad that much more.

Standing with her husband, Irene Hynes was fixing a flower arrangement when we entered the massive, towering main chapel. By some weird sense, she knew to turn, look our direction and, consequently, give me a pinched-face sneer. I pursed my lips and blew out some air. My every encounter with Kari's mom had been similar. Sadly, I had expected nothing less at her daughter's funeral. Dressed in a too-tight black dress and a gaudy display of pearls, she held out her arms and the two Thompson children did a bit of a jog to greet her.

Ryan, in his charcoal suit, which matched the tired color under his eyes, was still by my side. He was standing, but it was almost as if he was comatose. I followed his stare … straight to the open casket at the end of the aisle near the altar. He started walking that direction, and I just let him go. I knew it was something he needed to do by himself. She had been his wife and the mother of his children, and I did respect his feelings.

I teetered in place … not because of the black high heels I was wearing, but because I felt a little in limbo land—nowhere to go or anyone to be with. The children had their grandparents. And Ryan? I watched as he put his hand up to what I believed was Kari's face, but I couldn't see being so far away.

And then, after a moment, he turned and walked back to me. "I need to get the kids up there before people arrive." He noted why we had purposefully arrived to the nearly vacant church a little early.

"Okay." I felt like I was failing him with my limited verbal response, but I was at a complete loss as to what to do.

Leaving my side once again, he walked over to Sallie, Joel, and his former in-laws. I couldn't hear their conversation, but I did see Ed Hynes pat Ryan's back in a positive kind of way. And then Ryan and the kids were starting to walk past me and toward the casket. But Sallie, in a dark dress that did not match her normally bright personality, suddenly stopped. She didn't move.

"Sals, come on, sweetie, let's go see Mommy." Ryan let go of Joel's hand and bent to Sallie's level.

She didn't hesitate. She just looked him in the eyes and spoke her truth. "I don't want to."

"Tink …" He called her by the special fairytale name only Ryan used. "We talked about this. I know how brave and strong you are."

"Daddy, I don't want to."

Ryan had spoken with both of the kids that morning and right before we entered the church about what to expect. They had seemed okay. But then again, quiet was not really okay when it came to either of the Thompson children. As if to stake her claim and determination, Sallie then clung to my side. I soothed her silky, long, blonde hair and raised my shoulders slightly to Ryan. His gaze bounced from me to Sallie to Joel to his ex-in-laws greeting people at the entry. I was already beginning to understand that close friends and family might mean a hundred plus to the Hynes clan.

"Stay with her?" he asked me, then kissed the top of his daughter's head and reclaimed his son's hand.

Sallie and I both watched silently as Ryan and Joel made their way to the front of the chapel. Ryan helped his son stand on the kneeling stool and peer into the casket. I could see they were talking, but they were too far away for me to hear the words. In contrast, Sallie, next to me, said nothing.

When Ryan ruffled Joel's head, brought him to his side, and got him down, Sallie finally spoke. "Joel did it. He made Daddy proud."

Looking at the little girl, I realized that all her talent and smarts couldn't get her through the greatest challenge she had ever faced. "No matter what, Sallie. No matter what. Your dad and mom and brother and me are very proud of you. Stay here or—"

Taking my hand, she slowly, and then with determination, started us up the aisle. I hadn't intended to see Kari up close. It was something I believed others needed, but I didn't think it was my place. Regardless, there I was, on my way. Ryan and Joel had just taken a few steps away and were now taking turns hugging Kari's brother. When my fiancé spotted Sallie and me approaching the casket, he did a half step toward us, but I subtly shook him off. I didn't know if it was right or not, but the little girl was squeezing my hand so hard, I feared if there was even the slightest of disruptions, Sallie would back down. And if I provided her the confidence she needed to get through that moment, then I was blessed to do it. Thankfully, Ryan could see it, too, and nodded his approval and appreciation.

I let Sallie climb the little step to see her mom. I couldn't help but wonder what Ryan's ex would have thought of the scene—her sweet daughter relying on me … even simply me being there. I hadn't been Kari's favorite person or vice versa, but that was part of the expected dynamic of our relationship. Hopefully, she was at peace and could see what I saw—a beautiful young girl, making a choice to be her own brave self.

"Mommy is so pretty," Sallie spoke with such a softness, I almost didn't hear her.

But it was true. Someone had done Kari's makeup beautifully, and she was dressed in angelic white with royal blue accents, which I thought mimicked the color of Ryan's eyes. She looked like the rockstar version of herself, not the casual mother who picked up the kids, or the haggard and upset woman from the year before who had struggled with prescription drugs.

"Sallie, do you want to say anything?"

"Can I tell her I love her?"

"Yeah. Yeah."

After doing just that, she gave me a hug and scurried into her dad's waiting arms. Ryan pressed at his watery eye behind Sallie's back and told her how strong she was. He then secured my hand in his and reintroduced me to Maks, who, besides eye color, had the same facial features and similar hair hue of his sole sibling. We had been in each other's company before for the kids' birthday celebrations. And through those limited interactions, I knew Maks, thankfully, seemed to take on the kinder mannerisms of the male side of the Hynes family.

Ryan's attention was pulled as more and more funeral attendees started to filter in. He and Kari obviously once had a life together. So, he knew her friends, family, and, of course, members of the music world. He spoke with them quickly and considerately when they approached him, but he was extremely mindful of the kids. Everyone had the purest of attentions when it came to speaking with Sallie and Joel, but some weren't used to talking with children, especially during such an emotional time.

I simply did a lot of nodding. I was in Kari's world more than ever, and I didn't feel comfortable at all. My head was starting to hurt ... and not because of the head bobs. It was pure tension.

During one conversation, I offered to take Joel on a little walk around the interior of the church. He was getting particularly bouncy, and with the service about ready to begin, I thought it was important for him to get his energy out as best he could in the limited space. Sallie, in contrast, wanted to remain with her dad. Joel and I checked out the multitude of lit candles, an empty side room, and the bathrooms, which Joel claimed he did not need to use. When we were passing near the front, I heard a familiar voice trying to gain admittance from security. It wasn't any of the neighbors. They were not on the limited guest list—although Ryan had received some form of condolence from each of them in the days prior. It was—

"Uncle Dylan," Joel called out to Ryan's older brother.

When both Dylan and the guard turned their attention to Joel, I said, "He's—" I looked beyond to spot Dylan's wife and son, too. "*They're* with us."

I am pretty sure it was Joel's identification and not my declaration that allowed Ryan's brother and family admittance into the church because I hadn't exactly been invited either. *I* was with Ryan. Regardless, there was no denying little Joel Thompson's embrace of his paternal uncle.

"I don't think Ryan was expecting you," I said to my should-be brother-in-law.

I didn't just *think*. I *knew* Ryan wasn't expecting them. Ryan had made a point of telling his family not to come. There was no need, especially when they had to travel so far.

As if reading my mind, Dylan spoke of their home near Napa. "It's a few hours or so drive. I get the rest of the clan not coming in from Iowa, but we wanted to show our support."

I wrapped my arms around Dylan as Joel was doing the same with his aunt and cousin. "Thanks, Dylan. He'll … he'll be glad you're all here." I realized how much I was, too. It was nice to have someone there—besides the grieving kids and Ryan—who knew and actually liked me.

Music suddenly soared through the speakers and a church representative spoke softly to us. It was time. It was time to find Ryan and take our seats. The solemn reason why we were all gathered was set to officially begin.

# CHAPTER FOUR

After the eulogies, tributes, and prayers were delivered, Kari's own voice soared through the speakers. One of her older ballads, the lyrics seemed to take on a whole new, sadder meaning as the pallbearers stationed themselves alongside her casket. Ryan leaned forward and stroked both of the kids' hair as the body was lifted and started its way past us. On the insistence of Irene, Sallie and Joel were seated with her, Ed, and Maks in the front pew because they were "real family." Ryan had been "permitted" to sit behind them, and I wasn't even acknowledged, except by the only person who truly mattered, who held my hand during most of the service. Kari's tune couldn't drown out the sound of the sniffling, which, although it had occurred on occasion throughout the service, the finality of the march down the aisle seemed to bring it to a greater height. I pushed away the selfish thought of how I should have been walking down an aisle full of joy at that very moment and refocused on the two precious Thompson offspring who looked more confused than sad.

The congregation's sobbing dimmed to pure silence as everyone watched Irene stand up. She waited for Ed, who quietly directed the children to Ryan. And then Kari's parents followed their daughter down the aisle to the back of the church. Since Maks was one of the pallbearers, it was then our turn. Ryan blew out a huge gust of air and started us out the pew. He drew each of his children to either side of him and held on to their little hands. Sitting in the pew with us, Dylan and his family stepped out behind me. But Ryan had yet to start walking. I wanted out of there. There were too many eyes staring at us with a mix of pity and gawk. I wondered why he hadn't started down the aisle. The casket was out of sight and Ed and Irene nearly were, too. And then I found out.

Ryan bent down and hoisted Joel into his muscular arms, amid his son's protest that he was too old to carry. "We need to make room for Bethany."

The knotting pit in my stomach, which had only grown tighter throughout the service, loosened the teensiest of bits. The aisle was too narrow for all four of us across. I was prepared to simply follow behind like a lowly dog who had been punished. But Ryan's heart, in the midst of all he was dealing with, saved me from the banishment. He gave me the smallest of closed smiles, and I joined him to make our way outside.

Just as I thought we had finally made it out to the fresh, open air and could start back home—since Ryan couldn't see subjecting the kids to the actual burial—an obstacle catapulted itself in front of us. Not only was the press positioned at the bottom of the church's outdoor steps, but Irene was standing in front of them as if she was a famed conductor of a prized orchestra. Ryan immediately froze, causing the kids, me, and his brother's family behind us to do the same. After supposedly claiming she didn't want press, Irene—with Ed silently beside her—was actually thanking the media for being there. A low growl emerged from Ryan's throat. I refocused to hear her saying that Kari's music would live on forever. As she continued to talk, she seemed to actually be enjoying it more and more, and *I* wanted to growl. It was almost as if she was doing a media promotion instead of attending her daughter's funeral. I saw Ryan looking around, especially behind him in the direction we had come. More and more people were emerging, expecting to exit, just like we had hoped to do. It wasn't until Irene mentioned the kids and said she was going to personally make sure they would be stars as popular as their mother, that Ryan truly reacted.

As Ryan said Irene's name in obvious disgust, I grabbed his hand, and Dylan motioned to the kids. "Sallie, Joel, come back here."

Ryan let Joel down and the kids went to their uncle. Then Ryan's body seemed to broaden, as if he wanted to physically create a barrier between the kids and the media … and Irene. I did the same at his side.

Ignoring Ryan, Irene continued to talk about the kids, saying they would have her guidance. I squeezed Ryan's hand harder. Despite their differences, Ryan had never let the kids know about his terse relationship with their maternal grandmother. In fact, he was overly generous, even letting his ex-in-laws see Sallie and Joel when Kari had been out of town. But I knew neither Ryan nor Kari were necessarily enthusiastic about the kids going into show business. And even if that was what they wanted, it was much too early for such a proclamation to the media and certainly inappropriate at their mother's funeral.

Irene must have taken a mini breath or the press just got tired of her, since they started calling out to Ryan. Being connected to him, I could feel his whole body expand and contract before he reacted. I had no idea what it was going to be, so I geared myself up for anything.

He turned back to his brother. "Can you take the kids?" He lowered his voice. "Get them out of here. There's a side door. Meet us at the house?"

"Absolutely. That is where I'm parked, anyway. Come on, Team Thompson. We're looking for the escape route." I did a half chuckle at Dylan's attempt to create a bit of sunshine on an extremely mentally overcast day.

"Go with Uncle Dylan. I'll catch you spies later."

Joel seemed a little more of his energetic self as he gave Ryan a fist bump and the cameras clicked in unison. On the contrary, Sallie rolled her eyes, as if suddenly she was the adult among us. But she wasn't. In reality, she was a seven-year-old who had lived most of her life dealing with the spotlight. And that was the first time I think I saw her lose some of her innocence. They were not spies. They were sad, hunted, confused little kids.

Once we watched Dylan and the rest of the Thompsons diverge back into the church, Ryan started the two of us down the steps. I appreciated his strategy. We would forge straight ahead, bearing a few flashbulbs, just so the kids would be spared.

"Ryan," a member of the core called out. "Sorry about your ex-wife. Anything you would like to add to Mrs. Hynes' comments?"

"Don't engage," I whispered with emphasis because if there was anything that would egg Ryan on, it was Irene or something derogatory about the kids.

"I won't." Not letting go of my hand, he ignored everything else, including Irene, as we continued walking.

"Ryan?" Another voice called out.

"Please respect our privacy." He looked at them briefly.

"What about your wedding?" The voice continued anyway.

When Ryan did a shuffle in his step, I looked the few inches up to meet his deep blue eyes. It was my turn to curve my lips a little for encouragement. He breathed in through his nose, and we walked silently until we reached his car.

We cleared the church lot and the street before Ryan called Dylan. I wasn't sure if he waited because he thought the press might actually pursue us, or if he simply needed time to calm down. But, regardless, he did need to find out about the kids.

"You all good?" he asked once Dylan answered.

I heard Dylan's reply via the BMW's speakers. "We're good. All buckled and on the road. Say hi to Daddy, kids."

"Hi, Daddy," they seemed to say in unison.

When Ryan didn't respond right away, I glanced in his direction. The day had been emotionally draining for him—grief, anger, love. Hearing those two little voices and knowing they were safe, might have been his tipping point. He brought his hand up to his face and shook it a little.

I rubbed my left hand on his right thigh, and he managed the words into the car speaker. "Hi, guys." He then directed his comment to his brother. "They won't enter the neighborhood if you want to head over there now."

"Didn't know how long you'd be," he replied. "So, we already decided on ice cream and cookies. Or is it only frozen yogurt and tofu around here?"

When I did a half chuckle, Ryan let his out, too. "You sure?" he asked.

"Yep."

"Thanks for being here, Dyl." Ryan's words and the way he had embraced Dylan when he had first seen him in the church showed how much it did truly mean for Ryan to have at least part of his family there.

"Already had the full weekend scheduled for you, bro." Dylan was supposed to be Ryan's best man that day on completely different coasts. "Glad I can help. Sorry this was how it ended up being."

I knew Ryan was looking at me. I could feel him. But I had turned my head to the side window. He didn't need to witness any additional sadness.

"Yeah. All right. Bethany and I are heading home. We'll see you in a little while." Ryan disconnected his phone and then spoke with me. "We have plenty of food," he noted the neighbors' condolence contributions. "I guess we'll just set up the guest room for them. Levi can stay with Joel or on a sofa," he said of his nephew.

"They booked a hotel overnight and then are heading back tomorrow," I corrected Ryan, since he really hadn't had much time to talk with his brother when he arrived.

"Huh? Why?"

"Wanted to be here but not intrude." I relayed what Dylan had told me on the way into the church.

"They wouldn't be—"

"They're going to enjoy the sites. I like that we'll spend some time with them today, though. Dinner—" I stopped my thought as my phone rang. Looking at the screen and recognizing the name, I answered. "Hey, Ella." It was my sister—the maid of honor's turn.

I met Ryan's eyes. They still reflected his pain and sorrow. But his attempted smile showed me he knew my family meant the world to me, too.

Ella said she was the Opala family representative, making the call to find out how things went. Our parents didn't want to interfere but knew I would call if I needed them. And Garrett wouldn't know what to say. So, Ella was the logical choice, which at the moment was good for me. She wouldn't sugarcoat anything or make me necessarily overly sentimental for home. Yet, she was a good sounding board, being the closest to my age—less than two years younger.

We talked about the service for a little bit. While our conversation wasn't being broadcast via the car's speakers, I knew Ryan understood most of it through my dialogue. He did some sighing in the midst of the lane changes and curving bends in the roads. Ella said she actually saw a livestream of the impromptu interview Irene made. Then she brought up what was supposed to have been the other day's event—our nonwedding. She mentioned Carolina's weather and how they donated some of the already-made bakery items to a homeless shelter.

"It wasn't meant to be." I tried to sound at peace with it, and I trusted that would eventually be the truth. I knew our wedding would happen … just not that day.

I was glad it was a Saturday, so the commute from the church to Ryan's house wasn't as long as it could have been on a workday. When Ryan accessed the gate of his private housing community, there were thankfully no paparazzi camped out. I knew he needed to get home and out of the car. He needed to move around. The jittery way his body seemed to move in the BMW reminded me of his energetic five-year-old son ... and that was pretty much the opposite of the chill man I was used to.

"Ella?" I talked back into my phone. "If that's it ... if everything is fine, tell everyone we're okay and I'll talk some other time. We have some ... It's a hard day."

"Tell her I said thanks," Ryan added, and I did so, not questioning why but assuming he appreciated my family's support almost as much as I did.

"Tell beach-bod"—she used the nickname she had crowned Ryan with before even meeting him—"he's proving to be a good one."

"He is," I agreed, but didn't actually repeat it since we were in the garage and, as predicted, Ryan needed out.

The first few minutes we were in the house were shrined in silence. Ryan placed his keys on the hook in the breezeway and ventured through the hall to the living room. I trailed behind, allowing him to do or say whatever he needed to. And neither the subject of his words nor the fury in how he presented them surprised me.

"How could Irene do that?" Walking around in an ill-shaped circle, he contrasted my solid stance near the sofa and coffee table. "Family. Family! The kids are *my* family. Only family belongs in the front pew," he mimicked his former monster-in-law, causing Lyric, who was ready to greet us with affection, to back away to the edge of the room. "And then ... then to imply that Joel and Sallie are going to be mentored by her? Over my d—" He stopped himself, surely in ironic respect of the day. "Kari wouldn't have even wanted that. You know, in fact, there's no real reason for that woman to even see the kids. I bet I don't have to legally or otherwise. It's not going to be the same. I'm not going to sit by and allow her to mold my kids or … uhhh!" He partially screamed and then continued. "Or use them for sympathy or publicity. And the way she treated you? She couldn't even acknowledge you? Couldn't even say hello or, geez, nod her holier-than-thou head? She—" He suddenly stopped pacing and truly looked at me for the first time since starting his bashing-Irene rant. "Why aren't you telling me to calm down or something?"

"Because you need to get it out," I spoke simply, and then admitted, "And I don't disagree with you."

"Hmmm." He nodded ever so slightly.

"Go ahead, Ryan. It's the perfect time since the kids aren't here."

"It was—today was—hard enough, without … her."

"I know."

"Thanks."

"Thanks? For what?"

He walked the few steps or so over to me and brought me into his embrace. It was fiercely strong at first but eased as he spoke. "For being here, Lenay. For knowing what to say and what not to say. For helping Sallie. For having more grace than I will ever have. For being the mature one of the two of us, despite me having ten years on you. For loving me despite all my issues."

Well, I hadn't expected all of that, especially when I truly felt like I had failed in every aspect of the entire day. Not letting our bodies unlock, I placed my lips on his to show my appreciation for his kind words. And then I admitted my own disdain. "First of all, I was ready to tear that woman apart. Is my tongue severed?" I teasingly stuck it out at him. "I think I was biting it so hard, it has to be." When his slight smile emerged, I continued, "And, second, talk about knowing what to say, mister. I think I might need to write down those beautiful things you just said to me and make them into lyrics."

"Go for it, Lenay. I think your manager might

approve."

"Manager … cowriter … fiancé." I touched the cheek of all three rolled into one and could feel the tension that had been residing there since we had first set out on our sad day begin to ease.

"Any news from Carolina?" he asked, still in my arms.

"Well." I sighed. "It's raining. The church even has a leak. Everything … the whole world seems sad."

"Hmmm," he mumbled before pulling away. "Hold on a sec. Stay right here. I'll be right back." On his way out of the living room, he bent down and rubbed the dog. "Sorry, bud."

I only got to have a little Lyric love myself because Ryan was back in a matter of minutes. In his hands was a bouquet of magnolias with a red rose in the middle. It was an exact replica of what I had intended to carry down the aisle that day.

I tilted my head ever so slightly at my man. "What? What is …? How did you …?"

"I know this was supposed to be our day, and it's just a small, little thing. I didn't want to not do anything."

"Ryan, how did you get these?" I brought them into my arms, as if they were a cherished newborn child.

"I have my ways." His smile was legit enough to actually make his cheeks slightly rise.

"I love you."

"We'll say those words in front of family and friends, Lenay. I promise you. And you know how I am about promises."

"I do." My heart filled with appreciation and a little more hope. "Maybe you'll even kiss the bride." And due to the little tease in my voice, I got a preview of that act, making the day not completely all depressing.

# CHAPTER FIVE

"Aaaaaaa!"

Ryan's body shooting up in bed forced mine to do the same thing. Although, the sheer terror in the shriek had immediately woken me up as it had him. I quickly adjusted my nighttime eyes to acknowledge the worrisome features on Ryan's face. It hadn't been him who had spurred out the frightening sound. It was one of the kids. And since I had been in a sound sleep when it happened, I didn't know which one or why.

"Wha …?" I sat up a little better.

"I don't know." Adorning just red sweat pants, Ryan started getting out of bed. "I'll go find out. Stay here in case."

In case? Geez, did he think there was an intruder? We lived in an alarmed house surrounded by a gate inside a gated community. Nevertheless, I glanced at my phone, prepared to call for help if need be.

"Daddy?" That time I knew for sure it was Joel. But his voice sounded more sad or worried, not terrified out of his mind like the initial catapult-awake scream. Before Ryan could react or say anything in reply, the little boy—whose room was furthest down the hall—called out again,

"Daddy?"

Ryan pursed out some air and looked at me. "That sounds a little better. I'll be back," he proclaimed and exited our room.

The next voice I heard wasn't Joel's or Ryan's—it was a sleepy Sallie's. "Joel? Daddy, what's going on?"

I got out of bed then, too. Two of them. Two of them awake at three-forty-five in the morning—the morning after their mother's funeral.

Ryan was more than a capable dad, but I knew I needed to help. Shuffling into the hallway in my lengthy, oversized blue and white tank top, I saw Ryan kneeling in between the kids' rooms. Both Sallie and Joel were looking at him.

"Joel, you okay?" Ryan asked.

"I had a bad dream." The little boy clung onto his small stuffed dog, Eli, which I hadn't seen him play with in quite a while.

"Joel scared me, Daddy."

"Ry, if they need to come into our room ..." I offered.

Ryan had a rule about the kids staying in their bedrooms. It was more for their own safety when they were younger. But it was definitely for our privacy, too.

"Uh." He looked up at me from his crouched position. "Well, maybe let's try this first." He slid his back down the wall so he was in a completely seated position. Straightening out his legs in front of him, he patted both of them. The kids took a seat on either of their dad's legs without a second thought.

And, once again, I found myself teetering ... both physically and emotionally. I wasn't in heels or any shoes at all, but I felt like the outsider to their cuddled group of three. And maybe it was a case where I should have been. Even though I knew I was loved as part of their family, what they were going through—really, all three of them— didn't involve me. So, my swaying legs made a decisive move back toward the bedroom I shared with Ryan.

"Why are you leaving?" Sallie called out, making me turn.

Ryan looked up at me. "I don't have another leg, but there's always room."

With a grateful nod, I sat across from them, stretching my own legs out and allowing my left leg to rest alongside Ryan's left. A strange stillness swept through the hallway. It was quiet, reflective, and calming.

"You wanna tell me about the dream, Joe?" Ryan asked his son.

When Joel shook his head and buried it a little further onto Ryan's chest, Sallie used an adult, empathetic voice—not at all like the one she usually teased her younger brother with. "Was it about Mommy, Joe-Joe?" Ryan lifted his eyelids to look across at me, and I mustered a comforting smile as Sallie tried again. "It's okay, Joe."

Joel looked at his sister with what seemed like admiration. The dynamic was an awesome wonder to see. Complete opposites in so many ways, that all seemed to evaporate. They were then one. They had a connection like no other. It was both unbelievably sad and yet breathtakingly beautiful.

"I was in the bathtub, and I didn't know how I got there," the little boy started to open up. "And it kept going over."

"The water overflowed?" Ryan used a soft, middle-of-the-night voice.

"Yeah. And it was getting on my bed and everyone's beds. Then it was coming from the ceiling and the walls." His poor little voice was accelerating as he told the story. "I got some towels and buckets."

"Well, that sounds like a good idea," Ryan reassured, and I watched Sallie look at her brother as if he was retelling an action movie.

"And Mommy came and told me to run to the next house. It was dark outside, but I did. I could see you and Bethany in the kitchen, Daddy, and I was calling for you, but I couldn't get in." His eyes seemed to grow twice their size as he looked up at Ryan.

"Hey, I got you now, don't I?" He kissed the top of his son's head.

"Mmmm-hmmm."

"Was Mommy pretty, Joe?"

It was the first time I saw a legitimate smile from Joel that night as he answered his sister. "Yeah." Pause. "Yeah."

I wondered if Sallie was thinking of seeing Kari in the coffin. Pretty was the word she had used to describe her mother when we had been in front of the church. Pretty was important to Kari and, in some princess-like ways, it was to Sallie, too.

Ryan brought their two heads a little snugger onto him and hummed softly. I don't think it was a song in particular, but it might have been. It might have even been one of Kari's. It didn't matter. It was simply a way to calm both of his emotionally spent children.

The kids sat silent, listening to Ryan hum for nearly a half-hour. And me? Part of the time, I had my eyes locked on my fiancé, feeling, as if by osmosis, his pain, love, and appreciation. The other part of the time, I closed my eyes and let my own brain relax to his soothing tone. I knew the road of grief for those dear children was only beginning, and we all should cherish any serene moment we could, even if it was sitting against a hallway wall in the middle of the night.

\*\*\*

Instead of basking in the sun, sipping coconut rum, and saying Aloha, Ryan and I spent most of that following week hibernating in the house and trying to figure out how best to help the kids. Of course we had been planning on it. But Joel's middle-of-the-night awakening was a definite prompt to get things started as immediately as possible.

So, on Monday we ignored all forms of media—social sites, the internet, ringing telephones, and television. We worked on keeping the kids active inside while calling professionals who could guide us in the area of grief. Despite school being out for the summer, we were able to contact Sallie and Joel's elementary school counselor who recommended a child psychologist. Since she came very highly recommended, I couldn't help but wonder if the fact that she had availability the next day had to do with the severity of the issue or Ryan and Kari's star power. Sometimes fame had its advantages, and we weren't about to question it.

The meeting with the psychologist wasn't long at all. It was only a preliminary appointment to meet with us and the kids and to set up a schedule. For those, she wanted mostly to talk with the kids by themselves but would draw Ryan or both of us in as needed. While the kids sat in beanbag chairs looking at books, she emphasized to Ryan and me the importance of being flexible but consistent with schedules and expectations. The kids needed stability and normalcy more than ever. I couldn't help but think how Ryan had done just that, with adapting the stay-in-their-own-rooms rule the night before. Before leaving, the psychologist also gave us some pamphlets and recommended a special center for the kids to visit. It was only for children who lost close loved ones.

Thinking the psychologist visit alone was a lot for Sallie and Joel, we decided on the center visit the following day. It was located in an otherwise residential neighborhood. In a lot of ways, it reminded me of my family's one-hundred-plus-year-old home in Carolina. There were activities for the kids to do there—create art, sports, interact with animals, and more. Or, they could simply talk with other kids who were on similar sad journeys. It was obvious almost from the start that Joel would find a way to make friends there. But Sallie seemed hesitant, which then made Joel a little, too. I wasn't sure if it was a protective thing of his sister or that he looked to her for leadership. Not that he would ever admit to either. Regardless, Ryan decided to just keep the grief house on standby. He wanted to see how the kids did with the psychologist, as well as going back to their regular summer day camp. Besides, seeing as either he and/or I would have to stay at the center with the kids, he was afraid it would draw out unwanted publicity. And that was the opposite side of fame—the persistent thorn in your side.

That Thursday evening, I followed the sound of Ryan talking while his phone was on speaker. It led me to the game room, nestled in the unique downstairs of the house. On top of dealing with lingering press over Kari's death, Ryan was involved with some work-related things, too. I suspect even if we had been on our Hawaiian honeymoon, he would have still been on the phone a few times with someone at the office. Having your own successful talent agency kind of demanded that. As I was trying to determine who he was actually speaking with, Ryan, sitting at the desk, spotted me and waved me closer.

"She loved the kids," the other male offered.

"She did," my fiancé agreed. "She loved them … no doubt. She talked about them, with them, was concerned … I still remember how excited she was when we first found out she was pregnant with Sallie. Geez, that seems like a lifetime and two different people ago."

I watched as Ryan's eyes seemed to focus on a random, nondescript part of the edge of the desk. He was obviously lost in the past—one I knew only glimpses of. Sallie—who was named after Ryan's grandmother, Sally, and Kari's grandmother, Sadie—was planned. And they wanted another, but maybe not as quickly as Joel, who was conceived on the night Kari got to perform with the iconic Billy Joel.

As I leaned up against the desk, Ryan cleared his throat and continued to speak toward the phone. "Really, truth be told, she didn't have much of a maternal bone in her body."

"That wasn't only because of her career, though, Ryan." The male voice seemed to completely understand the Ryan and Kari relationship. "She didn't have much of a role model in the mom category."

"You said it, not me." I noted his nod and roll of eyes.

"I live it," he grumbled. "Having to give up her quote-unquote dancing career when she had Kari, and then having to keep trying for the male heir apparent. It—I—ruined her body!" On the mocking final words from who I then knew was Maks, I put my hand up to my mouth to resist bursting out in laughter. "I mean, what century do they live in? I wonder if Mama Irene got her tubes tied or just cut him off completely after me?"

"Geez, Maks, I don't want to know!" Ryan's face scrunched in obvious disgust.

"Anyway," he continued, "even though she was groomed to be our mom's mini me, Kari put her own spin on it."

"She did," Ryan agreed.

"So, honestly, how are my niece and nephew?"

"Hard to tell. I think there's still a bit of reality that hasn't set in." That was something Ryan had mentioned to the psychologist, too—the fact that when Kari was alive, she had been gone so much ... the separation and divorce and her extended tour. He worried that the permanency of Kari being gone still wasn't really registering to the kids, despite the funeral and viewing.

"For all of us," Maks admitted.

"Yeah." Ryan reached out and touched my hand.

"How's Bethany?" Kari's brother asked, as if he was on video chat and could see me instead of just a regular call. I couldn't help but think how incredibly unselfish his question was. After all, I had not been his late sister's favorite person in the world.

Ryan rubbed my hand. "She's been our rock."

"Good," he answered, and I truly believed both men

meant what they said. "So … just you and me at Kari's place. Go through what she would have wanted the kids to have?"

"Without your folks joining us?" I'm pretty sure that was relief in Ryan's question.

"Let's do it this way. I mean, I am the executor."

"Your sister was very wise when it came to business."

"Agreed. Saturday?"

Ryan raised his eyebrows in my direction and, understanding the implied question if I could watch the kids, I nodded back. "Yeah, okay. Hey, sorry." He was looking at his phone's screen. "I gotta go. Anamaria is buzzing in on the other line. There's something wrong with one of our clients, and they are insisting on talking with me. She's been trying to side-sweep it, but I don't think it's working."

"No prob. Good luck. See you on Saturday then."

Ryan ended the call and immediately put the next one on speaker. "Hey, sorry. I gotcha. Can you give me two minutes, Ana?"

"Yeah. Yeah. Sure, Ryan." I recognized Anamaria's voice. Ryan's loyal secretary had been around for my first meeting with him at his office and had subsequentially watched our relationship grow, even when she was oblivious that it was not only professional but personal.

He put her on hold and walked around the desk to sit on it next to me. "It's one after another."

"I know."

"You sure you're good with the kids Saturday?"

"Of course. Your parents are coming in, though."

"Yeah. I should be back by the time they get in. I want my 'Someone went to Hawaii and all I got was this lousy T-shirt' T-shirt."

I chuckled, glad to hear him able to joke. There had been very little of any humor since leaving Carolina. "I'm glad our honeymoon didn't go to waste. It was a wonderful anniversary gift for them."

"Forty-five years. Makes me feel old."

"Oh, geez, *you're* not even close to that!" I kiddingly smacked him. "And you have three older siblings. Take your call. Talk with Anamaria. She sounded stressed. I just came down to tell you I was going to start dinner."

"Yeah? What are we having?"

"Meat ravioli with dried fruit and a sweet and spicy—"

"I love you." He kissed the top of my head, and I knew right away he had made the connection.

The ravioli recipe was the first meal I had ever made for him, even before we were dating. It all seemed so safe and innocent back then. Could we get it back?

***

Ryan ended up going into the office and the building's gym for a couple hours Friday morning. So, he dropped the kids off at their summer camp for a sort of abbreviated test run. They should have already started that Monday, when we were supposed to be in Hawaii and Kari had them. But ... well ... that didn't happen. Kari was actually the one who had enrolled them and had the year before, too. That was the good part. Since Sallie and Joel had gone there previously, Ryan knew the rather elite facility and trusted it would be a free-from-gossip zone. And even though Ryan said the kids were clingy and sad on drop-off, they both saw friends and camp counselors they recognized and were okay with being there for a shorter than usual time.

Because I was a little leery the press might try to bother me, I had decided not to reclaim any of my shifts at the coffee house that week. Since becoming engaged to Ryan, I knew I didn't need to keep working at the independent coffee shop. But I liked to. It was a personal, separate part of me I had since first arriving in LA as a wide-eyed but determined college grad just a couple years before. The manager, Gracie, allowed me to sometimes sing my original pieces for the customers. Plus, I couldn't ask for a better schedule. Since I had proven myself to be a valuable employee, I was rewarded with a regular, weekday opening shift, which coordinated perfectly with both the kids' and Ryan's schedules.

So that Friday, I decided to hang out at the house with Lyric, who needed a good grooming. The doodle part of him definitely was high maintenance. But brushing him was cathartic for me, and he actually liked the one-on-one attention.

I also legitimately looked and reacted to some of my social media sites. It was something that had quickly gotten pushed aside after the news of Kari's death broke. All of my sites had gained followers. I wished it was because of my songwriting talent—and still hoped that maybe some of it was. But the burst was surely, unfortunately, because I was mentioned plenty of times in association with Kari's death. As Bethany Lenay—the professional name the world knew me as—I very rarely posted anything personal. But it didn't matter. The gossip mongers felt like they needed something ... anything. Similar follower boosts had also happened when my relationship with Ryan initially broke in the media and, of course, when he first contacted me via Twitter.

Because of that, I knew whatever I posted next would receive lots of attention. What I said or didn't say—just like Ryan's press release—would get positive and negative feedback. No matter what I did, some would think I was being self-serving or hypocritical. But I had to do it. At some point, there had to be that first post after her death.

Grabbing a notebook, I penciled down some words as possible themes. I then looked up relatable lyrics, quotes, and photos. But nothing seemed right. And then I realized that was exactly it. I took a photo of my brainstorming list and posted it without any explanation besides the hashtag of "priorities."

*Faith*

*Family*
*Healing*

A number of likes immediately emerged on the forums. Prayer hands, regular hearts, and broken hearts flooded the screen, too. And there were comments—overwhelmingly positive—telling Ryan, the kids, and me that they were thinking of us, asking how the kids were doing, and wondering if my post was possibly a new song title.

I didn't respond to any of them, except for the one who wrote, @Bethany_Lenay Mine, too.

My reply? @RyanThompsonMusic xoxoxo

\*\*\*

Going to an album release party was not originally on our plans for that evening. Soaking in the last day of our honeymoon had been. But God laughs when you make plans, right?

Since we were in town, though, and it was the first album for a client in Ryan's firm, he thought it would be a good idea to attend. We happened to luck out that Vail—a fifteen-year-old neighborhood kid—was free to babysit. And Sallie and Joel knew and liked her, which definitely helped with transitioning out the door.

It was nice to actually get dressed up and go out, even if the event was casual. I wore a simple, white, spaghetti-strap dress. And Ryan purposefully coordinated with a relaxed white button-down and jeans. It wasn't the fashionista in him but instead his music, publicity-mogul brain at work. He wanted our first official outing since the funeral to represent a light feeling and unity.

It didn't really matter, though. There were still a lot of questions and condolences from not only music colleagues but, of course, press representatives. Ryan just tried his best to deflect and keep everyone on point with the current, hopeful chart-topper we were there to celebrate.

In a way, I was glad my phone alerted me of an

incoming call. It gave me an excuse to momentarily excuse myself of the constant buzz of the evening. I squeezed Ryan's hand, pointed to my cell, and exited.

"Vail? Hey. Is everything all right?"

She had exchanged numbers with me and not Ryan because, even though she was a neighbor kid who understood privacy issues since her mother was a news anchor, she was also a teenager. And, well, teenagers tend to like telling their friends things. We didn't want TV Judge Ryan's cellphone number to be one of those.

"Yeah. It's fine. Mrs. ... uh ... Miss ..."

I breathed in a little relief on her initial answer and then corrected her. "I appreciate the nice manners, but it's Bethany. Please. Really."

I was actually closer to Vail's age than that of most of the homeowners in the exclusive neighborhood. And even though I was old enough to be married, in a lot of ways I didn't feel it. "Mrs." sounded even older. And, yet, I ached that I actually wasn't Mrs. Ryan Thompson like I should have been.

"What's up?" I refocused on the reason for the call.

"I really tried not to bother you guys, but you said to, and my mom said to, too. She's at the studio prepping things before going on air. And my dad went out for the night."

Rumors of the Bartons' marital affairs and swinging lifestyle were not only neighborhood gossip but were starting to bleed into the public forum. I wondered if their daughter—an only child—knew anything of it. I vowed to hold Sallie and Joel close. Even though they weren't mine, I felt the responsibility. I felt like I needed to protect their innocence, and if I couldn't, then at least I could help keep an open dialogue for them to talk. Because they were most certainly a product/victim of LA scandals and media, too.

Live music started coming from the room I had vacated as I reassured Vail that calling was the right thing to do. "It's okay." Taking a couple more steps away, I decided not to sit on the nearby velvet lime sofa until I knew everything was definitely all right.

"It's ... well, Joel started telling lots of stories about him and Kari."

It didn't slip past me that Vail felt comfortable calling Kari by her first name. But she had been a national superstar who everyone "knew." I was just a struggling songwriter.

"And then Sallie got upset. I tried to, you know, do things ... play with them, but it didn't really work. And I know it is past what time they are supposed to be in bed. They want their dad."

As if on cue, Ryan entered the lobby and did a heads-up nod as a silent query into what the phone conversation was about. When I mouthed Vail's name, Ryan's eyebrows furled a little in concern. I held up my hold-on-a-minute finger to him and resumed talking on the phone.

"Yeah, he's right here. Can you put them on?" As Vail agreed, I handed my phone to Ryan. "The kids want to talk with you."

"Sals? Joel?" Ryan spoke into my phone. "Hey." He paused to listen to his children as I sat. "Hey ... hey ... slow down." Ryan shook his head. "Quit arguing and tell me nicely what is going on. Sallie, you first." He sat next to me, watching as I peeled my feet out of my strappy heels and rubbed them—I definitely wasn't used to wearing those. "He's allowed to—Joel, wait. That's what I am saying." He listened for another moment and then said more calmly and sympathetically, "I know." A sigh. "I know. We're going to head home now, okay?"

Ryan looked at me with a part-sorry/part-question shrug. I tilted my head onto his shoulder and nodded in agreement. In reality, I was ready. We knew what would happen with the public and press the first time we truly emerged from the sanctuary of our home. And perhaps it was good we broke the seal so to speak. But, even more so, it was good we had an excuse to leave.

Ryan told the kids he loved them before hanging up and handing me back my phone. "Sorry or not?" he asked me.

"About leaving?"

"Uh-huh."

"Not sorry," I admitted.

His chuckle was so slight it was barely noticeable. "Me, too. Today was a lot for them with camp and us being out. I think they just need to see me."

"It's all good, Ryan. Except for the fact that I'm hungry. Will you make some of your infamous mac and cheese for me when we get back?"

"You mean my *gourmet* mac and cheese?" He smiled, surely recalling the first lunch he ever made me at his house, which was by far gourmet but a comfort food for sure.

"Debatable."

"You're on." He stood up, holding out his hand for me to do the same. "Let's go in quickly and say our good-byes."

"How about I meet you at the car?" I suggested, not wanting, now that I was out, to go back into the flashiness of the main room, even if for only a few minutes.

He scoffed in a joking manner. "Bailing when I need you most. Thanks a lot, Lenay." He pecked me on the lips. "See you in a couple minutes."

Ryan handed me the car keys and then made his way back into the boisterous room. In contrast, I found my way out to the peaceful nighttime air. The silent walk to the car was a perfect opportunity to give my mind a chance to have thoughts of its own ... and not just what was appropriate to say in a room full of music movers-and-shakers.

It took a little more than a couple minutes, but Ryan finally met me at the BMW. "Home it is," he said as he slid into the driver's seat and went for his seatbelt.

"Ry?"

"Yeah?"

"Don't start the car yet."

"Okay …" he said slowly.

He watched as I carefully climbed over to his side and sat on his lap facing him. The parking lot was full of cars but not people. It was really early for anyone to be leaving the party but late for even fashionably latecomers to arrive. But, in all honesty, I didn't care if anyone saw us. We shouldn't have needed to hide. We had done that before, and I never wanted to do it again. Besides, my car action wasn't anything dirty.

"Hi?" he said, and I laid my head on his chest, feeling the tautness of a man who appreciated fitness and hearing his healthy heart beating steady.

"I needed a second of this—you and me, silence, our own private shelter—just a second or two."

"I need a million more." He partially sighed.

"I will never bail on you." It was something else I had done once and never wanted to do again … even though, in the long run, it was what we had needed. When he lifted my head to look at me directly, I clarified, "I know you were teasing, but I wanted to let you know that for sure."

"Well, if you haven't yet, I'm thinking I believe you." His smile was slight and soft but I knew full of truth and appreciation.

***

The weight of Ryan's body reentering the bed caused my partial sleep status to become a little more awake. I hugged my pillow, turned, and curved onto his side. I couldn't see him well since it was dark in our room, but I could hear the sigh in his voice.

"Sorry, didn't mean to wake you."

"Hmmm," I mumbled. "You didn't. How is he?"

I felt his breath expel on top of my head before he answered. "Finally asleep again."

"At least he didn't wake up screaming this time."

"No. No. There's that. And he didn't wake up Sallie, either."

"Did he tell you about it?" I rubbed my hand along his washboard abs, hopefully as a way to soothe.

"That's just it. He says he doesn't know why he's awake."

"Not a nightmare?"

"No. He said he didn't like sleeping, and he wanted to see me." Ryan's hand running down the length of my long, dark brunette locks felt good.

"Hmmm," I hummed. "The way he jumped into your arms when we got back tonight ... He held on so tight. It was like you had been gone for weeks."

"Sallie pretty much, too."

"Yeah," I agreed, but hers had been a little slower and reserved ... Sallie-like.

"Joel asking for me in the middle of the night ... bring back any memories?"

"Yep."

My mind traveled back to the first night Ryan and I had ever spent together. Joel had called out for his father similarly back then. He had been going through a tough sleeping pattern with the adjustment of Kari being on tour for so long. Things had been stable since, though. But, now ... well ... Kari wasn't on tour.

"Damn her."

It was like I froze. I had heard him correctly. But it was completely unexpected, especially because I was pretty sure he was referring to the same woman I had just been thinking about. Slowly, I propped myself up on my elbow to face him.

He looked at me the best he could in the darkness. "Damn her for leaving them. No matter if she did it on purpose or made a stupid, stupid mistake, it was her choice. And she altered those kids' lives forever." He shook his head as if trying to make himself stop. "Maybe

… you know what? Maybe"—he threw his one arm up—"it is for the best."

"Ryan!" I immediately admonished.

"I'm sorry." He covered his mouth with his hand momentarily. "I didn't mean that. I didn't. I would never want … Geez." Another huge gust of air. "I, God, don't know what to do or think."

Neither did I. I didn't know how to help the kids or him. He was experiencing a loss, too, although he hadn't really acknowledged it. Whether that was for the kids' or my benefit, or whether it was self-denial, I wasn't sure. The only thing I did know was he needed my love and support more than ever. So, I rewrapped my body around his, and it was my turn to hold on to him extra tight.

# CHAPTER SIX

"Out of all our kids, Ryan is the one who really did things his own way. I think he always felt a need to."

It was neat having a chance to truly talk with Ryan's parents ... especially when he wasn't present to argue or dispute the truth. But what Mrs. Thompson had just said really wasn't news. Ryan, himself, had told me, as the youngest of four, he had always felt like he was in competition to do everything the others were doing but better. And that drive was what led him to his successes in life—honor roll, athletic scholarships, band manager, and now owner of a very prosperous talent agency. He never stopped.

"Want to know something funny?" Ryan's dad chimed in. When I nodded and the kids gazed at their grandfather with even greater anticipation, he continued. "So, yeah, Megan is a teacher like her momma was, and Teagan does things with the farm with me. And what is a vineyard? A wine farm."

"Ha! I never looked at it that way." But it made sense.

"Yeah, here Dylan thought he wasn't part of the family business." He chuckled. "And your betrothed?"

"What does betrothed mean?" inquisitive Sallie

61

interjected.

"Person to be married to." Ryan's mom shook her head. "Your pappy likes to throw out big words every now and then to prove he knows more than just pig and cow talk."

"Oh, shush, silly woman." He smiled at his wife. "So, anyway, don't tell our youngest, but he takes after his papa, too."

"Yeah? How?" I mean, physically, I could totally see the resemblance—both had strong chiseled cheekbones and similar eyes—but professionally?

"My garage band." He drummed on the kitchen counter and joked, "I've been … What's that called when you try to sell your product to a company?"

"Pitching," I answered.

"Yes. Yes. I've been pitching to him for years. No such luck."

"Did he tell you there are lots ahead of you and you aren't mature enough?" I jokingly replayed the words Ryan, as a judge, had told me at my *Singer Spotlight* audition.

"Not many more mature years after sixty-seven." He chuckled over his age.

"Sure there are." Mrs. Thompson was *tsking* her husband while helping her two grandchildren spread icing on the cake.

Along with a last-minute card, hand-painted rocks/paper holders, and a frame for other artwork the kids drew, that was going to have to do for Ryan's Father's Day gifts. The next-day holiday had kind of snuck up on us between the wedding-that-wasn't and Kari's death. And it had been something Kari had helped the kids with the year before. So, I hadn't originally planned anything at all.

I walked across the kitchen to where my phone was ringing on the dinette table. Recognizing Ryan's ring and number, I answered. "Hey, where are you? I expected you home by now. We need to talk about your dad's talent."

Ryan's reply was partially overshadowed by his father's

bellowing laugh. "Um … yeah, sorry. It's gonna be a while. My folks are there, huh?"

"Yeah. Where are you?" I repeated.

Ryan had texted earlier, saying he was going out for a beer with Maks since they had gotten through Kari's things rather quickly. I had wondered if the speed of the task and the consequent drink afterward were both due to the men's emotional states. Regardless, he still should have been home for his parents' arrival. But he had not been. And when I found out why, at first, I was scared, and then I was angry.

It seemed like he sucked in his breath before answering. "I'm getting checked out just as a precaution to make sure I'm all right, and then I need to go to the station and see how we can settle this."

"What? What does that mean 'getting checked out'? Are you hurt?" I hadn't realized my worried reaction came out so loudly until both Ryan's mother and father turned in my direction.

But I focused on Ryan's response. "I'm fine. It's procedure—documentation—so no one sues anyone." He sounded calm but tired and annoyed.

"What are you talking about? What happened? And what do you mean the station? Are you talking about the police?" I rattled off my list of questions, only then piecing the second part of his original statement together.

He gave the answer I was hoping he wouldn't. "Yeah. It's nothing. Really."

"It's not nothing!" I screeched, not caring who was looking at me. "What happened? Why are the police involved?"

"I can't get into all of it. I went to the bar with Maks and there was a little altercation with Olsen." As soon as he said that name, his speech pattern got quicker. "Scuffle. Everyone's fine. No serious charges. It'll take a bit, but I'll be home." And then he stopped because it was obviously my turn to say something. When I didn't, he cautiously called out my name. "Bethany?"

"Fine. I'll see you later."

Click. End call. Enough.

***

Physically, he looked all right. There weren't any noticeable marks from the confrontation or whatever it was. Emotionally, though, was another story. Ryan appeared beat and concerned. I knew because his eyes hadn't left mine since entering the house and room. I refused to let the straight line my mouth had formed budge. I hadn't talked with him since hanging up and, even though I was happy he was home and safe, I was still upset with what had happened. And he knew it.

"We signed you up for wrestling so you knew how to properly let go of aggression," Ryan's dad broke the beyond chill in the air.

"Yeah, well … this was a little different than teenage angst." Ryan vocally acknowledged his father but still looked at me.

"Doesn't seem all too different to me."

Under other circumstances, I would have laughed at or high-fived Mrs. Thompson's comment. Ryan's mom was a straight shooter. I suppose she had to be, as the mother of two boys and two girls, and being a retired teacher and high school principal. I hadn't had many opportunities to really get to know Ryan's parents since they lived in Iowa, but everything I had gotten to know portrayed real, true, wholesome love.

"What about any charges?" Mr. Thompson asked.

"A mutual, off-setting kind of thing. Paid a fine for the police being involved and disturbing the bar."

"Ryan Lucas Thompson, honestly, what were you thinking?"

Ryan's eyes swung to his mother then—her tone had dictated it. "I didn't even see him at first. He approached us. You know, sympathies to Maks," he attempted to explain. "And then he had the gall to taunt me … with what happened … with Kari and him … like it was the best thing ever." I closed my eyes and tried a calming breath through my nose as Ryan asked, "The kids … they're asleep?"

I opened my eyes just to give a nod. I wouldn't even give him the satisfaction of hearing my voice. Believe me, he didn't want to.

Mrs. Thompson added to my response about the kids. "Not too long ago."

"Why didn't you walk away?" Ryan's dad got back to the original topic with a question, but he immediately followed it up as a directive. "You walk away."

"I would have. Maks … he started it so—"

Mrs. Thompson interrupted her son. "Mercy … it's like when you all were children. It doesn't matter if someone started it. You be the one—"

"When you wallow with pigs, expect to get dirty."

Even though I didn't want to show it, I was amused by Mr. Thompson's farm analogy, but Ryan wasn't. He was only concentrating on me. "Bethany?"

"Are you all right?" Although bland in presentation, I managed to have my first words to him be out of concern.

"Yeah," he confirmed. "All checked out."

That was all I really needed right then. I was already mad, and the more he explained, unfortunately, the worse I was getting. But I did want to make sure he was physically all right. And then I really didn't want to hear any more. So, I promptly walked out of the room.

He found me only moments later, standing on the backyard patio. It had been the location of our first date and had always held a special place in my heart. But more importantly right then, it was separate from the confines of the house … far from where the children were sleeping in their rooms and no one would see or hear how upset I was.

"You don't want to be near me right now," I said as he closed the patio door.

"Yes, I do." He sounded wounded or tired or older … or all three.

"Ryan, no … you … don't. Really, you should give me some space."

But the only space he allotted was a less-than-a-minute pause in the conversation. "I'm sorry."

"For?"

My question seemed to throw him. "For … for getting in the fight."

His answer only infuriated me more, and I let him know. "Over her," I cried out. "Over her. She's still coming between us."

"She—"

I was too upset to cry but not to state what I was feeling. "No. It's the truth. From when we first got together … we couldn't even be together … because of her. Because Kari's social standing was more important than the world knowing we were in love."

I know he tried to halt his disappointed sigh, but he couldn't. "Betha—"

"And when she OD'd the first time and you went to her side?" Honest to goodness visual flashbacks of us cutting our romantic weekend short and tearing into the hospital parking lot a year before seared my brain.

"The kids were with her." His voice rose a tad.

"I know. I was going to say I understood. I did. And after rehab, she settled down. But it was always a passive-aggressive thing with her toward me. I know you know that. And I understood. I understood that was the dynamic. I could live with it because I knew you loved me." Dang … the tears weren't visible, but they were marching their way to the starting line.

"I do," he practically pleaded.

"I've put up with a lot, Ryan."

"I know you have, Lenay. I know." He sounded

defeated.

"You know what's sad?" My rapid dialogue and emotional eyes were no doubt because of everything I had been trying to hold back for a week and a half in order to be a supportive fiancée and future stepmom. "May God send a lightning bolt down right now to strike me. A little terrible part of me thought, well, she's gone, I won't have to worry about her interference."

Ryan's slightly bulging eyes made me feel even worse for the words I meant but shouldn't have said. It wasn't really that much different than him damning her the night before. I guess we both needed to get some things out. And I was on a roll.

"Now you get in a fight in a bar over her. Geez! What do I have to do? I'm never good enough. I'm always just so close ... but second best ... not worth—"

"What? That's not true. I know you know ... not with me." He spoke with determination.

But I knew otherwise. It was my life, after all. And it had been one full of almosts but not quites. I hadn't known it at the time, but I had simply been a placeholder for the guy I dated in college. I was good enough to have around until it was time to go back to his high school sweetheart. I moved to Los Angeles because I was offered an entry-level job in music media. But, oh, no. Almost. Sorry. They decided to give it to someone else at the last minute. And rejections in the music field? Ryan was even a culprit in that one. I was good enough to try out for *Singer Spotlight*. But it was definitely a no to move on. *There are others way ahead.*

I shook my head, feeling my life bombard my brain. Everything was getting to me. I had been able to hold it all together because Ryan and the kids needed me to, and I knew the real tragedy wasn't that we didn't exchange a couple of rings. But he was off fighting over *her* when he was supposed to be home with me? I just couldn't.

"I told you, you should have let me be."

"No." He sighed. "No. I'm … no. As far as tonight … it wasn't over her … not like … With what that jerk was saying … what he said happened? Honestly, Maks had every right, and I had a couple beers in me. I wasn't—"

"Bad decisions drunk," I recited, letting the statement hold its own for a second or two.

I had made a couple of those before knowing Ryan. And he knew it. The momentary pause at least calmed me enough to offer a solution to the merry-go-round of hurt and blame we were riding.

"I really don't want to be arguing with your parents in the next room." When he blinked, I continued, "It's only a night layover before they go home. Spend some time with them."

"What about you?"

It didn't go unnoticed that I was his first concern. But, nonetheless, I needed to put some distance between him and me for all of our sakes. If his parents were not there, it might have been a different story. I could have retreated to a different area of the house or we could have hashed it out. But, no … not with the Thompsons nearby. And to sit in a room with them and pretend everything was all right? Nope. I was not good at pretense. I considered it a lie.

"I need to take a drive."

"I think I liked it better when you didn't have a car."

I tried a smile at his reminisce of the days when we had first met and started to get to know each other. I never owned a car in California. I couldn't afford one when I first arrived, and it wasn't a necessity. I could walk or get a car service to anywhere I needed.

My shoulders dipped as did my lips. "It's your car."

"Come on …" he tried.

Ryan had bought a new, additional car, which just happened to be the car I had teased about getting when I initially dreamed about making songwriting money. We both knew the silver convertible Audi was for me. And, indeed, I was the one who drove it. But it was technically his car.

"Go be with your parents." I used a softer voice. I needed to. I needed to not let myself get too emotional and overreact.

"There's more I need to tell you."

"More?"

That did it. The last time he said something similar, our wedding was canceled. And his "more" sounded just as ominous as then.

"I definitely need a breather."

"Bethany …" he started.

But Ryan knew. He knew to let it go right then. We rarely argued, and, if we did, it was over silly things like hair clogging the drain or not replacing a light bulb. But he knew when I needed my space to give it to me because me digging in would not help either of us.

"Don't be long," he said, and then added, "Please."

\*\*\*

Even though I was upset, I was responsible and considerate enough to let Ryan know where I ended up, and to reassure, true to my word, that I was not bailing. I just needed a break. I found myself in a dark movie theater ten-plus minutes into the actual film. It was really ideal— no one could see me, and I didn't need to focus. I could let my mind go blur.

*Movie?* Was his text reply to mine. When a screenshot was my only response, he texted back, *OK. Thx for letting me know. C U after.* And when I didn't reply, he followed with, *For Real.*

I looked at my phone screen and then buried it into my purse … deep down. I shouldn't have been texting during a movie. And … I didn't want to.

\*\*\*

Silence in the Thompson abode was a rarity. Between the kids, dog, music, and much more, we normally lived in a lively residence. But silence was exactly what I returned home to much later that evening.

Figuring everyone was asleep, I started toward the staircase, only to spot the light coming from the floor lamp in the living room. "You're still up?" I asked as I entered the room and spotted Ryan on the sofa softly petting Lyric. "And with the dog."

I wasn't really shocked. Ryan pretended Lyric was an annoyance, but he loved the puppy as much as the rest of us did. And even though Lyric loyally followed me around—especially during my early-morning-rise routine—and was so sweet with the kids, he constantly looked for Ryan when the music mogul wasn't home and lavished up his approval when he was.

He looked up at me. "Yeah. He seemed a little lethargic … a little whiney. And, I needed someone to listen to my woes."

As if knowing we were talking about him, Lyric made his way off Ryan's lap, onto the floor, and to me. I picked him up and gave him a cuddle. He did seem a little sleepy but loving just the same … most likely picking up on all the sadness and confusion in the household around him.

"How was the movie?"

Ryan's question was an obvious effort to keep everything between us on an even keel. And I played along. We had learned over the year-plus of being together that the tactic worked best with us.

"You would have liked it—good old-fashioned chase scene." I hesitated but then went for it, knowing it would surely break the niceties, "And the couple had more problems than us. Can you believe it?"

When he stood up to meet me, I noted he had changed clothes since I had left. He no longer had on the plaid shirt and slacks he had been wearing at Kari's condo, the bar, the station ... He was now wearing a casual, all-black ensemble, which I hoped didn't represent his mood.

"I'm sorry." He nodded slowly and methodically before really explaining why he was apologizing. "Not just for the fight at the bar. But for worrying you that I was hurt. And for making you think you aren't enough or you have to rival her. I need you to know ..." He dipped his head so his eyes would exactly meet mine before he started again. "I need you to know I love you."

I answered immediately, not only because I had no doubt but because I realized he truly did understand why I was so upset. "Ryan, I do. I know you love me." I expected to see his shoulders drop a little ... to ease the tension, but they didn't.

Instead, he said, "And ... you feel the same way, right?"

"Yes." Of course, I loved him. "Why would—"

"You've never not 'for realed' me back," he spoke of our texting, and I placed the dog on the floor. "You did it on purpose. You know you did." Even though it was accusatory, he didn't say it in a mean way. He was just hurt.

"I did," I admitted with a puff of regretful air. "I was upset and, yes, coming down from being scared about you." I made sure to meet his eyes, wanting him to know the sincerity in my words. "But it's not at all how I feel ... will always feel. I'm sorry. I guess I'm not the person you told Maks I was. I'm not a rock or even a pebble. I allow myself to break and be weak when it comes to Kari. I always have a little."

That was the truth. My insecurities about not being good enough definitely festered and multiplied like nothing else when it came to being compared to an international singing superstar. And, even worse, a woman Ryan had loved.

"You *are* the person I told Maks you are—even better." He softly and briefly caressed his hand on mine. "And you are second to no one."

I smiled at his sentiment and then let out a little air I hadn't known I was holding in. "What exactly happened with Olsen? You said there was more to it. I'm ready to listen." I was. I had time to cool off, and Ryan had said all the right things. I not only *wanted* to know what had transpired with the man whose affair with Kari had broken up Ryan's marriage, I felt like I *needed* to know.

"He was the one who gave her the drugs." He clasped his hands a little at his sides on his revelation.

"Wha …"

"Yeah." He swallowed and took in a deep breath before continuing. "She was hooking up with him again. He came over to, y'know, taunt me a little about it. That alone didn't bother me." When I tilted my head slightly, knowing Olsen's revelation had to disturb him a little, Ryan continued to deny it. "Really, Lenay. That is … was"—he corrected his tense—"her personal choice and one I couldn't care anything about. She didn't interfere with our relationship." I know he noticed my eye roll but ignored it. "And her life was hers. But Olsen was trying to get a rise out of Maks and me. And when he didn't, he slipped with the fact that he gave her the shit. He said he had no idea it wasn't going to mix with her anxiety meds and how much she was going to take. He wanted to help her out since she was upset about …"

"About?" I prompted when he hesitated.

"Our wedding."

"He said that? She said that to him?"

"Yeah … I don't know. Both. I'm sure it wasn't exactly a day she was looking forward to. I probably should have talked with her or tried to—"

"Ryan, you know what happened wasn't on you." What had he said the night before—it was *her* stupid, tragic choice.

It was hard not to connect the dots of our wedding and her overdose, though. But it wasn't our fault for being happy, and it wasn't Ryan's responsibility to check on how his ex-wife felt about everything. They had coexisted well for the children, and that was what mattered, but otherwise had separate lives.

"I know … I guess."

I immediately recognized how his response was riddled with hesitation and uncertainty. So, I tried another way around the same subject. "But it sounds like she didn't take her own life, right? She just made the wrong decision."

"Again. About a couple of things. One too many." He stifled a growl.

"Can Olsen be charged with anything? I mean, with the drug supply?"

Gosh, how easily those words rolled off my tongue. Living in LA and not sheltered in rural Carolina had definitely changed my perspective and knowledge of certain things. Although I would never trade how things were, my previous self could have never imagined the person I had morphed into. Bolder and wiser had both its advantages and disadvantages, but I was proud to have kept my integrity intact.

"That's up to her family. It's not my business. But I suspect they won't pursue. They don't want Kari's name tainted anymore."

I offered up my own apology. "I'm sorry I didn't stay and listen before. Your parents probably think I'm an insensitive drama queen. I'm going to have to apologize for being so rude and leaving."

"First of all, no one would ever accuse *you* of being a drama queen," he stated, and I wondered if the emphasis was about Kari and/or her mother. "And my folks? They are ready to give you their prize farm animal and pie or whatever. They lit into me for tonight. I'm in my mid-thirties and they lit into me about all of it—the bar, how I should treat you … I felt like I was a kid being sent to my room."

My laugh was more like a breath through my nose accompanied by a closed smile. I could picture the scene he described and appreciated his parents' support, but also knew I was still a little at fault. "So, you think they'll still let me go out to Father's Day brunch with all of you before they leave?"

He touched my arm. "After church?"

"Yeah ... yeah. Is everyone going?" I asked, knowing I attended regularly and Ryan did most of the time, but the kids had usually been with Kari.

"Yeah. I think it would be nice. I know my folks would like that. And me, too. Priorities." He winked his remembrance of my hashtag.

I took his hand solidly in mine. "Ry? Just so you know ... for real. Absolutely, positively, always for real."

# CHAPTER SEVEN

"Hi, there." I entered the family room with a slight bounce in my step.

"Hey," he returned my greeting from the sofa. "How was work?"

"Good. It was good being back." Leaning over, I gave Ryan a quick peck on the lips.

It *had* felt good to be back at the coffee house. Putting my mind on something else besides Kari's death and the grief that came from it was a good thing. No one really bothered me, and the unworthy feelings residing in my soul dissipated. I even got to preview a song I had been twiddling around in my head.

"How's everything here?" I asked, knowing Ryan had worked from home since he took the kids to their first official session with the psychologist.

"We're good." He had texted me after the session to let me know everything went fine. "And there's no backlash from the whole—" He stopped to look over at Sallie, who was coloring at the nearby table. "The bar incident."

"Still nothing in the press?" I couldn't help my astonishment.

"Nope. Since it was kind of early, the place was pretty

empty and not the normal bargoers who want any kind of action. They seemed more scared or perturbed than interested in who we were or taking pictures or videos. And if it isn't out by now—two days later—it's not going to be."

"You're lucky, Ryan." I sounded like my mother … ugh!

"I know." His remorse was evident, and I didn't mind that it still clung a little.

"Where's Joel?" Time to change the subject.

Ryan lifted his chin toward the open door of the patio, where I saw the little boy with headphones up to his ears and a tablet in front of his face. "A new game. Entranced."

"All right. I won't bother him. Sallie's gonna love this so much more, anyway." I turned to the blonde seven-year-old only a few feet away. "Sals, guess what I got?"

"Huh?" She looked up slowly. She didn't have headphones on like her brother, but she may as well have. She seemed lost in her own little world.

"I got tickets to the *Princess Perfection* movie premiere." I smiled waiting for hers.

But all she said was, "Oh."

Ryan, who was shockingly more interested than his daughter was, stood up. "How'd you get those?"

"I make a good cup of java and my customers like me."

"That's some tip. Is he expecting something in return?" The left side of his mouth scrunched.

Both of mine went up. "First of all, how do you know it is a 'he'? But you're right. And second, you're cute when you're jealous."

"Mmmm-hmmm," he mumbled. "I'm gonna get even cuter if—"

"Palmer Walker." I recited the name of the gifter, who was a regular customer of mine.

"The movie critic?"

"Yep," I acknowledged his recognition of the honest and fair reviewer, who also happened to be happily married to a male artist. "He knew the kids could use something nice." On Ryan's accepting nod, I teased, "Come on, still be cute."

"You mean I'm not always?" he joked back before turning to his daughter. "Sals, what do you think? Pretty cool, huh?"

"The princesses are going to be there," I tagged on.

"I don't care. Princesses are stupid. They're not real."

A little thrown by the girl who usually lived and breathed all things princess, I took a second and then rationally disagreed. "Sure they are. Our country doesn't have them, but the—"

"I don't wanna go. It's dumb." As she sprang out of her seat, Lyric was forced to jump from her lap, too.

"Sallie Belle Thompson!" Ryan called out in shock, and then with a little more determination as she started out of the room. "Sallie! You need to apologize."

"Ryan, it's okay." I tried a soothing voice, even though, admittedly, I was completely taken aback by the little girl's behavior, too. Never ... ever since I had met her—even when she wasn't feeling well—did Sallie remotely act that way.

"No, it's not." His voice didn't raise, but he was determined to have his children always use good manners. "Tell Bethany you're sorry," he instructed when the girl stopped and turned. "That is a really big thing she got for you."

Sallie suddenly looked even smaller than her young age as she looked up at both of us. "Sorry." She obeyed and then started to downright bawl.

It took both Ryan and me off guard. Of course, the previous few minutes had done that, too. Even Lyric started lightly barking at her, obviously upset by the odd behavior. But before we could say or do anything, Sallie put her hands up to her face and ran from the room.

Ryan's eyes swung back in my direction. "What? What was that about? She loves princesses. She's always—"

"I know." I shook my head, trying to still piece the series of events together. "Tell me what happened today."

"I don't know." He shrugged and looked in the direction of which she fled.

"Start with the psychologist." I picked up the dog and was at least able to calm one living thing down.

"You know the doc wanted me to sit in on this first session with the kids."

"Yeah."

"So, they answered all her questions. We talked a little … about all kinds of stuff … normal stuff. They said what they like to do and shared what makes them scared. Joel mentioned the nightmare and that he sometimes wakes up in the middle of the night. Sallie didn't say much but, you know, that's Sallie. I reinforced how proud we were of them. They both seemed okay … good," he corrected. "And they went to summer camp for a little bit and that went well, too." He burst out a gust of air in obvious frustration of not knowing what went wrong. "I guess I'll go talk with her."

"Let her be for a sec," I suggested, placing Lyric back down.

"Yeah?"

"Didn't it help giving me space the other night?"

"That's a female thing? She's too young to be hormonal." I resisted rolling my eyes, and he was kind of fortunate we were interrupted by the ringing of his phone. Picking it up, he looked at the screen and said, "It's my sister—Teagan."

"Bethany!" Joel called out my name with excitement. "Look. I got to the next board!"

I put my finger up to my smiling lips. Joel didn't realize he was talking so loud with the headphones still in place. Ryan, who had just said hello to his sister, put his hand up to his other ear and started exiting the room. Lyric decided to follow him, and I went toward Joel.

Getting to the next board … making a step forward …

doing something fun ... seemed like something we all needed to do. But as it turned out, Joel's game seemed to sadly mimic the game of life the four of us were sloshing through. The next board proved even more challenging with scary mazes, which often led in the wrong direction or to a place you kept repeating and not being able to get out of.

When I saw Ryan reenter the family room, I should have been instantly aware of his distress by the look on his face, but it took me a moment. "Your son is trying to show me how to play this but—" I stopped and started again. "What's wrong?"

Ryan tilted his head at Joel and tried a smile, which was not convincing at all. I touched the little boy's shoulder and rose from the floor where we had been playing. He didn't seem to mind my departure—he was too occupied trying to chase off the zombies.

Ryan and I walked to the opposite edge of the family room before he told me the news that his sister had obviously delivered over the phone. "My mom ... she needs surgery."

"What? For what? What happened? We just saw her yesterday."

"Yeah, and they didn't say a word." His sentence was coated in frustration. "They even knew before the ... right before the wedding."

I hated that every time our upended marriage was discussed it was done with sadness and hesitation, but I pushed it aside and concentrated on the real concern— Ryan's mom. "What's wrong? Is she all right? What—" My breathing was partially erratic, and she wasn't even my mom.

"She needs a pacemaker. I guess she's been having some fainting spells. I don't know ... Brady ..."

"Bradycardia," I clarified and breathed a little easier. "Irregular ... slow heartbeat. My great uncle had that done. It seemed like a pretty routine procedure from what I heard. He's still—maybe even more so—a real spitfire."

"Oh, great. My mom could actually calm down."

I partially chuckled. "Are you okay?"

"Yeah." He ran his hand through his hair. "I'm just a little pissed they didn't say anything. And now Teagan is on my back to come out, and I'm sure Megan will be, too, especially because Dylan can't go because of the harvesting conference they're hosting. But I didn't know. They thought Mom told me. Teagan said Mom's trying not to make it a big deal, but she's older, and I guess anything can happen with any surgery."

"When is it? Wait … the harvesting thing is soon, right?"

"Yeah. This week. Her surgery is Thursday."

"This Thursday?" As he nodded to confirm, I asked, "You're going, right?"

"No. I told her I couldn't."

"Why? You should."

"You said it's pretty routine."

"It is. But it's your mom, and your dad will need some support, maybe even at the farm."

The tension that had been momentarily eased, revved slightly back up. "I can't. I can't take the kids." He looked in Joel's direction. "They can't … No. They don't need to see people in a hospital or worried. Not now. Not with everything … In fact, I don't even want them to know."

"Well, apples and trees."

"What?" His eyebrows scrunched.

"An apple doesn't fall far from a tree. You are doing the same thing your parents were doing with you—protecting their child by not telling them."

"I'm an adult!"

"Okay." I reached out and squeezed his hand in an effort to calm him. "I know you don't lie to the kids, but I understand where you are coming from. I do." We both knew those little ones had enough on their emotional plates. After a calming pause, I refocused on his eyes and reiterated my original thought. "I still think you should go."

"Bethany." He was back to exasperation quickly. "I just said—"

"You go." I exaggerated the first word. "I'm here. I've got the kids. We'll be fine. *You* go."

He physically see-sawed around for a second or two as if his feet were mimicking the thoughts in his brain. Then he took a deep breath and said in the same indecisive way, "If I go, I'll be there a couple days."

"I'll be *here* for a couple days. Well, even more." I tried a smile that time for encouragement.

"Really? Yeah? You wanna do that?"

"Sure. It will help every—" I cut myself off, beginning to laugh at a sudden memory.

"What?" His scrunched brows showed his confusion.

"I feel like we've had this conversation before … um, a while back. We were talking about the kids and then you started grilling me about my life goals."

Ryan instantly shook his head, and I knew he, too, was remembering one of our most important conversations. It was when we were first becoming a couple. In fact, when I thought about it, it was probably that conversation that had pushed us from dating to knowing we were serious.

"I wasn't grilling you about your life goals." He *tsked*.

"Life goals is actually what you said!" I jovially bellowed.

"I … I …" What a guy.

"You wanted to know if I was worthy of letting yourself fall." His intense, deep blue eyes burrowed with adoration as I spoke the truth. "It was big for me, too." I smiled.

"How about heads I stay or tails I go?" he offered.

"No," I denied him immediately—family was too important. "Go to Iowa. Be with your mom … your dad … your sisters. The kids and I will be here. We—"

"You're leaving?" We both swung around to face Sallie,

who had, unbeknownst to us, joined us from the hallway.

"Just …" He looked at me for a second, as if to confirm, and then back to his daughter. "Just for a couple days. Okay?"

"Why?" Her one word was riddled with obvious trepidation, and I wondered how Ryan was going to handle not only her disposition but the answer itself.

"I'm going to see Grammy," he answered truthfully in his most calm dad voice.

"I wanna go," Sallie offered immediately.

"Uh …" He hesitated only slightly. "Not this time."

Again. "Why?"

"It's not a regular farm visit. It's boring … like business stuff," he tacked on at the end, and I admired how he held on to his integrity of not lying.

"I'll behave. I won't get in the way," Sallie instantly offered up, and before either of us could react, added, "I'm sorry about before."

I'm not sure my eyes ever got that instantly watery. My heart broke for the little girl. She was obviously taking on so, so much. And it hadn't dawned on me when I proposed the idea, how seeing a parent—their only remaining and always consistent one—leave for a faraway destination would confuse their psyche. Geez, us just going out for a couple hours on a Friday night had sent their emotions on a tailspin.

"Tink, sweetie …" Ryan bent to his daughter's height. "It's … I know you are. Bethany knows, too." He looked up at me briefly, and I stroked the little girl's golden hair. "You can't come this time. I won't be in Iowa for long. A couple night's sleep. All right? You don't want to miss day camp. There are so many activities. And you know Bethany will need help with Joel, right?"

If Sallie was anything, she was her brother's boss—not that easygoing Joel ever acknowledged it. "He's a handful." Sallie's eyes seemingly got big as she nodded and Ryan let out a legit chuckle. "Will you call us?"

"Of course." After our Friday night out attempt, Ryan learned the importance of the kids at least hearing his voice. "I can even video chat with you. What do you think, my brave, smart little girl?"

"A couple night's sleep? That means two and no more, right?" She wanted confirmation.

"Yeah. Yeah. Two." He stood back up. "Let me work it out, but I still have two nights here and then two nights at Grammy and Pappy's."

She didn't say anything for a moment, and with her unpredictable behavior that late afternoon, I had no idea what to expect. Certainly not, "Will you be gone when the princess thing is?"

Ryan looked at me for confirmation—we hadn't even gotten as far as when the premiere was before Sallie had run out of the room earlier. "I don't know." He said it tentatively because we both knew the topic was obviously a sour one with his little girl.

And I answered the same way. "It's Thursday." Recognizing that was the day of the actual surgery, I knew the definite answer. "Yeah."

"Oh." Pause. "Can we still go, Bethany?"

Ryan's entire body seemed to instantly relax. He needed her to be his princess. He needed her to still have that innocence. "Yeah?" he asked hopefully, while rubbing the top of her head and looking at me.

"I'd love to if you want to."

"Yeah," she admitted shyly.

"Great. Yeah. I'll see if my friend Willow will go with us then. She can help us dress up as princesses and"—I nodded across the room where Joel remained oblivious, taken in by his game—"we can embarrass Joel."

I actually got a smile out of Sallie. "Okay. Daddy? I'll make you proud."

"Thanks, baby. You always do."

\*\*\*

83

It wasn't until later that night when we actually had a moment to truly be alone again. Ryan had gotten on the phone with his siblings and then made travel arrangements. And then we had eaten dinner and played Frisbee in the backyard. Girls won, but I'm pretty sure normally extremely competitive Ryan missed a few easy catches on purpose in order to give his daughter a positive ending to the day. And Lyric didn't help the boys' side as Joel had hoped. The puppy, who usually rivaled Joel's energy, seemed to tucker out quickly and wanted his water and comfy pillow. But the sweet dog deserved a break after running around in the California summer heat and being up with Joel the night before with another late-night awakening.

Finally, with the kids in bed, Ryan and I laid in each other's arms on the family room sofa.

"You always thought *I* would be a tough negotiator." I moved my index finger around his well-defined, T-shirt-covered chest. "I think Sallie is definitely one in the making with her 'two and no more sleeps' confirmation." I let out a light chuckle.

I felt his head shake back and forth above mine. "She almost broke my heart and made me change my mind."

"I know," I consoled and then teased with my Ryan voice. "There's no emotions in business negotiations, though." I reiterated something he had told me a couple times regarding his job. Even though I knew he felt strongly about what he was trying to accomplish with every business deal, I understood how he had to keep feelings out of it.

"That is not how I sound."

"How did you know I was pretending to be you?" I laughed lightly and looked up to meet his eyes. "I still think it's good for you to go, though. And, what did I tell you about giving Sallie a little time to herself?"

"I know," he admitted and softly touched my face with

the back of his finger.

"Good call with using the big sis tactic on her, by the way."

"Hmmmf, that's because I just had *mine* pulling it on me."

"I love every part of you." I clarified as I sat up a little straighter, "Son, dad, brother, business exec, future husband …"

"Ah, sheez, how was I so lucky to have you step on that stage that very first time?"

"Well, Mr. Mean," I teased a nickname Willow had assigned Ryan when I had auditioned on *Singer Spotlight*. "I just hope when we *do* get married and you get asked, 'Do you take this woman,' you don't echo the words you said to me when I was on that stage."

"Huh?"

"'It's definitely a 'no.'"

Ryan pushed out a burst of air and shook his head. "Lenay …"

I placed my hands up to his cheeks and kissed him with a bit of hunger. "Yeah?" I questioned.

The nearly two weeks since our world got turned upside down had been terribly emotional and draining. We had been either falling asleep at different times or quickly out of pure exhaustion. I needed us—our closeness … our connection … in every which way.

"God, I want that so much right now." He kissed me back with the same passion. With the appreciative groan I knew and loved, he started on the buttons of my top. When he stopped, I thought maybe he was going to say something about the color of my now-exposed white bra or a song he was thinking of like he sometimes did. But that wasn't the case. He said, "You were never meant to be a singer." It was a fact we both knew. "A phenomenal songwriter? Yes." And then he added something even more emotional and much more important. "The love of my life? Without a doubt. Come on, upstairs …" And he swung me into his magnificent strong arms and carried me to bed.

# CHAPTER EIGHT

"Uh, Ryan?"

"Yeah?" He called out from our upstairs bedroom, where I knew he was finishing packing for his trip to Iowa.

"Come here a sec."

"Okay ... be right down."

I just stood and waited. I wasn't sure if it was a big deal or not. But ... yeah. Uh ... yeah.

"What's up?" He found me in the family room.

"Well, I think we know why Lyric hasn't been quite himself."

"Yeah? What? Why?"

I walked Ryan a few steps to a spot about maybe five feet from the patio door. Laying right there on the floor was doggie doo-doo. And a good amount of it.

"Awww, geez, what?" He jerked his head back a bit. "Lyric! Where is he?"

"I don't know," I answered. "Ry, he's usually so good."

Lyric knew his routine. He knew when and how to get us. He also was good at holding it in when our sometimes-chaotic lifestyles didn't match up with his potty needs. That day had not been one of those, though. We had as normal of a day as we possibly could have. I went to work.

Ryan brought the kids to camp and went to work himself. I picked up the kids, and Ryan returned for dinner. Normal as normal could be for the Thompsons and me.

"Lyric!"

"Ryan ..." I touched his arm. "He wasn't feeling good. You know that. He wouldn't do that inside. Look," I said. "Look at the poop a little more carefully."

Ryan took the additional step and saw what I had seen. "Oh." Ryan scrunched up his nose. "Is that ...?

Not only was there a lot of it, but it also contained bits of ... LEGOs. As Ryan straightened back up, Lyric made his way into the room. He truly was such a good dog. He always came when he was called ... even when he knew he was in trouble. He slowly walked over to me but, I swear, looked wearily the whole time at Ryan. Dogs and humans. Humans and dogs. We really weren't so different from one another—the feelings and emotions.

"Joel!" Ryan's pause wasn't even noteworthy. "Joel, come here!"

"K!" the younger Thompson responded from *his* bedroom, where he was supposed to be getting his things ready for summer camp the next day.

In the meantime, Ryan picked up Lyric and brought him over to where he left his deposit. The dog whimpered. Again, they are such smart creatures. The furry animal understood he had done wrong. But I knew he couldn't help it.

"No!" Ryan forcefully told the dog. "No. No eating toys and no pooping in the house."

He held him there a second. I don't think Ryan was necessarily really mad. I think he simply wanted to teach the dog a lesson. And that was confirmed when he stood back up and gave Lyric a little ruffling of the hair on his head. Lyric readily lapped kisses on Ryan's bare, chiseled face.

And then, Joel walked in. "I'm done. I was making an airplane picture for you," he announced, unbeknownst to the doggie drama.

Ryan placed Lyric back on the floor and walked a few steps toward his son. "What was the reason—for the longest time—that I said we couldn't get a puppy?" Joel's eyes seemed to get big as his dad continued. "Come on, you know."

"I didn't clean my room." Joel most definitely knew.

"Yep." His voice punctuated. A mini staredown happened between the two as I reclaimed Lyric in my arms. "You know what happened, Joel? You know what happened to Lyric because you didn't keep your room clean?" Ryan's irritation was rising. "Guess what happened."

Joel shifted those large eyes. Besides when he was actually sleeping, I never recalled seeing him so quiet. "Huh?"

"Lyric. He ate some of your blocks. It made him sick."

Before Ryan even finished, Joel swung his head straight over to Lyric panting in my arms. "Is he okay?"

"I'm not sure," Ryan answered with straightforwardness. "We'll have to call the vet. But, Joel, he is under your care. Do you understand me? You need to be responsible when taking care of something that young. I'm so disappointed. You need to get some rags and bags right now and clean up the dog poop he left on the floor. You will have to prove to me you can keep your room clean again."

"Okay." He looked down and then back up at Lyric and me. "I'm sorry, Lyric. I don't want you to be sick. I'm sorry."

Lyric bounced in my arms. I did feel a little bad for Joel. While he needed to, yes, keep his room clean, the rambunctious little puppy was one we all had to keep an eye on as far as eating things. He once went head-first into a freshly baked pie I had cooling in the kitchen—even though Sallie was holding him tightly. And in the yard, he loved chasing after other animals. If a bird would ever dare swoop down too low? Oh, look out. We had learned to even keep a tight lid on the garbage cans after he tried desperately to knock one over to get into the contents.

"Go ahead. Go do what I asked, please." Ryan nodded in the direction of the kitchen and the cleaning supplies. When Joel started that way, Lyric followed him and Ryan said with a sigh, "All right. I'll take him to the vet."

"Do you think that's necessary?"

His eyes closed for the smallest of seconds as he shook his head. "I mean, what if something is blocked or any of those sharp edges did any internal damage? We had outdoor dogs growing up. I'm sure they got into all kinds of stuff and managed just fine, but I —"

"You want to make sure he is okay." My smile was part smirk at his kind, dog-loving heart. When he rolled his eyes back at me, I made the offer. "I'll take him. You finish packing. And who knows how late it will be. You have an early flight tomorrow."

"Exactly. All I have to do is sleep on a plane. You have to wrangle two kids to camp, produce pleasantries to noncaffeinated customers, and be with my two precocious offspring nonstop in the evening for two days."

"What!" I mocked. "I'm doing all that?"

He smiled softly and kissed me on the forehead. "I'll take him. I'm finished packing, and if it runs late, you get to sleep. Let me go get the mutt."

"Hardly a mutt." I t*sked*.

"Purebred mutt." He turned to walk out of the room.

"Ry?"

"Yeah?" He faced me once more.

"Shit happens."

His full belly laugh was so fun to watch. "It sure does."

\*\*\*

Lyric's visit to the vet did take a while. Ryan kept me informed via text of all that was going on during his time at the animal hospital. Since he didn't have an appointment and it wasn't an emergency, there was a slight wait. Then, they took images and made some assessments. The goldendoodle's prognosis was the best we could have hoped for. There didn't seem to be any damage and everything was to pass.

When Ryan returned home, the kids were already asleep, and I might have been also had I not wanted to stay awake for his return. I trusted all was right with our curly four-legged critter. But I wanted a chance to say goodnight and close my eyes looking at my fiancé, especially since his flight was super early the next morning and everything would most likely be crazy in those moments.

He entered our bedroom with an initial brush of air coming through his mouth. And then the ends curled up when he spotted me sitting up in bed waiting for him. "Next time we flip, Lenay."

"What?"

He was unbuttoning and pulling off his shirt as he answered, "Who goes to the vet."

"What? You offered. I told you I would."

"Yeah." He took off his shoes and hung his pants over the nearby chair. "Not being noble anymore. A twenty-four-hour veterinary hospital is way too stimulating, and someone, seriously, came up and asked me for my autograph." He placed his wallet on the nightstand and started to crawl into bed with me.

"Sorry," I consoled with my word and a kiss. "Lyric's good, though, right?"

"Yeah." He sounded and looked tired. "Do you know how much a vet bill costs for something as simple as that?"

I crinkled my brows at the LA music manager who, while not an extravagant over-the-top spender, did not need to worry about money … at all. "No. But I'm sure you're fine with it."

"Yeah, yeah. I was thinking of the people in there who

might not be."

"Probably hocking your autograph for cash."

His laugh was short but legit. "Well, that certainly wouldn't pay the bill. You know, it reminded me of you going to the ER for the brownie nut reaction and not having good insurance."

"It's the whole reason I agreed to marry you," I teased. "Your insurance."

"I thought it was my uncomplicated life," he joked back.

"Ha! Yeah."

He sat quietly for a second or two before speaking again. "Do you think the kids ... do you think they know the advantages they have? Do they understand all that they don't have to worry about?" Introspective Ryan was clearly taking over. "They've never had hand-me-downs or watched us buy with coupons or whatever. They've never wanted for anything." Not like Ryan or me growing up. He knew he was speaking for both of our childhoods—his rural farmland and mine as a small-town preacher's daughter.

"No," I acknowledged. "I'm sure they don't realize it." Before his grumble lasted too long, I continued, "But they are also not *those* kids. They are kindhearted, respectful, compassionate children." While I had his direct eye contact, I added one more thing, "And, quite honestly, because of who they are, they have other, different worries." Before and after Kari's death, I thought.

"Yeah." He breathed out his sad, accepting breath again. "There's not much I can do about that."

"Nope. It's their world ... their reality."

"I was thinking of finding some way of having Joel pay me back for Lyric's bill. Not the real amount or cash, of course," he quickly added.

"Cleaning out the chicken coop?" I smiled a tease, thinking of his own childhood.

"You laugh, Lenay, but it was not fun work."

92

"I'm sure it wasn't, farm boy. To give Joel credit, he was very concerned about Lyric and did a good job cleaning the mess up ... both Lyric's and his room."

"I saw it." Ryan, I'm sure, had peeked into his children's rooms as he had made his way to ours. "And you wanna know something?" He poked my arm. "Those chickens were never appreciative!"

I laughed legitimately that time. "*I* appreciate you."

"Well, thank goodness someone does."

"I'm pretty darn sure there would be two little hands and a paw raised in addition to mine, Ryan."

His whole body seemed to rise and fall slightly. "I worry about them—their world, as you said."

"I know you do." I elongated my body and rested my head on his torso. "And you have legit reasons to. But how they are turning out as human beings is not one of them." I kissed his strong, sturdy, beating chest a couple times and did what I wanted to all along—tilted my head so I could look into his eyes and fall asleep.

\*\*\*

We did a Thompson family video chat Wednesday afternoon. Well, it was the afternoon for the kids and me. It was dinner time in Iowa. All of the Thompsons—minus Dylan's clan—had gathered for dinner at Ryan's parents' house. Mrs. Thompson's surgery was midmorning that next day. So, Wednesday eve was our one chance to live chat.

I had barely gotten my greeting into Ryan when Joel piped in next to me. "Daddy, do you see where we are at?"

"Huh? Uh, the house?" Ryan responded.

"Where in the house?" Joel further questioned.

"Spin the phone around a little, Joel. It's too close," I suggested, but he did so in the same speed Joel did everything—super fast. "No. Slowly. You are going to get your dad seasick."

Once he did, he immediately looked back into the phone. "Do you know now? It's my room!" He immediately gave the answer away with excitement. "I bet you couldn't tell because it is soooo clean. I told you I would keep it clean."

I couldn't help but laugh. It hadn't even been twenty-four hours since he cleaned it. And he had barely been in the house, nonetheless his room, for one awake hour of those. But Joel was proud. So, Sallie and I had appeased him with our location central to call Ryan.

"Uh-huh," Ryan acknowledged. "Great. Now, you just need to keep it that way."

"I will!" Joel said as I gained control of the phone again and Ryan spoke.

"How's the dog?"

"He pooped another one!" Sallie exclaimed, a little grossed out.

"Well, that's actually a good thing," Ryan responded.

"Hey, hey, hey, Bethany." The image of Megan wrapping her arms around her younger brother from behind filled our screen. "Hey, kiddos!"

"That's Aunt Megan!" Joel called out.

"Yeah, Joel." Sallie looked at her brother incredulously. "They're at Grammy and Pappy's." Duh!

"Hi, Megan." I decided to properly answer for all three of us. "How is everything there?"

"Did you see Cotton Candy?" Sallie asked about her favorite animal at the Thompson farm—the white horse.

"What about the piggies?" Joel chimed in.

"Your dad is going to clean the pig pen out for Pappy." That was Teagan, who was now also in view from Ryan's end.

"Oh," Ryan immediately shot back. "*He* is not."

"I cleaned my room, Daddy!" Joel countered.

And Sallie called out, "Hi, Aunt Teagan!"

"Make sure he does the chicken coop, too," I told Ryan's sisters. "He was just talking to me about that last night."

"Lenay ..."

"So, I'm sure we have you to thank for getting baby bro back home, huh?" Teagan was obviously talking to me.

Rolling his eyes at the screen but very much meaning them for his sister, Ryan emphasized the first two words as he said, "Baby bro can make up his own mind."

"So, yeah, I got him to." I stuck my tongue out at Ryan, who winked at me in return.

"Totally a better man because of you," Megan added.

"Can't argue that," Ryan agreed, prompting both of his sisters to gush and awe at him.

It was fun watching Ryan, who always claimed to hate being the youngest and therefore picked-on sibling, interact with his family. It made me long to be with him and them. But I knew and understood the reasons why I couldn't. I also noted Megan's last comment. It had never been told to me directly—and certainly not in front of the kids—but when Ryan was married to Kari, his relationship with his family, while not necessarily strained, wasn't as present. And that made me sad because we all needed family. We all needed support from wherever we could grab on to it.

Soon after, we wrapped up our conversation with everyone saying they missed and loved one another. And I knew that was most certainly the case. Even though I kept their routine pretty much on target, the kids missed their dad a lot. They weren't used to him being the one who was away. It had always been Kari. So, it wasn't just Joel, but both of them who had trouble falling asleep that night. But we made it through.

\*\*\*

Thursday was another story. Our schedule ... routine ... balance was completely thrown off, but it was for a fun reason. We went to the *Princess Perfection* movie premiere.

After getting the kids from day camp, we picked up Willow and all her creative cosmetic and fabric elements. My best friend loved the idea of going to the premiere. She had even gotten props from the fashion magazine she worked at and was able to leave work early to act as a correspondent for the event. After she swooned over the house—which she did on every visit—Willow made a fashion station in the family room. While I prepared dinner, she enhanced the clothes for Princess Sallie and Knight Joel, which included homemade wands, crowns, sashes, and more. Makeup would wait until after our meal. We were on a tight schedule, but it was a good thing—it kept us all going. It was particularly fun to see Willow interact with the kids. She was far, far from wanting to be a mom herself, but she most definitely warranted the fun "aunt" status.

Between parking, the red carpet, photo ops, snacks, and, of course the movie itself, by the time everything was done for the night and we made it back home, it was much later than Sallie and Joel's regular bedtime. Joel had even fallen asleep in the car, which was probably a result of resisting sleep for so long the night before. I couldn't help but think if Ryan had been there, he would have carried him. But I wasn't that strong. So, I woke the little boy up enough to get him to his bedroom and didn't even bother to ask him to change clothes.

When I next entered Sallie's room, she was in her pajamas and in bed. Her droopy eyes and unicorn stuffed animal against her chest told me she was moments from falling asleep, too. More than anything, I hoped the evening had been a good one for her.

"Hey, Princess Sallie Belle, you all set for dreamland?"

"Yeah. Thank you for taking me today, Bethany. It was a lot of fun."

"It was, wasn't it?" My internal beam surely equaled the one on my face. "You know what I thought was so super special?"

"Huh?"

"Meeting the real princess."

Sallie momentarily closed her eyes as if reimagining meeting one of the European princesses who flew in for the event. "She was so nice and just like a regular person."

"That's what I was saying. Princesses are real, and we can all be them. I'm gonna send your dad the photo of the two of you so he sees it first thing when he wakes up."

"Yeah. That will make him happy." She smiled a little in her sleepiness. "I miss Daddy."

I touched her cheek, still rosy with extra Willow blush. "I do, too."

Particularly since we hadn't had a minute to talk with him the entire day. And by the time we had gotten home, it was too late, especially in Iowa. Although, he had texted while I was at work to tell me that all went well with his mother's surgery.

"I miss Mommy, too." The little girl was getting sleepier with her words and eyes, but her brain was very accurate. She glanced to her bedside table where a photo of Kari, among others, sat. "Do you miss her? I know Daddy doesn't."

Huh? Wow. What? And, how to answer?

I chose two out of three. "I know you miss your mom, Sals. If you're sad and want to talk about her, you can. And your dad? Yeah, sure, he misses her."

Why would Sallie think he didn't? What gave her that impression, and it was obviously a concern of hers. I thought of Ryan and how cautious, caring, and protective he had been with the kids, especially since Kari's death ... how he tried to keep things sunny and bright. Was it too much? Did Sallie see what I did, too—that Ryan hadn't vocalized any of his own feelings on Kari's death?

As I thought about all three of their grieving processes, Sallie said, "He misses Mommy?"

"Yeah," I reiterated and added, "Sometimes adults

don't really know how to say or show it, though."

"Oh." Her heavy eyelids flickered.

Then after a moment or two, I leaned over and nuzzled my cheek up against hers. "Sweet dreams."

After making my way down the hall and into the master bedroom, my thoughts were much more subdued and sentimental than a few minutes before. Sallie's words had done that. I took off my own princess dress, removed my makeup, and started putting on my blue shorts pajama set. But I changed my mind. I might not have missed Kari— although, I would have never wished her dead—but I did miss Ryan. And I missed him even more so since talking with Sallie and looking at our empty bed for the second night in a row—a bed that seemed so much larger and lonelier without him. So, I traded my pj's for one of his shirts—a record label graphic T.

Snuggling under the bedcovers, I was prepared to forward the photos as I had told Sallie I would. But I decided on a simple text instead. Even though it wouldn't wake him up—and I didn't want it to—it made me feel somehow like we were connected.

*Pang. Pang.* I wrote.

I placed my phone on the nightstand and started reminiscing about the first time, over a year before, when Ryan had said he had pangs. He had been in a meeting and suddenly had an urge—a pang—to call me … out of the blue. And, ironically, I had needed to talk so much right then. I think it was the first time we both knew there was a connection between us different than most.

The present-day phone ringing made me jump a little. "Ry?" I answered. "Hey, why are you calling? It's so late."

His smooth, late-in-the-evening voice sang across the line. "Can't sleep."

"Like father, like son," I jested. On his partial grumble, I continued, "They're both wiped out and asleep from the movie premiere now, though."

"Good. It went well, then?"

"Yeah. No one recognized us." I knew that was a fear of Ryan's, but he didn't want to disappoint Sallie after she decided to go, after all. And it wasn't as if I didn't know how to avoid questions. "Wait until you see Sallie's photos," I continued with a more positive thought. "She's totally one hundred percent all about princesses again." I left it at that, thinking her words about Kari would have to wait until a time when Ryan and I were face-to-face.

"Thank goodness." I "heard" his smile.

"Everything all right? Is your mom okay?"

"Yeah. Yeah. All good. No reason for you to have any pangs. That's one of the reasons I called—so I could tell you that."

"Pangs are only for when you think something is wrong?" I didn't give him a chance to answer. "I was just thinking of you. I miss hearing your whistle breath as you sleep. I miss you. That's what my pang text was about."

"Well, if that was the case, there wouldn't be a second in the day when I didn't have pangs."

"Ry … geez." I swear I actually felt my face heat and flush in a matter of seconds. "Melt my heart, why don't you?"

"Just speaking the truth."

I brushed a dang tear away. Our hectic day, him being so far away, and those sentimental words definitely warranted a straggler or two. But at least they were warm, welcomed ones.

"What was the other reason?" I recovered with a question.

"Other …?"

"You said *one* of the reasons you called."

"Because as much as I miss you, we don't get moments like this."

"What? Being able to sprawl across the bed and take every pillow and blanket for myself?" I went with humor.

"Don't get used to it." He chuckled out a mock-stern voice. "And I am on, I swear, the hardest mattress ever. I feel every spring. So don't tease me with all the cushy comforts of home."

"I won't mention what I'm wearing then."

His moan was much more audible. "Please don't. What I meant was, talking to you like this."

"Hmmm. I'd still rather be in your arms."

"Me, too," he concurred. "For sure. But, do you know what I mean?"

I thought for a second. Yes. Nighttime talks on the phone involved soft voices, no immediate distractions, and listening to purposeful words instead of touches or gestures. It also enhanced the longing. Yes. In a strange way, it was nice.

"It reminds me of when I was in Carolina last year." I used *my* soft voice and then tugged the sheet more snuggly to my body.

"Well, that wasn't the best scenario."

"No," I agreed. When I had gone home for Ella's college graduation, things were extremely strained between Ryan and me … to the point I didn't know if I would return to either California or him. "But it was those late-night talks about nothing that made everything all right," I said out loud.

"Yeah."

"Everything's going to be all right again."

My words were meant to comfort and reassure him, but they were as much for me, too. We weren't currently in any kind of relationship danger, but the sadness and seemingly never-ending drama were draining and straining in other ways. I knew there were still things to plow through. And, yet, I had faith we would. Even though I missed him desperately, he was where he needed to be, and I was where I needed to be, too. Everything *would* be all right again …

***

I said it, and I meant it. But life had other plans. Suddenly, it seemed like we were once again in the scary maze of Joel's video game. Because out of nowhere, that very next day, we bumped smack, head-on into a wall. And we fell ... hard.

# CHAPTER NINE

Admittedly, I had other things on my mind. I was thinking about the obnoxious customer Gracie had to kick out right before I left work. I was trying to remember all the ingredients I needed to get at the grocery store on our way home from camp. And I was thinking how glad I was that Ryan would finally be home for the special welcome-home dinner I was going to prepare.

So, when Zander said the kids weren't there, I was only half-listening. I just kind of assumed they were in the back area. Then I realized the summer camp assistant was saying something about the emergency cards.

"Wait. What?" I swear I physically shook my head as if erasing an image from a screen. "Why were you using the emergency cards? Where are Sallie and Joel?"

"We, of course, called Ryan first, but it went straight to voice mail. And then, well, Kari is listed because when the kids were signed up in May, we were told all of last year's info was correct."

When Kari was alive—I got it. "Yeah, Ryan, he's ... he's midflight. The kids? Is something wrong with the kids? Where are they? Why did you need the cards?"

"Mrs. Hynes—she's the other contact number. She

headed straight to the ER. Hazel and Sallie rode with Joel in the ambulance."

"What?" My voice rose on the news that an ambulance was called ... obviously for Joel.

"It wasn't too long ago. Even though I probably shouldn't have, I was trying to look up your number since it's not on the cards. But the only two Bethany Lenays I could find was one living in Minnesota and the other was ... I forget, but it wasn't you."

The summer camp worker had spoken the truth. Bethany Lenay didn't exist, since it wasn't my real name. Hardly anyone in California or the entertainment field knew my true last name. Because I had used Lenay professionally and on my infamous *Spotlight* appearance, they just assumed that was it. The anonymity worked for so many reasons, except, obviously, the type of emergency situation I seemed to be in.

"I know you pick them up and, well, we know you and Ryan—"

"Yes, the whole world knows about Ryan and me," I shouted in my stress and then practically cried, "What happened?"

"So, I wasn't there, but ..."

Oh, flip, I was going to lose my marbles if I didn't find out something soon. "What—"

"They were at the pool. Joel saw one of the older kids, and he was running or something and fell in."

"Oh ... oh ..."

"Look, I don't know the details, and I probably shouldn't be telling you this since, you know, you're not on the official record. All I know is ... they needed the ambulance."

"You don't know anything else?"

"I can't—"

I didn't have time to try anymore. I needed to be where I could definitely know what was going on. "Where?"

"Children's," he said, and I bolted out the door.

In a way, I was glad I had to drive. It kept me from being online and searching all the possible things that could happen with young children at a swimming pool. Drowning, of course, was top in my mind. Joel could swim, but if he had fallen …

My stomach was flipping and flopping so bad. I thought for sure I was going to have to pull over and vomit. But I couldn't. I needed to get there, and I had never been to that hospital before. So, I needed to figure out directions and manipulate through the crazy traffic, which seemed, if possible, ten times worse than usual.

I tried Ryan's cell to no avail, getting the same voice mail I am sure the summer camp did. I wondered if they had left a message. I chose not to. I would keep calling. Besides, if he saw it was me, he would call, anyway. I wanted to call Irene, but I didn't have her number. Never in my wildest dreams—or nightmares—did I think I would ever have wanted to do that. And Sallie. She had started pleading with Ryan around her March birthday for a cell phone of her own. Even though we both thought it was ridiculous at her age, I wished right then that Ryan had appeased his little girl. At least I would have been able to get ahold of her.

And I drove on. Somehow, I managed to do it tear-free. Most likely because I was still in a state of shock and determined to get where I needed to be.

When I arrived, I did a very quick scan of the emergency room waiting area. No one I recognized was there. Not Joel, Sallie, Irene, or even Hazel—the director of the summer camp. I didn't allow myself enough time to wonder if it was a good or bad sign. Maybe I should have given Zander my number and had him call me if he heard anything. But he had been cautious about telling me anything. And I hadn't been thinking straight. Gosh, I was glad I could even comprehend a little of what was going on.

I next raced to the main desk. It was an emergency

room and, of course, people should be panicked and frantic, especially when it involved little children. But, even with me in that state, the woman behind the desk remained calm.

When I asked about Joel, I got an almost robotic reply. "Relationship to patient?" she prompted me when I blanked on what to say. "Aunt, maybe?"

"No," I replied. "No. I'm engaged to his father."

"Oh. Sorry. I'm sorry, we can't give out any information then."

"What?"

My mother took medication for anxiety, which also helped her blood pressure. I didn't. But right then, I needed to pop one or two of those pills. I had never felt my nerves even remotely close to the prickly sensation that was covering my body, even when I had been on live television in front of thousands and thousands.

"I live with them," I tried again. "I take care of him. I … My name's Bethany. Please, I—"

"I'm sorry. I'm sure you do. We're following policies and procedures—both the hospital's and the rights of the family." She gave me a sympathetic smile, and I wondered if I got the one person who either didn't know of my relationship to Ryan or was simply a rule follower.

"Please," I said one more time.

But … nothing. I turned around. I would say I started to walk around in circles, but that would mean I had some kind of control over my body. At least I was still standing and moving in a haphazard fashion. I decided the only thing I could do was try Ryan again. He should have landed by then.

Thank goodness, he, indeed, picked up. "Hey. Just right this second turned on my phone. Not quite a pang but—"

"Ryan, where are you?" I interrupted with haste.

"In line for the cabs. I should have probably driven. Such a world of everyone having things done for—"

Ryan sounded like Zander, babbling on. He needed to stop. I needed to talk.

"Come to the hospital. Come straight to the hospital."

His jovial tone changed instantly. "What? Are you all right? Did you eat something?"

"No. It's not me." My allergy to nuts was something he held very close in his mind and one I wished he didn't. I was very careful and responsible.

I don't think he was completely listening to me, though, as I heard him obviously speaking to someone else on his end. "Excuse me, excuse me."

I could actually hear people grumbling at him in the background, and I imagined he was pushing his way through the cab line. "Ryan? It's Joel." In order to get a quieter and more private place to talk, I stepped outside to the immediate entrance of the hospital.

"What?" His voice boomed with panic across the line. "Bethany …?"

"We've tried to call you, but your phone's been off."

"Yeah, yeah, yeah." I thought he was speaking to me, but by his next words, I could tell he was still trying to manipulate his way at the airport. "My son is in the hospital. I need to see him. What's wrong?" He had switched back to me and then reverted again. "I need that taxi. Please."

Listening to Ryan's panicked state was not helping me. I was ready to cry or scream. The helplessness and not knowing were eating away at me. But hearing his anguish on top of …

I heard someone on Ryan's end tell someone else to let Ryan get the next cab, and then as the background noise became a little quieter, Ryan said my name again. "Bethany? What hospital? Where?" I hardly had the answer out of my mouth before he was repeating it to the driver and then, once again, speaking to me. "Okay, tell me … tell me what's wrong. What happened?"

"I don't … I don't know." I knew he would react the

way he did, but I had no other answer to give.

"What do you mean you don't know?" His unnerved voice escalated.

"The hospital won't tell me. They won't let me see him."

"Bethany, what happened? You have to know what happened!"

I took a breath and started relaying what information I did have. "I went to pick up the kids from camp, and they weren't there."

When I completed the tale to the current point of me standing there in front of the hospital, he asked, "You still don't know what's wrong?"

"No. I just got here—the hospital—and called you. They won't tell me anything because of family rights. I'm not family." The word stung a little coming out, as I recalled Irene's similar stance at the funeral. It also made me wonder where she was and if she had anything to do with what information was permitted. Pushing the thought aside, I continued, "I'm lucky the day camp did."

"Geez!" He let out a long exhale as if he had been holding it in since he first picked up the phone. "Where are Sallie and Irene?"

"I don't know, Ryan! Hazel doesn't even seem to be here."

"All right ... all right ... crap." Somehow, I knew he was trying to be a little calmer just for me. "Hey ... hey, can you drive faster?" I realized he was once again talking to the cabbie. "I'll pay you double, triple ..." And then back to me. "Bethany, can you give the phone to someone at the desk? They have to tell *me*."

I started to reenter the building, not only because of his request but because I did want to be present in case something happened. I spoke honestly into the phone. "I don't think they will. They won't believe me. Why don't you call, though? Call, Ryan. And if you find out something, call me back, please. Please?"

"Yeah. Yep. Yeah." And we were disconnected.

Being in the waiting room, which was painted with bright murals and housed games for waiting children, was a tough task. It was hard for me to sit still with such uncertainty looming. So, I would periodically get up and do my own Bethany parade up and down the narrow hallway, sometimes going in the restroom and spinning around in circles in there. I felt like people were watching me, as if I belonged in a psych ward instead of a hospital for sick little ones. I'm sure some of them were awaiting news like me—whether it was their own child or a relation of other means. And I am sure they were worried, too. But they probably at least had some idea how the kid ended up in the emergency room and/or what the current status was.

I didn't hear from Ryan and, even though I was tempted, I didn't try to call him again. I knew he would let me know what was happening as soon as he could. And he needed to concentrate on what facts were hopefully coming at him.

Finally, after an agonizing amount of time, I spotted someone who could provide the answers to the questions I most desperately needed. It definitely wasn't the first person I would have chosen. But she was far better than not knowing. Or, so I thought.

"Irene." I approached Kari's mom as she was entering the lobby from a long hallway. "How's …? What's going on?"

"What are you doing here?" She seemed to hiss more than speak.

"I'm here for Joel," I stated the obvious. "How is he? Did he hit his head? Did he take on water? Is he okay?"

"I don't need to tell you anything. What are you doing here? Go home … like that camp person. I made her go away."

"I'm—"

"You're nothing. No, you know what? You are an

immature tramp … a whore who ruined my daughter's life. You have no rights. They called me because I am responsible and his blood."

I knew blood didn't make someone family and age didn't make someone responsible. And I knew all the other words she was saying were malicious, mean, and untrue. I could take the verbal insults if only she would let me know what was going on. "Please. I need to know if he is all right. What—"

"Damn it, Irene, stop harassing her. Geez!" Ryan's voice startled me yet brought me such relief. Knowing he was there made the situation the teensiest of bits bearable. "Where is Joel?" Standing directly with us then, he was staring down his former mother-in-law. "Irene … I am going to blow up. Tell me where my son is." I had never, ever seen Ryan even remotely that upset, but I knew it was with due cause.

"Ry, is he all right? Did you talk with—"

His voice calmed when speaking with me. "I talked with the hospital and just got off the phone with the camp, too. He's okay from what I gathered."

Swish! Breathe. Breathe.

"Oh … oh, thank goodness." I actually felt a little lightheaded with the pure adrenaline rush of relief.

"Irene …" Ryan was still on his ex-in-law.

"I was coming out here to see if there is someone better in charge so we can take the kid home. He doesn't need to be near all these germs." Her head scanned the area and her nose scrunched as if there were a thousand skunks lifting their tails, and I wondered how she ever dealt with being a mom to young children.

"*I'll* find out." Ryan took charge. "But I understand they need to keep him for a little while just as a precaution observation."

"He's fine," she protested before relenting that Ryan should actually be the one who should do the questioning. "They'll need your insurance information, anyway."

"You can go," he stated simply while adjusting his overnight bag on his shoulder.

"I—" she started.

"Go. I mean it. I got this, and you are not welcomed when you can't be civil."

I admit, I was a little shocked by Ryan's comment. Not that Irene didn't completely deserve it … and possibly more. But, in the past, Ryan would have at least acknowledged his appreciation for Irene being there. I think along with everything else thundering down on his life, she had pushed him one too many times.

By the piercing of her eyes, I knew Irene fully blamed me for her ostracizing. But I ignored it and focused once again on who we all should have been—the kids. "Where is Sallie?"

"Irene …" Ryan's growl was at best tolerable when she didn't answer.

"She's with her brother and a nurse person in the room area place," she spit out and sported another scowl at both of us. "I do all this work, and I get no thanks." And with that, she stomped off in her red stiletto shoes because what else would she be wearing.

I know Ryan needed to take care of paperwork and, more importantly, see Joel. But I selfishly took a minute of him to myself. I adhered my body to his and felt a good part of my anxiety strip away.

# CHAPTER TEN

Since Ryan was Ryan—a.k.a. recognizable television judge—we were ushered, without any further questioning of my status, straight to Joel's curtained-off section, located in the depths of the hospital's emergency room. Ryan hugged both of his kids extra tight before a doctor greeted us. It was then that we found out both the details of the accident and the medical prognosis.

Joel had been running to show one of the older boys at camp something when he slipped and fell into the pool. He hadn't hit his head but was disoriented in the deeper water. Having his regular clothes and shoes on hindered his ability to swim, causing an even more panicked situation in the pool. At first it looked like play, but luckily a lifeguard took note when the flailing turned to more of a floating. They were ready to start CPR, but Joel coughed up the water himself. Luckily—thankfully—that was it. He was going to be discharged from the hospital with a clean bill of health. But we did have to wait a little while in case of any side effects of the water and his lungs. I didn't mind. He was okay. That was all that mattered. And I knew the importance of secondary reactions. It was a similar protocol for me in the emergency room after an allergic reaction.

While we waited, the kids listened to Ryan's tales of the farm and thanked him for the little gifts he picked up for them at the airport in Iowa. They then played some games on my phone. Ryan was on his own cell, but I am sure it wasn't games he was playing. That was when I noticed what Sallie actually verbalized.

"Daddy, that girl keeps pointing at you."

Ryan looked up from his phone and glanced across the no more than three feet of walkway separating us from the patient across from Joel's dedicated space. Ryan briefly and softly smiled at the petite, dark-haired child who looked to be around Joel or possibly Sallie's age. If she had been pointing at me, I would have automatically wondered if my pants were split or I had something in my hair or teeth. But it was Ryan, and that could only mean one thing.

"I'm so sorry," the woman, who I could only assume was her mother by their similar features and her age, apologized and gave the little girl a narrowing of her eyes. Yep, she had to be a mom. "She recognized you from TV. She watches *Singer Spotlight* all the time."

That was the problem, in general, with being a male public figure. Unless you wear an actual disguise or a deep riding cap and eyewear, you look like yourself. Women? They just need to not put makeup on and no one would ever be suspect. Like it or not, it was the truth.

"It's all right." A now calmer and relaxed Ryan stood to walk a little closer to the woman and her child. "You're a music fan?"

The little girl's eyelids expanded instantly at Ryan speaking to her. "Yeah."

"What kind is your favorite?" he asked as I joined them.

"Pop," she answered.

"You must like Jorja then, huh?" Ryan mentioned his fellow judge.

"Yeah." The little girl's eyes, if possible, were even

larger.

"I'll let her know," he offered.

"Cool! Mom, did you hear that?" She looked at the woman to confirm my suspicions of relation.

"Yes, Darlee," she answered. "That is pretty cool."

"That's a beautiful name," I jumped into the conversation. "I hope you're feeling better soon. It's hard being in the hospital, isn't it?"

"I have seizures." She said it with a bit of melancholy but just as matter-of-factly.

I looked at the woman. Her expression was much more solemn than melancholy. It was a solid mixture of fear and pain.

"This one was longer than the others," she started only to be interrupted.

"Do you have them, too?" Darlee was looking directly at me.

"Me? Uh, no. Why?"

"You have a necklace like me."

Darlee's comment made me reach for my chest. My medical alert necklace had found its way to the outside of my shirt. While I didn't necessarily hide it, I did usually keep it beneath any garment. There were times when I wondered why I even wore it. After all, any attack I'd ever had, I had been alert enough to speak and inform medical personnel of my allergy. But I had promised my parents I would wear it, and, just like Ryan, I kept my promises.

"Yeah," I admitted to the little girl. "We're twinsies but for different reasons."

I was going to explain further, but one of the doctors approached. "Mr. Thompson, we should be about ready to discharge your son."

"Oh, uh, great. Great." Ryan shook the doctor's hand as he had with every doctor who had joined us that evening. His manners were surely a complete contrast to how Irene must have acted with the dedicated staff.

"Let me go over some things with you … and Joel."

He started toward Joel.

"Why do you wear your necklace?"

"Darlee, they need to talk with their little boy's doctor now. You need to say—"

I interrupted the mom but spoke to Ryan. "Go ahead. I'll be there in a sec."

"Okay." Ryan agreed and did a positive thumbs-up to Darlee.

I didn't end up joining Ryan, the doctor, Joel, and Sallie right away. I thought I was just going to explain to Darlee about my nut allergy, but I ended up talking with the little girl and her single mom about so much more. And it made me appreciate all I had in that little room only feet away. Not only did I have someone by my side to help me through the rough times, but Joel was going to be fine. We were lucky. We needed to count our blessings no matter how frightening and sad things seemed around us.

***

Ryan kept checking the rearview mirror to the backseat as we finally started on our way home later that night. I didn't blame him. I was looking, too. Getting so incredibly close to losing the precious little boy made you want to stare at him all the time. And now in the quieter setting of the car, I think the reality of what happened was truly sinking in for all of us. Well, at least Ryan and me.

"Daddy, I'm hungry," Joel called out.

"Huh?" Ryan looked backward again. "Uh, yeah. I guess you guys haven't had anything to eat. How about we do a drive-thru?"

"Ice cream," was his response.

To which his sister echoed, "Yeah, ice cream."

"Well, okay, ice cream." Ryan chuckled. "But we still need some protein. What do we eat for that?"

"Turkey? Pork?" Sallie suggested.

Ryan looked at me sitting in the Audi's passenger seat

and smiled. He knew I taught the kids so much about food and health. "Yeah, those are good. But what protein do we usually get at a drive-thru? What's the only thing Joel will eat?"

"Tenders! Barbecue," the boy himself called out.

Ryan was pulling up to put in the order. "Sallie? What do you want?"

"I want a burger, please."

"Okay." Ryan announced the kids' choices and turned to me. "You're good here, right?"

"Yes." I would have scoffed more at his overprotectiveness of my allergy issue, but I knew he had too much on his mind, and the love and concern behind his question should have been cherished not berated. "Get me a chicken salad. I might eat it later." I wasn't hungry, but who knew. When he repeated my order and started toward the payment window, I asked, "You're not getting anything?"

"I'll finish Sallie's. She won't eat everything," he replied, but I had a feeling his stressed-out appetite was about as vacant as mine.

***

Between the ice cream and having to sit so long at the hospital, Joel was not at all ready for bed when we got home, despite it being almost that time. He was zooming around the hallway like a hypersonic jet. And it did not impress Ryan ... at all.

"Joel, stop running!" It was already the second request, and with his mom's surgery, the flight, and the harrowing experience with his son, Ryan did not have the patience for a third. "Joel! What did I say?"

"I'm Flash!" He zipped once more.

"You are not a superhero! Damn it, I said stop!"

His voice really escalated, and he actually grasped on to Joel as he attempted to race past. Joel kind of glanced at his dad like it was more of a bother being caught than anything else. Sallie, though, froze and looked at me with her eyes wide. I knew why. Ryan very, very rarely got upset with the kids, and, if so, he certainly didn't swear and hardly raised his voice. They knew if they did wrong without any of those harsher devices—sort of like the Lyric and eating toys incident.

I tried to be the calm one. "Ryan …"

He seemed to ignore me, though … his eyes still fixated on Joel. "No. You understand? You are not invincible. There are reasons why there are rules. You … Dang it, Joel. Go. Go to bed. No electronics."

"Daddy …" he whined.

"Now."

On his father's command, the youngest Thompson burrowed his eyebrows and declared, "You are the meanest daddy ever!" before stomping up the stairs. At least he didn't run.

Joel's stunning reaction made the remaining three of us pause. With the way Ryan's gut seemed to retract, he looked like he had been physically attacked instead of emotionally. Sallie's eyes swung from her brother to her dad. And I had no idea what to say to help any of them.

It wasn't me, though, who made the first attempt at making the situation better—it was Sallie. She took the few steps to Ryan and gave him a hug. "I missed you, Daddy."

Even with him noticeably mad, Sallie needed her father near. She wanted him to know that. She needed him. We all did … even stubborn, active little boys who voiced otherwise.

Ryan held his lips on top of his daughter's head for an extended moment and then managed a smile. "I missed all of you, too. Do you think you can maybe—"

"I'll go to sleep," she answered before he even got a chance to ask the actual question.

"Thanks, sweetie."

After Sallie's more amicable, peaceful retreat up the

stairs, Ryan covered his face with both of his large hands and then ever so slowly dragged them down so only his eyes were showing … and looking at me. His head-nod said it all. The last couple of hours were just too much.

Before I once again tried to find something reassuring to say or do, we both heard Lyric crying. The sound obviously coming from near the patio doors, I realized he hadn't been left out. He was completely off his schedule like the rest of us. And, goodness knew, we didn't need another poo accident.

When Ryan's eyes shut and he slowly shook his head, I offered to at least take care of Lyric. "I'll get him."

"Thanks."

The poor neglected pup did his business outdoors rather quickly, and I petted him for being the one with the most patience in the household. His reward was to be allowed a little more outdoor time to roam and play. But, in reality, it was a reward for me, too. Sitting on the bench, I did some relaxing Yoga breaths, took in the crispness of the late-June air, and watched as the stars seemed to appear as if by magic.

Ryan came out after another minute or two, carrying my salad, a bottle of wine, and two glasses. "Thought you might need some nourishment."

The food and beverage choices were similar to our first date in that same locale, but our moods certainly were not. When he sat next to me, I grabbed for the bottle. "I'll definitely have some of this."

"I'll pour it for you," he offered like the gentleman he always was.

But I simply took it, wiggled out the cork he had already loosened, and tipped the bottle to my lips. After a good gulp accompanied by an appreciative "hmmm" by Ryan, I pointed the bottle in his direction. Taking my lead, he set the salad and two empty glasses on the ground and then took a mighty swig of the sweet red liquid himself.

"Did you talk with him?" There was no additional

reference needed to my question.

"No. I was going with your give-him-a-minute-to-himself strategy." He referenced my suggestion with Sallie a few days before and then took another sip of wine.

"Ah," I acknowledged. "Yeah, good choice. I think you both need a minute ... or two."

"He doesn't get it. He has no regards for what happened ... how it happened ... how he was running ... how he almost ..." He verbally stumbled and couldn't come to say his son almost died. "He doesn't get it."

"No. He's five. He doesn't."

After putting the bottle down, Ryan marched on with his thoughts about what exactly did happen that afternoon and how seconds made such a difference. "How long can you go without air ... minutes, right? I mean, thank God he was in the water less than three and then only seconds without ... But, oh geez, had someone not seen him or had they thought ... Geez. Oh, man. I couldn't. I couldn't live if something happened to him. And what did I just do? I yelled at him. I yelled! I *am* the meanest dad ever."

"Ryan, he didn't really mea—"

"And on top of that, you know what I was thinking the whole time in the taxi ride over? I kept thinking, the last time I saw him in person I was mad about the dog. And if that was the last time ..." And then he started to cry. It was something I rarely witnessed from that strong, positive man, and because of that, he immediately tried to hide it. "Sorry," he said. "I'm sorry."

"What? Why? Don't be sorry." I reached out to touch his hand covering his face.

"You don't need me to be like this." He managed to look at me, while stopping his even more ablaze than usual deep blue eyes from tearing.

"What? As a man who loves his children ... who would do anything for them?"

"I can hold it together. In fact, all good." He pushed out his hands to either side to signify completion.

"Ryan!" I nearly bellowed. "You do *not* need to hold it together all the time—not for me and not for the kids. Yes, you are their hero and they know they can count on you, but they need to see it's okay not to have it all together sometimes." My little monologue had him looking at me as if he was hearing something brand new. "They need to know they have responsibilities to their rooms and animals and rules. They need to see things scare you, and it is all right to be scared … and mad … and sad." I knew Ryan's uncharacteristic temper with Joel had been his fear on display, and his tears with me were when he just couldn't suppress anymore. "I'm afraid they're doing the same … holding feelings in. The princess thing … when Sallie cried? I realized yesterday that it was the first time since Kari passed away that she cried. I know the psychologist said there might be grief bursts." Come to think of it, wasn't that what Ryan basically just did, too?

"Yeah."

"But then she felt bad. She felt bad that she let herself break. That's why she came back and apologized. She didn't want you disappointed with her. She is always trying to make you proud and happy."

"Disappointed?" He was even more taken aback. "Why would I be? I'm so proud of her. She never does anything wrong."

I blew out a gust of air. That was something else I had realized when I thought of Sallie. "Here's the thing—I was Sallie. I still am a little bit. My mom put on this happy face when I was growing up and wanted everything to be normal for me, despite not going to school with the other kids and despite not being able to eat things everyone else could. I thought I was wrong for feeling upset or sad about it because she and my dad weren't."

"But they were," he connected the verbal dots.

"Yeah. I started to figure it out, but then didn't want to make her sad knowing I was sad. Ry, some of the things Sallie is saying makes me think she feels exactly that same way. She's confused on how to feel." I was relaying Sallie's nighttime talk with me, even if it wasn't word for word.

"Oh, man." He covered his eyes again. "How could I have messed this up so bad. I can't fail at this … with them. I can't—"

"No, no, no." I touched his thigh and tried to redirect as he looked at me again. "I'm sorry. I'm probably just projecting my own issues. And I've only had this bottle of wine to eat or drink. All I'm saying is, you all need to not hold things in. They lost their mother. And I know *you* have to have feelings about Kari's death. She was the mother of your children. You loved her at one point."

"Bethany, I—"

"It's okay." I actually didn't want him to deny it. "You wouldn't be the guy I love if you hadn't." He brought his lips together tightly and looked at me with the slightest of accepting nods … and I continued, "And what happened today with Joel? Gosh, Ryan, I … I understand how upset you were." My own eyes let a tear cascade down my face in remembrance. "I was so scared when I found out … and at the hospital. I'm sorry I let you down." And right there was the little girl Sallie still in me.

"What? How? How could you have let me down?" It was his turn to touch me—hand-to-hand.

"Joel. You trusted your two young kids with me and look what happened … under my care. Just like Joel with Lyric." I hadn't even realized I had been thinking that, but out it came, and I knew it was true. I guess I was holding in a little bit, too.

"They were at camp," he said instantly. "And you did everything you were able to do … everything," he reiterated and then sighed. "Kids? They get sick. They get hurt. Every photo of me at that age? I have some kind of bandage or scratch or am completely mud-covered. Just like you see yourself in Sallie?" He did a one-nod, as if to make sure I was listening. "I was Joel—the younger brother trying to do everything everyone else did and shouldn't have been—sometimes my choice and sometimes their dare, by the way." By the ease of how he said his final words, I realized he was not only rationalizing with me, but he was getting calmer and accepting everything himself. "Hey, thank you for being here for me ... for us. It's ... it's all good. We're good."

While those last words seemed like he was still in denial of any bordered-up feelings, I did appreciate his acknowledgment of me. And knowing we very much needed a light moment, I replied with, "Thank *you* for the wine."

How long had it been since we had been able to be our easygoing selves, full of sassy, quick, sarcastic one-liners? It felt like forever. And that seemed wrong.

Ryan straight out laughed, which was also nice to hear. "I missed you something fierce, Lenay. I didn't like you being so far away."

I climbed onto his lap, facing him. "Any better?"

With a final tug so I was that much more intimately close to him, he said, "All except for the damn dog."

I laughed at both Ryan and Lyric—who seemed to be chasing and barking at something in his own imagination. "I think he's going to think that is his name," I teased with a smile. "And you love him."

"Still ... Lyric, hush!" Ryan called out to the dog and then with sweetness to me, "I love you, too."

# CHAPTER ELEVEN

I had been standing there for a good minute or so before Ryan caught my reflection in the extensive master bathroom mirror. He didn't turn. He just slightly raised the left side of his face, which was still covered with shaving cream.

"Hey." When I offered nothing in exchange, he directly questioned my gaze. "Something up?"

"Neh. I like watching you shave," I admitted. I rarely had the opportunity, since on weekdays Ryan was only waking as I was heading to work.

Both sides of his cheeks lifted that time. "Oh, good. Was afraid you were going to complain about counter space or something."

As he finished his last few strokes, I pondered what he said and then softly verbalized my feelings on the matter. "There are imprints of her everywhere around here, huh?"

He stopped rubbing his face and turned to me. To his credit, Ryan didn't try to deny knowing who I was referring to. "Kari?"

"I've never used more than a few inches of the counter." And I had seen Kari's extensive makeup collection spread on the very same space.

"I wasn't talking about her specifically. I meant it as a joke."

"It's okay. I know she's on your mind." Our conversation seemed to be almost directly picking up from the night before. "She should be. She—"

"Bethany, really. I feel *you* here. And …" He sighed. "I've tried to make the house yours."

"I know you have. That new bed over there"—I let my eyes shift toward our bed so many feet away—"was the best housewarming gift I could have ever asked for." And we had christened it well. "I didn't mean that. I'm—"

"So, watching me shave is a turn on, then?" He smirked.

I'm pretty sure every one of his preemptive verbal cut-offs was because he knew I was going to say something about me being concerned about him. But I went with his conversation detour because it was also the sexy truth. "You know I like you clean-shaven."

He closed his eyes and nodded before saying, "I draw the line at my legs, though."

My body bounced at his humor. "Okay. On that note, I'm leaving. I won't be long … just a few things at the grocery store." I tipped up the tiniest of bits to hold his smooth face with my hands and kiss him. "Good luck with Joel."

"Yeah. We'll be fine. I know he didn't really mean what he said last night, and I'm sure he's sorry. We both needed some space and sleep."

While that statement was undoubtedly true, I knew Ryan hadn't really done the latter. Before the two of us had gone to bed the night before, and even once after, Ryan had ventured into his son's room to make sure Joel was still breathing … alive … as if he was a newborn. I wondered how long the trauma of almost losing his son would resonate in Ryan's psyche. And then I thought of my parents. The answer was crystal clear. That kind of scare never goes away.

\*\*\*

I hadn't planned on going there. But it was as if the car was on an autopilot of sorts. After buying the ingredients for Ryan's welcome home dinner—the same ones I had meant to get the day before prior to our world doing a somersault—I found myself in a parking lot about a block or two from the grocery store. While I had never been inside that particular building, its concept was far from unfamiliar.

I made my way up the sidewalk, pulled on the wrought-iron door handle, and slowly walked into the church. I didn't know exactly what to expect. It wasn't my usual place of worship. It was also midmorning on a Saturday. And because the church was nondenominational, I wasn't sure if there were services or anything else that might be going on. My regular church wasn't open on Saturdays, just as my dad's church wasn't. He had office hours during the week and, of course, was there on Sunday mornings.

After a little entryway, I discovered the main chapel. Pews aligned either side of a fairly lengthy aisle, which led to the raised altar area. It reminded me of our church in Carolina. But the one I was standing in was bigger and done in more neutral tones in comparison to ours with stained glass, white wood, and red bricks. There wasn't anyone in the room itself, although all the lights were on. I did a second glance and decided to do what I had intended to in the first place. I sat in one of the pews off to the very left-hand side. After a moment of looking at the altar, I closed my eyes, bowed my head, and tried to allow my mind the luxury of easing into peace.

It was only when I heard a muffled sound, that I lifted my head. Looking around, I saw a few women entering from the back. Having been completely focused on recalling the terrifying moments at the hospital, I hadn't even realized until then that I had been crying. I swiped at my face, knowing in a way I had been doing the same thing I feared Ryan was. I wanted to be strong for the kids and for him because they needed me to be. But I needed a release. The church's steadfast walls were providing me with that. But what would help Ryan? Because, despite his brief letting go the night before, I knew he was still definitely holding back.

I didn't quite make out what the women were saying, but when they spotted me, they stopped. "Sorry." The younger redhead, who was carrying a basket, nodded in my direction. "We didn't know anyone was in here."

"No. No." I stood. "My fault. I don't know what the proper, uh, protocol is here. I wanted a place to think for a couple minutes and saw cars in the parking lot."

"You are welcome to, dear," the older woman told me. "The church isn't normally open, but we're setting up for a wedding this evening."

And then I laughed. It wasn't a soft, breathy one-huff. It was a downright, full-blown laugh, and it burst straight out, as if I was a legitimate crazy loon.

Of course, it was a wedding. And I bet the bride would actually walk up the aisle covered in the crash I saw in the hands of the third woman. And I bet the happy couple would say their vows surrounded by their treasured guests. And most of all, I bet there would be joy and love and forevers.

"Sorry," I apologized, picking up my crossbody purse. "I'll get out of your way."

"Really," the older woman said. "I'm the minister's wife. You're welcomed to stay. You are not in the way at all. If you need to—"

"No. No. Thank you. These few minutes helped. It's a lovely church. Best wishes to the bride and groom." And I made my way back out to the natural lighting of the clear California sky.

The temporary serene setting of the church gave me what I needed in order to release and refocus. It also made me realize that I not only wanted to, but needed to, talk with another minister and his wife. I called my mom and dad via the car speaker once I was on the road. Since I hadn't had a chance to talk with them for a few days or so, I first recounted the harrowing experience we had with Joel. On their own speaker system, my parents both said they would pray and thank God for providing Joel with the help he needed and for sparing his life. I asked if they could also keep Ryan in their prayers.

"Of course," my dad answered. "Is there anything specific, Bethie?"

"There's just so much going on with him." I pulled the car into the garage.

"It's a lot for one person to handle," my mother stated, as I reached up to the visor to hit the remote and shut the garage door. "Goodness, one thing after another."

"Yeah." I sighed my agreeance. "You know, all three of them are grieving but in different ways. And I don't know if Ryan understands what I'm trying to tell him about letting things out."

"Remember, grief is not an event. It is a long, complex process. They have to come to terms with the loss." My dad's voice soared across the speaker.

"I know." I internally recalled some of the thoughts, feelings, and physical issues the psychologist had told us to look for. "I want to help them and not make things worse."

"You cannot make things worse," he replied. "You are you. And that already makes things better. Ryan may or may not be able to react to everything you are saying. But he knows you're there. That's what's important. God has you all in his hands. You know that."

"I do."

"But, Bethany, you need to make sure you are looking after yourself, too," my ever-cautious mom chimed in. "It's beautiful you are thinking of everyone's needs. But don't neglect your own. Be careful. And you know I mean your health—"

"Yes, Mom."

"Don't dismiss what I am saying."

"I'm not. My own needs. Yeah, I know."

"Bethie?"

"I gotta go. I'm here and need to unpack the groceries. Talking helped. Thanks."

It did, and it didn't. The pep talk revitalized me to keep doing what I needed to in order to help the kids and Ryan. But not knowing exactly what that was seemed to be the challenging part.

The sudden, unexpected knock on the driver's car window caused me to jump in my seat. It should have. I had disconnected the call and had been looking at the center dashboard, not seeing anyone approach. When I turned, Ryan was on the other side of the glass pointing for me to open the car door.

After I did so, he immediately asked, "What are you doing? Are you okay?"

"Yeah."

"Bethany, turn the car off."

"Wha—"

"Geez!" He reached across me, pressed the ignition button to turn it off, and then unfastened my seatbelt.

"What's going on?" I asked as he took my hand and got me out of the car.

He walked the few steps to reopen the garage door and then came back to me. "What were you doing?"

"I was talking with my parents on the phone. What's wrong?" I know I had to have had the most perplexed look on my face because that was certainly how I felt.

"Geez, Bethany! My heart practically flipped out of my body. The car was running and you are inside a closed garage," he noted at the last second. "Carbon monoxide just takes a couple minutes. You take it in … you don't even realize it is happening, and you're gone."

Oh, man. I went from talking with a nervous mom on

the phone to an overprotective fiancé in the garage! And then Ryan's words dawned on me. It just takes a couple minutes to die. I got the connection. It was like drowning … or maybe even an overdose.

"I was okay," I tried to reassure. "Ry, really. I right now finished my conversation and was ready to turn the car off. Ryan?" I tried again.

"Sorry. I may have overreacted. Sorry." He brought me into his arms.

"Mmmm," I murmured after a moment of utter peace. "This hug more than makes up for you showing me you love me."

Because that's what it all came down to—wanting to protect and help and heal … wanting that person's hurt to be gone. It's because you love them. But sometimes it isn't as easy as putting a bandage on a scraped-up knee. Sometimes it takes a lot more time and patience and understanding.

\*\*\*

Weekends had always been Kari's time with the kids, unless she was on tour. On top of that, she was expected to have them for extended times during the summer. But all of that had obviously changed. So, Ryan and I made an extra effort to do special activities with the kids on Saturday or Sunday. It wasn't so they would forget Kari. It was so they could see there were happy things in the world, too. The week before, Ryan's parents were in town for pure grandparent fun. But that Sunday, we decided on the zoo.

Once we were on our way, I turned slightly from the passenger seat of Ryan's car to face the kids in the back. "What animal do you want to see the most?"

Sallie started, but Joel hijacked her thought. "I wanna see the wolf!" His little eyes seemed to grow and brighten in anticipation.

"Oh, no!" his sister shrieked as my face scrunched in disgust, too.

Ryan did a slight chuckle and peered quickly into the rearview mirror. "Why, Joe?"

"For Wolverine!" he stated in the "isn't it obvious" kind of way.

Ryan shook his head at his predictable son. "What about you, Sallie?" When she didn't answer immediately, both Ryan and I turned to look at the little girl, who was staring out the window as if in a daydream. "Sals?" Ryan tried again.

"Mommy liked the giraffes. She said they could almost reach the sky. I want to see those."

Ryan looked at me before glancing to the back seat again. "Good choice, Tink. We'll go there first."

Sallie beamed brightly and said, "Then your pick, Daddy."

"I choose the fish," he said confidently.

I literally *tsked* at the man and his fondness of fishing. He had even booked us a side fishing excursion during our not-to-be honeymoon in Hawaii. Although, admittedly, I hadn't complained. After all, the first time I had ever been fishing was with him, and it was one of our most favorite, peaceful, just-Ryan-and-Bethany-alone memories.

"Why don't fish drown?"

Joel's more subdued than usual voice instantly stopped Ryan's smirk at me. In fact, the question stopped almost everything in the car. It wasn't that we didn't know the biological answer. It was because the question and who asked it, obviously, had a much deeper meaning.

"Because they don't run and have shoes on." Sallie seemed to huff.

"Sallie ..." Ryan started but must have realized, as I did, that the little girl was only repeating what she surely had heard a couple times. "It was an accident."

"Was it scary, Joe?" his sister asked him.

Thank goodness Sallie hadn't been directly present at

her brother's pool incident. Riding in the ambulance and being in the hospital was probably traumatic enough for a seven-year-old. But to see her only brother almost die on top of losing her mom? Oh.

"Nope," Joel punctuated.

I looked over at Ryan upon his low grumble. It had been beyond scary for me. And it most certainly had been for Ryan, too. And we hadn't even been witnesses.

"It should have been," Ryan said in a bit of a corrective tone. "You just really don't understand. You're going to be much more careful now, right?" That time it was full-on dad-mode.

"Yeah," Joel agreed, and I was glad Ryan's talk with his adventurous son the day before seemed to bring understanding to the seriousness of the situation.

"Fish have gills," Ryan reverted back to the original question. "That's what lets them breathe under water. We don't have those."

"Joel," I turned around. "You know who a real superhero is? A lifeguard."

"Yeah," he agreed, and Ryan reached over and squeezed my hand in appreciation. "I want to be a lifeguard when I grow up."

The other three of us laughed. Joel seemed to change his mind on what he wanted to be as often as Willow changed outfits in a fashion show. I took a deep breath. Our day had hardly begun. Who knew a casual conversation about animals could bring up so much?

"Hey, Joel, let's sing the zoo song," Sallie suggested, continuing us on a more positive note.

"What zoo song?" His little voice sounded perplexed.

"You know. How's it go? Zoo tomorrow, zoo tomorrow ..." she sang.

"But, it's today! Today!" Joel announced and then they both burst into more of the lyrics. "We're going to the zoo, zoo, zoo, how about you, you, you?" They were pointing to each other and to Ryan and me as they sang.

However, when they didn't know any of the individual versus, the two siblings just started repeating it over and over again until Ryan had enough … and, admittedly, so did I.

"All right. All right," he called out. "How about if I turn on the radio for a little while? We're almost there, anyway."

Without waiting for a response, Ryan did so. And I silently prayed a Kari Thompson tune wouldn't happen to play during the remaining time to the zoo. I wasn't trying to be malicious, and I knew Ryan felt the same way. He purposefully had not been putting the radio on when the kids were in the car because of that fear. It wasn't that hearing Kari's admittedly stunning voice wasn't inevitable and should be heard. It was just because it was too raw yet. We knew Sallie sometimes played her mom's tunes in her room and neither of us was going to deny her. She was actually lucky to have that remembrance. But our zoo trip really didn't need one more mental U-turn. At the same account, I think Ryan was willing to risk it to not have to listen to the zoo song one more time. Judge Ryan was giving that song two thumbs down.

There was some type of commercial on when he first turned on the radio. So, he flipped to another station, and we started listening to a song that was on top of the charts because of its crossover status. It was a unique mix of rap, country, and pop.

"It's gonna take someone mighty to kick that one off the throne," Ryan commented as the song ended and started to fade into the next.

But then *that* song? It sounded familiar … so familiar. It was only the opening notes and not a word was sung yet, but it was very familiar.

"Ryan!"

He took his eyes off the road for the tiniest of seconds to beam proudly at me. I moved in my seat in order to turn toward the radio. It was really happening. The words were starting to be sung.

"Ryan! Oh, my gosh. Oh, my gosh. It's—" I was bouncing as I screamed.

"What's wrong? Daddy, what's wrong with Bethany?" Sallie's concerned voice came from the back seat.

"Nothing. Shhh! This is Bethany's song. It's the first time we've heard it on the radio."

"It's a guy. That's not Bethany!" Joel interjected, as if Ryan had gone crazy.

"Bethany wrote it. A man named Finn is singing it," he corrected.

"Like Mommy sang," Sallie said.

"Yeah. Mommy didn't write her own stuff. Bethany does," Ryan stated and hit the volume up a few notches. "Shhh! Let her enjoy it."

As the kids hushed, it was taking a lot for me not to sing along. After all, I knew the words more intimately than even Finn Murphy did. And even though he had sent me his final recording, I didn't know when I would have the experience of hearing it like the world was. It was my first song ... my first break. And I knew since a few others were sold after that song, I would get more experiences like the one on the way to the zoo. But nothing was going to ever top the emotional feelings exploding inside my body at that moment.

"Oh, my gosh. Oh, my gosh. Oh, my gosh," I murmured over and over again as I continued to bounce in the car.

"Lenay." Ryan lightly chuckled. "Do I need to pull this car over?"

I laughed at his dad comment and tried to stop my movements, as well as my near hyperventilation, as the song came to a close. "I—"

"I liked it," Sallie chimed in from the back seat as Joel pretended to play air guitar.

"Wait, listen to what the DJs are saying." Ryan actually turned the volume up a little further.

I caught the male disc jockey's voice midstream. "That's his latest … just-released single. Sure to be another bona fide Finn Murphy hit."

The female DJ seemed to agree. "Y'all, there's something special about that one, though. The lyrics? They really got to me."

"I think he worked with a different songwriter, maybe?" the other radio personality suggested. "But, anywho, you know what we have to do right now? Right now, what we need is caller number twenty. Be caller twenty into the station and you'll win a pair of tickets to Country Fest next weekend. Good luck."

As the station went to commercial, Ryan turned the radio off completely. "How do you feel?" he asked me.

"Excited … nervous … in shock," I admitted. "Like maybe you really should pull the car over because I am going to pee my pants."

"Gross!" Joel screeched.

"She's not really going to, Joel!" Sallie vehemently denied but then added, "Are you?"

"No." I laughed. "No."

"You *should* be excited, especially with the comments after. People will be searching online to find out who wrote it." Ryan rubbed my leg.

"That's the part that makes me nervous." I felt a cringe ripple through my body.

"Good," he surprisingly agreed, and I looked over at his sweet but serious face. "Don't lose that. Remember what this feels like. Keep loving it for the reasons you do—the magic … the power of how you put words together with music."

"I don't care if anyone searches me. *I* know. I know those are my words. And I know it has made people happy. That's exactly how I want it."

Ryan actually did pull the car over to the side of the road. The kids started asking if we were at the zoo. But we weren't. We were in the park and nearly there but not actually. I guess Ryan couldn't wait, though. He leaned in my direction, put both hands on my cheeks, and kissed me so dang sweetly.

I looked into his sparkling eyes and then back to the kids, who were used to us smooching but maybe not that dramatically. The weekend was seeming to turn around. One step ... one day ... one surprise song on the radio ... at a time. That was all we could hope for.

# CHAPTER TWELVE

Ryan got home from work later than usual that Monday. Since he had taken off most of our "honeymoon" week and also for the impromptu trip to Iowa, he had a lot of catching up to do. Plus, he had a catered dinner meeting.

He found me in the kitchen, where I was finishing making a lasagna for our dinner the following day. "Hi," he cooed, wrapping his arms around me from behind.

Before I could echo, I noticed the small box in his open hand. "Ryan, what is that?"

"Come on, you know by now."

I turned around so we were face-to-face but still very close. When he officially presented me with the box, I said. "There isn't a special occasion."

"Oh, yes, there was."

"Wha—"

"Open it up, Lenay."

I smiled softly and opened the box. I loved getting his special charms for my rapidly growing bracelet, and I think he enjoyed picking them out almost as much. A tiny silver and blue radio lay flush on the cotton inside the box. It was perfect—just like the key representing the house, the heart for our love, the ring for our engagement, the guitar for our meeting, and the original Napa wine bottle.

"First song on the radio," I acknowledged. "How'd you get it so fast?"

"Had it ready and on standby in the desk at my office."

I slightly shook my head before kissing him. "I love you."

"I love you, too." He smiled. "So, what's going on here? Everything at camp go okay?"

"Yeah. I thanked Hazel for everything on Friday. I guess you did, too, when you dropped the kids off this morning."

"Uh-huh." He opened up the refrigerator door, seeing I wanted to slide the lasagna in. "Did she tell you—"

"That you put my name on the emergency cards?" Food mission accomplished, I closed the fridge door. "Yeah. Thanks, Ry. I felt so helpless when everything happened."

He kissed me again. "I got rid of Irene, too."

"What?"

"Yeah, Maks is the third contact. Enough of her bull."

I couldn't blame him. For as much as Irene supposedly cared, neither she nor Ed had tried to contact Ryan all weekend to double-check on Joel. Of course, she knew before leaving the hospital that her grandson was okay. But if it were me, I would have followed up or at least tried to. Being dismissed by Ryan the way she had, though, surely riled Irene's stubborn feathers up.

"Come on." I took his hand. "Something else came up, and I need to show you."

"Awww, really? On a scale of beer to wine to hard liquor, how bad?"

"Water's not even an option anymore, huh?" I joked.

"No." He sighed. "It doesn't seem to be."

We walked into the living room, and I pulled up the information on my tablet. I wanted Ryan to be able to see it on a large, clear screen. And while I could have forwarded it to him while he had been at work, I knew it was something we should discuss in person.

"Oh," he practically whispered after reading it.

"Yeah. I overheard one of the moms—I think it was someone in Sallie's class—talking to Hazel about it at camp today. It sounds like a lot of kids are going. You didn't know anything about it?"

"No." He stared at the screen again, as if he didn't believe it the first time.

"I mentioned it to Rebecca. She texted the principal. They're in some group or something together."

"Uh-huh." I'm sure Ryan wasn't interested in the social dynamic of the situation but rather if our next-door neighbor would have the connections to fix the latest Thompson dilemma.

"The principal told Rebecca that Kari signed the kids up for it."

Ryan reached his hands to the back of his neck and cracked. "Do the kids know about it?"

"I don't know. They haven't mentioned it, right? So, either they forgot, or Kari never said anything. I'm sure it was right before she … she died." It was even hard for *me* to say those words. "But it's this Thursday."

"Is it only moms? No dads?" He was asking the same questions I had.

"No dads. Your reading festival date is later in the summer. This one is just for moms. Or, if not … a grandma."

"Oh, heeeeck no." His face practically jerked up in disgust. "The thought of Irene—"

"I know." I paused for the slightest of seconds and then asked what I had been tossing around in my mind since shortly after I found out. "Ry? I don't know if they'll let me or if you would want me to, but *I* could do it with Sallie and Joel."

I wasn't their mom or grandma or aunt or even stepmom. That had been well documented at the hospital and by Irene herself. And I knew no matter what outcome would be decided, a mommy-and-me afternoon at school to promote summertime reading would surely stir up emotions. But seeing my fiancé's face instantly relax into a warm, serene smile, helped.

"Even if they don't know now," I continued. "I think they're going to find out when all their friends go and talk about it. I don't want them to feel different. I want them to feel loved. I can leave work a little early, pick them up, and go to the school together. I just didn't know how you wanted to handle it. Or, if it is even the right thing to do. And I didn't want to step on anyone's toes."

"You are not stepping on anyone's toes," he said vehemently. "You are a—"

"Daddy!" Joel entered the room in typical Joel style— with lightning speed and excessive energy.

"Hey ... hey ... hey ... hold on a minute." Ryan put his hand out. "I'm talking with Bethany. At least say, 'excuse me.'"

"Excuse me," he obediently replied, standing in front of the two of us.

"All right." Ryan looked at me and then gave in to his son, knowing our conversation had to be put on hold. "What's going on?" But when the five-year-old shrugged and almost comically scrunched the one side of his face, Ryan shook his head. "You don't remember?"

"I came to see you."

"Oh, okay." Ryan ruffled Joel's moppy hair that needed a cut. "How was your day?"

"Good," he answered simply.

"Always good," Ryan replied.

I wondered if he realized the kids had already learned how to respond to that question like adults—a generic "good," which was not always the truth. And what *was* good for the Thompson kids? Would their world ever truly be good again?

To further add to my analysis, Ryan acknowledged the

quieter—by far—of his children, who had snuck in behind her brother. "Hey, Tink."

Sallie, who was standing a little off to the side, walked up and adhered to her father. "Hi, Daddy."

It was her turn to be thankful that Ryan had returned once again. It was the little things that showed vulnerability and fear and loss. It was the unspoken things.

"Where are the Radcliffe rugrats?" Ryan asked as he released his hold from Sallie.

"What's a rugrat?"

"It—" Ryan started to answer his son only to be interrupted by him.

"Like the cartoon?"

"No. Well, yeah." An exasperated Ryan decided to drop it. "Nothing, Joel."

"They're in the family room." Sallie spoke of our next-door neighbor's two children, similarly aged as Sallie and Joel.

"Rebecca and Kingston said they should be back around nineish," I added.

"Who knew they were such Trekkie fans to celebrate their anniversary with a satire cabaret?" As Ryan shook his head, I wondered when our new anniversary date was actually going to be and what we would do—it seemed so out of reach right then with everything happening nonstop. "Come on, kiddos. You're not being very good hosts. Let's all go to the family room." Ryan touched my hand and whispered, "I'll talk with their school if you're sure."

"Yeah." I nodded but then made a request. "Can you deal with the kids right now for a little bit?"

"Huh? Sure. Why? What's up? Kids, go ahead. I'll meet you in the family room."

As Sallie and Joel scuttled off—secure once again—I answered Ryan, "I want to go for a run."

Ryan's eyebrows shot up in clear surprise and amusement. "You're gonna run?"

I admitted to a more realistic version, since I had never tried running as a sport or any form of exercise before. In fact, the most I did was walking, some light weights, and Yoga. "Jog ... try ... whatever. Just around the neighborhood. I'll take Lyric. He already needs out with the overstimulation of now four kids."

"Yeah, don't know how my parents did it. Two are already enough to manage."

"Right?" I gave credence to his thoughts. "All right," I continued. "Need that jog. Having this dream kitchen at my disposal all the time is threatening to add miles to my hips. And I don't want you teasing me when I'm in my thirties," I recalled the comment he made to me at his brother's winery, which was my first indication he truly saw us in for the relationship long haul.

"But I like teasing you." He smirked.

"Right back at you." Before I went upstairs to change into suitable running gear, I smiled and said, "'Tennessee Whiskey.'"

"Huh?" He had yet to move.

"Not about what kind of drink level the school news was. It's what song I'm feeling right now."

His smile was as smooth, sweet, and warm as the lyrics I was referring to. "You win," he admitted. "Much better than what I was literarily humming in my head."

"What?"

"It's just another manic Monday."

I laughed. "But equally as true."

*** 

It felt nerve-wracking—like every neighbor was watching me, although few were out. It felt exhilarating listening to the tunes invade my ears as my feet pounded the pavement. It felt exhausting. It felt good. It felt torturous. It felt like a breath of fresh air.

Running felt like all of those things. And even though I

legitimately might have put on a pound or two, the real reason I wanted to explore the outdoors was that I needed a short Bethany escape. I needed a chance to be by myself—and my furry frisky friend—to relax, think, and release my thoughts.

The summer reading event was the latest in the domino effect of how Kari's death changed everything. I knew offering to take Sallie and Joel was the right thing to do. But it *was* another stress. It was something that should have been an easy and fun event for the kids to attend but was now riddled with possible sadness and isolation. Because of my allergy, I knew how it felt to be different from your peers, and that was the last thing I wanted for Ryan's kids. I hoped the decision for me to attend would be the opposite ... but one never knew.

I felt better after my experimental run ... at least mentally. But, physically? First of all, I was a sweaty mess. And, second, as I climbed the steps to the master bedroom, I could already tell there would be residual pain the following day from using muscles that were infrequently tested. I gingerly sat on the edge of the corner chair to take off my shoes and socks. Lyric, who had followed me upstairs, decided to then exit. He was my little protector. And after seeing I was safe, he most likely needed to rehydrate himself via his water bowl in the kitchen. So, I continued on with my mission.

"Second thoughts?" Ryan's voice made me look up to see him standing a couple of feet away. The confusion must have shown on my face, since he followed up with a clarification. "Your ring ... you're staring and fiddling with it." He crouched in front of me, and I stopped looking at my engagement ring. "I know this isn't what you signed up for. Not being married, attending reading programs, having the kids all the time. We didn't—"

"Ha. Well, no. But then nobody knows what they're signing up for in life." I went a little philosophical, thinking he hadn't signed up for any of it, either, but it didn't matter or deter him. I needed him to realize it went for me, too. "Yeah, I'm so okay with it. Promise." I leaned over and kissed him.

While I didn't necessarily think he was legitimately concerned that I was second-guessing our engagement, I could tell my reassurance helped by the look on his face and his next words. "Then your new hobby"—he looked purposefully at my now discarded shoes—"won't be for running away."

"Oh, geez no. Believe me, I'll be lucky if I am even walking tomorrow."

"So, running is a little different than all the walking you used to like doing?" he teased.

"Uh … yeah," I recalled my pre-car days.

He nodded toward my left hand. "What's up with the ring then? Are you sure you like it? I can totally get a—"

"Stop it. You are not. I told you I love this ring and where you got it from. Besides, no one is getting it off me. My darn fingers swelled in the heat of running. That's why I was fiddling with it. I can't get it off to go in the shower."

I shook my head and looked at my finger again. There was a part of the engagement ring story I had always wondered about but never brought up. Honestly, I was a little afraid that asking might taint the tale. But *not* asking was almost like there was something between us, and we were much too close and honest of people for that to occur. *And* the topic had pretty much presented itself.

"Ry, why didn't you give Kari this ring when you proposed to her?"

"It wasn't offered to me, for one thing," he answered immediately.

The engagement ring had been Ryan's mom's mom's, and she had passed away before he and Kari were engaged. And her husband—Ryan's grandfather—had died before her. So, Ryan's mom, as an only child, had it in her possession. Why didn't Mrs. Thompson offer the ring to her son when he was going to marry the woman he loved back then?

"And, Kari? Yeah, uh … even if mom would have given me the ring, I wouldn't have." I tilted my head in question, and he continued, "Kari, well, she wasn't subtle."

"No kidding."

He verbally ignored my sarcasm, but the slightest of smiles crept on his face, nonetheless. "Anytime we were near a jewelry store, she made sure to let me know what she liked. It wasn't my taste. It wasn't a classic, graceful beauty like you … I mean the ring." He glanced at my gold band with simple yet significant-in-size cushion-cut diamond. "But she was the one who was going to wear it. Affording what she wanted was a little out of my league at that time, but with a little compromise, I was able to get something she liked and it didn't totally bankrupt me."

"And you don't think that was a sign the two of you weren't the best match?"

"You would have thought." He shook his head. "When she upgraded it a few years later and didn't tell me, that should have been the bigger sign. She changed. So much changed … so, so much … both without noticing and in the blink of an eye."

Having seen her upgraded ring when she and Ryan were "still married," I knew it had bordered on ostentatious. Ryan had told me plenty of times about how much had changed since he and Kari had gotten together and were first married … and how that was the initial breakdown of their relationship. And I knew that mental scar wasn't buried too far under the surface.

"So, what were you first thinking of when you were considering a ring for me?" I decided on a more positive twist to our conversation. "Just you asking and knowing we were going to be together … I didn't even need a ring." My heart seemed to be beating slower because it was finally regulating from the run but, at the same time, beating faster thinking of our love.

"That's what made it difficult. There was nothing as perfect as you."

"Please," I scoffed.

He ignored my denial. "And then my mom offered."

"She didn't even really know me." That was the part I didn't get.

"But she knew how much I loved you, and so she loved you because of how happy you make me."

I mentally shoved the Kari comparison aside. I did too much of that. It was my pointless, silly insecurity. I needed to let it go and realize there really wasn't—or shouldn't be—any comparing. We really were two completely different people. And I inexplicitly trusted my love for Ryan and his love for me.

So, I said just that. "I love you so much." And then I tagged on something *his* little insecurities might have needed. "And I love my ring. And, you know, I even love this hot mess of a life we are living right now." As I concluded my statement, I lowered my body onto the floor and kissed him.

"I love you, too, Lenay, but, good grief, I'll love you more if you get a shower."

I proceeded to smother my body right on top of his, landing us both flat on the ground. As if he were the kids, a couple mocking "ewwws" escaped from his mouth. But they were quickly replaced by a few loving kisses. I would then shower, and he would go back to the collective group of kids, and our crazy life would continue. But for as much I had needed my Bethany-break, I was also equally glad we had those few minutes of Ryan-and-Bethany time.

\*\*\*

"Hey, everything all right?" Ryan answered my call the next day in a way that made me think he was flashing back to the call I made to him when he arrived at the airport.

"Yeah," I reassured while sitting on the bench behind

the coffee shop—the perfect, sunny, secluded spot for my work break.

"Good. Good. What's up?"

"I wanted to run something by you. You have a minute?"

"I'll make it happen." I smiled at his answer. Ryan was just that guy—he had his priorities straight. "For you, even two."

"Thanks."

"Hey, but before you do … I talked—well, messaged—with the school. They put you on with Joel and Sallie for the reading gig and said there's no signage or anything with 'mom' written on it. It's really casual. I mean, they're not even usually open in the summer."

"Oh, good. That should help."

"Yeah. All right. Your turn. Go." He definitely sounded in his work mode.

So, I dove right in. "I was thinking about everything that happened … with Joel." I realized I needed to clarify because, goodness, so much had happened in only a few weeks, never mind our entire relationship.

"Yeah." His response sounded part question but mostly reflective.

"Remember when you asked me if the kids realize the privileges they have?" I couldn't help but think of the one we had just spoken about—a small, private, exclusive primary school. "I think they do, but in a good way. It doesn't hurt for them to be a part of helping others, though."

"No. Sure. Absolutely."

"I thought of a way we can thank the hospital for helping Joel the other day and for what they do for so many kids. But there are a lot of factors and people who would need to be involved and probably a little upstart money."

"Great. I wanted to find a way for Joel to pay back Lyric's bill. We'll break into his piggy bank," he jested.

When I *tsked* at him, he made another offer. "No? Then, you better start writing another song."

"Ryan!"

"Bethany, really, you know I'll help if it means something for the hospital. I told you I wanted to do something to thank them."

"I know. That's what got me thinking. But you still might want to squash the idea."

"I don't even know what it is in order to squash it. You have to tell me first."

"Okay, I'm getting there." I was suddenly a little nervous about bringing it up, and, at first, I couldn't figure out why. Then I realized it was because it was really the first time I was truly stepping out with my own platform of sorts as Ryan's pseudo-wife. Sure, we had been to social events and were recognized as a couple. But what I had in mind was different—it felt and meant something different. I had never truly been in that role, and I wasn't sure what to make out of it or, for that matter, what Ryan's feelings would be.

"Lenay?"

"Sorry."

"Time is money. Your two minutes are almost up."

"Ryan!"

"I'm kidding. Come on, tell me about your idea and why I might squash it."

"Having a fundraiser," I started, only to be cut off by his light moan. "Not a stuffy suit and tie thing," I amended right away at his deflated response. "Something where we invite kids and their families and have the animal shelter bring some critters to play with. It would potentially help the animal shelter by sparking some interest for those who are looking for a pet. And the ticket price would raise money for the hospital. It's a dual purpose. There shouldn't be much of a startup cost or whatever. I'm sure I could get Gracie to donate coffee and pastries from the shop."

"Okay. It's sounding better. What exactly am I going to squash?"

"Well, it will work better—launch better—if I personalize it. And I know you don't want the kids exposed."

That time, I could legitimately hear the hesitation in his voice. "Exposed how exactly?"

"I really don't know how to go about organizing something like this or really getting the right people interested. But using Joel's story—putting it out there on social media—I am pretty sure would touch people's hearts and make them want to be a part of it. And then I could see if other families who have kids at the hospital would like to share, too. Maybe like Darlee. But I completely understand if you don't want … if you don't want me to do any of this. Maybe you simply want Joel to write a thank-you card."

I heard his breath and couldn't quite navigate how to interpret it. His equally as elusive response wasn't any more help. "All right. Let me think about it. I really do gotta go, though. Can we talk about it later?"

"Yeah. Yeah. Sure. I know you're busy."

"All the time." He sighed.

"Go ahead. I love you."

"For real." His words warmed my heart as I hung up the phone.

I sat for a few more minutes in the midmorning sun and thought about my grand plan. It really had just come to me during the opening hours of my shift. And I know I had presented it to him in a similarly disorganized manner as I had dreamed it up. Sitting there rethinking it through, I realized it probably wasn't feasible at all. Besides making sure the animal shelter and hospital were on board, I didn't know the first thing about organizing something of that caliber. Our wedding was even easier to plan—and, well, look what happened with that. Gathering strangers and asking them to donate a significant amount of money to make the purpose worthwhile? Who did I think I was? Ella was good at that stuff and … Kari. Kari would have been able to do it with a snap of her fingers. Ugh! After sulking a little over my own inferiority, I made my way back inside to caffeinated central, a little less lighthearted.

\*\*\*

Ryan rarely found his way to the coffee shop, but if he did, it was a surprise. That was the case a couple hours later. Instead of ordering his cinnamon Americano, though, he walked with purpose right over to my end of the counter.

"Hi," I acknowledged with a tilt of my head.

"Hi," he echoed.

I passed the iced caramel coffee over to the waiting customer and added the final touches to the next espresso. "Give me a sec.?"

"Yep." He walked toward the wall at the end of the counter, which housed upcoming events and led to our back room.

When Gracie nodded and smiled in my direction, I knew I could take a few minutes to legitimately talk with Ryan without beans and milk and syrups in between us. "Hey, you want to go outside or—" I started saying on my approach.

"You have the most generous heart of anyone I have ever known." His deep blue eyes could not have been more focused on me.

"And it belongs completely to you," I answered the compliment, not really understanding why I deserved it or what exactly prompted the words or his unexpected appearance. When he flanked his hands on my cheeks and kissed me, I smirked. "I remember a time when we couldn't do that in here. We had to hide in your car."

He shook his head as if he was clearing the demons of our past hidden relationship. "So, so wrong."

I instantly felt bad for bringing up something that no longer had any relevance on our current situation, especially when he had greeted me with beautiful words and an equivalent kiss. "I'm s—"

"You okay with having someone perform at this fundraiser shindig, too?"

"Huh?" I tried to catch up to his question.

"I'm getting one of our up-and-comers to perform. Kid-friendly, of course."

"Yeah?" I pierced my eyes at him. "You're good with it?"

"I talked with the hospital and the animal shelter. They are completely on board and grateful."

"Ryan …"

I hadn't even been sure if he thought any part of my idea was doable, and there he went and orchestrated most of it already. Of course he had done it that quickly. He had the connections. It really wasn't his money the project needed. It was his influence.

"I got some contact names and numbers for you to coordinate a date. But a little while off, okay? You need time to get the word out and, uh, to be honest, I'm not really in the social mood. But we'll find a way to tell Joel's story. It's important on a lot of levels. And, you know, a thank-you card from both of the kids with the final check is a must."

I managed to close my gaping mouth at his revelation before saying, "I didn't mean for you to do all of that."

"I know you didn't. But it's a great idea and, again, only one you would think of. Can I have my coffee now, with maybe an extra shot? I think I'm gonna need to work at a little quicker pace. I somehow managed to get roped into a side project and am behind."

"You better look in the mirror when you are considering generous hearts, Ryan."

"Don't let that get out. It would kill my Mr. Mean reputation."

I shook my head, kissed him quickly, and went back behind the counter. I added an extra touch of cream to the top of his coffee so I could make heart art. He smiled at my creation before securing the lid and making his way out the door.

# CHAPTER THIRTEEN

Ryan texted me so many times during the reading event, I teasingly told him he should have come in drag if he wanted to know about it so much. I got a hysterical *Mrs. Doubtfire* GIF in return, but he did slow down his correspondence. It did go remarkably well, though. There were enough activities to keep the kids, for the most part, occupied and not concerned about who showed up and what their relationship was. Of course, there were children calling out for mommies, and while Sallie and Joel looked up on occasion, they remained focused on reading with me. The other women were all respectful to what the Thompson children were going through. They either completely gave us our space or talked about anything but Kari. The buzz, actually, was more about Joel's water tumble the week before. Thankfully, they had found out from their own kid-witnesses—not any kind of press. Both the camp and hospital had strict policies when it came to their clients. And even though Ryan and I had talked more in-depth about how to have Joel's story be one of the launching boards of the fundraiser, we had yet to actually post it.

With just enough time for a quick kiss and passing off

kid-duty, Ryan got home from work a little earlier than usual so I could set off for my local songwriters group meeting. Held once a month in a community center basement, the meetings were casual for the most part. There was a topic of discussion, time to showcase what we were working on in order to get similar-minded feedback, sharing successes or events, and dinner delivery in between. I had joined the group before *Singer Spotlight* and, therefore, of course, before meeting Ryan. And I was grateful that once I got my fleeting opportunity on the television show and my relationship with Ryan was revealed, no one treated me any differently. And, by that, I mean, tried to use me as a connection to him. Because the fact was, we all were in the same boat. Every one of us still had to find the right words and the right music to even get looked at.

The news about the song I wrote for Finn Murphy being released definitely found its way to our songwriting group. There were others who had some success in the past. But at that meeting, it was my turn to shine. And even though it was a bit overwhelming and embarrassing to a shy, modest person like me, I needed it. I needed a little lighthearted, feel-good pouring of congrats. The song was, indeed, getting a lot of social media buzz and airplay. And the singer himself reached out to congratulate me, which I thought was incredibly kind, considering, without his name tied to it, there would be nothing to even discuss. It also motivated me to work on new songs. With things having been so hectic and stressful, creative writing and music were pretty much squelched where I was concerned. But maybe I was ready to actually write about some of it. So, once my peer songwriters left, I stayed a little longer to write in the solitude of the center's basement.

When I returned home, it was around nine-thirty. The house had the unique stillness of sleeping children. I found Ryan in bed, too, but he wasn't asleep. His sidelight was still on, and he was doing something on his tablet.

"Hey," I met him with a kiss as I sat on his side of the bed.

"Hey, yourself." He dutifully put the tablet aside. "How was your meeting?"

"Great." I smiled, feeling every truth in my word.

"Good."

"What did you three do? Did the kids tucker you out, old man ... already in bed?"

"Pretty much." He laughed but also agreed. "We were all wiped. Just waiting up for you."

"Thanks." I stood to walk toward the master bath with accompanying walk-in closet. "It was a busy day. Did they say they liked the school reading thing?" I started shedding myself out of my jeans and putting on some sleeping attire.

"They did. Thanks for doing that. I know it couldn't have been easy."

"You are very welcome, Mrs. Doubtfire," I teased. After brushing my teeth, I reentered the main bedroom, stretched out alongside him, and threaded my leg through the middle of his two. "So, you gonna tell me? How was your evening? What did you guys end up eating?"

"You think we would starve without you?" His smile told me he was joking.

"Maybe," I teased back.

"Thank goodness for takeout." He chuckled.

"Really?" I don't know why I was surprised—on our first date, Ryan had ordered out. "Takeout or delivery?"

"Takeout. They wanted the place where Kari would always order from—Thai Temple—and they don't deliver."

"Hmmm." I had to admit, Thai was a favorite cuisine of mine, especially if I could find a nut-free friendly establishment. It was one thing Kari and I had actually had in common. "Do I get any leftovers?" I decided to stick with the food part of his statement.

"Yes." He smiled and touched my nose, knowing me so well. "I may have gotten you some pad thai and eggplant."

"Mmmm," the foodie in me pleasantly moaned. I swear my mouth instantly salivated, despite having had pizza at the meeting.

Lightly laughing, Ryan teased, "I think maybe we *should* have had you do jingle writing for those eateries when they offered that very first time I tweeted you. You really would know the target audience."

"Ha! Ha!" I sat up to sit pretzel-style next to him. I wanted to get back to the underlying part of Sallie and Joel's dinner choice. "So, the restaurant Kari really liked. There was a reason why they picked it today, huh?" When he sat up straighter to meet me more equally, I continued, "There weren't any outwardly Kari comments at the school today, but I know the kids felt it ... being there ... with me."

"Yeah," he admitted. "Yeah. I think so. They didn't say anything about it directly to me at first either. But the Thai place is right next to where she lived. When we got there, they wanted to know who lived there now." On my piqued look, Ryan replayed the answer he told the kids. "All I know is that it was cleared out. So, Joel asked what happened to all her things that were in there."

I could feel the topic turning a little more serious and could only imagine what it would have been like for him with Sallie and Joel. "And? What did you tell them?"

"We talked about how most of it will be theirs when they get older and might appreciate them more."

I actually started to tear up a little. Once we had gotten past his bar encounter with Olsen, Ryan and I had talked about what he and Maks were going to do with Kari's things. So, it wasn't like I didn't know. It was picturing Sallie and Joel's faces listening to Ryan and understanding even more so how much they had lost. And, yes, how much Kari was losing out on, too. Not the silverware, jewelry, or artwork, but how she was not going to have the chance to watch her babies grow and thrive—to see Sallie giving up the training wheels on her bike, or Joel playing on the T-ball team, or graduations, or falling in love themselves. She wouldn't get to see them becoming their own spectacular people.

"Lenay ..." He obviously noticed my sentiment.

"Sorry." I tried to laugh it off. "Me getting teary-eyed over Kari. Well, that's a new one." I dabbed my eyes dry and continued. "What else did you talk about?"

He rubbed my hand. "I explained that Maks has everything in storage. I told Sallie we could see about maybe a piece of jewelry for special occasions or a little perfume."

"And Joel?"

"He wanted to know where their things were—their own personal stuff ... the things they had at her place for when they stayed there. Joel wanted his Captain America figure and his pillow."

"His pillow. Hmmm. Did you give them that stuff?"

I knew Ryan had them. He had personally brought those back and didn't have Maks put them in storage. He just hadn't known when or how to proceed with the subject. But I guess it wasn't really up to him. The kids dictated when.

"I did."

"Wow. You had a night, didn't you? Sorry I wasn't here."

"You were doing something good for you." He gave me a soft smile I knew was heartfelt. "You needed and deserved that. You do so much for all of us all the time." He didn't realize it, of course, but his words reminded me of my mother's. "So, no," he continued, "I hadn't expected to get into any of that today. I thought we were going to have a totally relaxing night. But, you know, it worked out okay. It was time, and they seemed all right with it and, really, it gave them a—I don't know—a better understanding of everything. They weren't ever going back to Kari's. All of their things are here in this house with us."

"Hmmm … yeah. How are you?"

"Me?" His eyebrows rose in shock of my query.

"You. That was an emotional couple of hours."

"Uh … well … yeah, I guess. I guess I'm relieved." It was like he only gave himself permission to consider his own feelings since I asked. "A little at peace since they seemed to be." And those words brought *me* peace. "And," He let out a small chuckle. "exhausted!"

"You *are* an old man!"

"What!" He reached over and started tickling the white fabric covering my ribcage. "Take it back!"

"Uh-uh." I squirmed at his touch.

"Take it back, Lenay!" He might have been laughing even more than me.

"Uh-uh. Old. Old. Old," I punctuated.

"Daddy?"

Ryan's whole body seemed to sigh. Mine just relaxed. And we both stopped laughing. No more tickling or teasing.

But, really, after the day and night the fair-haired Thompson siblings had, it was no surprise it was going to be one of Joel's nights to call out. Ryan leaned his head back, took a second, and started to slightly move his legs as if he was going to get out of bed. I put a hand on his arm, though.

"Let me," I offered. When he looked at me as if an internal debate was going on in his mind, I spoke again, "You know, I can take a turn every so often."

I couldn't help but wonder if we were mimicking what parents of newborns did. The infant wakes in the middle of the night and whose turn was it? Did they play rock-paper-scissors? Or—I laughed internally at my sudden thought—do they flip a coin?

I thought about asking Ryan for our special quarter, but I didn't want to risk losing. So, I pecked him on the lips. "Go to sleep, Ry. I deserved a night out. You deserve a night staying put."

"You sure?" The way those two little words came out, I knew he was appreciative but would have gone to his son, anyway.

"Yep. Besides, afterward, I might want to get a little taste of that pad thai. You're the best, Ryan."

"Food ... that's all it takes," he teased, shaking his head and smiling.

"Thinking of me is all it takes," I rephrased most correctly.

And he answered in his true, sweet Ryan way. "Like I said ... all the time, Lenay. All the time."

"Daddy?"

"Okay. Love you. Get some sleep." I touched his lips before kissing them, crawled out of bed, turned off his light, and went to check on the one who should have been sleeping, too.

***

Ryan decided to hold a family meeting the next day. We needed to devise a strategy for Joel's sleeping issues. Because if either the fighting off going to sleep or nighttime callouts continued, all of us were going to have to invest in continuous intravenous caffeine drips.

"All right, Joe, we have to come up with a game plan here," Ryan started the discussion off.

"I pick Twister," Joel announced and would have bounced to the game closet had Ryan not stopped and corrected him.

"Not that kind of game." He looked at me and then back at his son. "We need you to try your best to sleep, okay? Meaning ... going to sleep at bedtime with no arguing, and if you wake up, maybe trying something like counting sheep or—"

"We don't have any sheep." His little curled-in eyebrows and the exclamation in his voice was priceless.

But Sallie's was classic. "Joel!"

"Not real sheep." Ryan was being patient, which I internally applauded him for. "It is pretend. Count whatever you want. Let's say you count those funny creatures that are in your video game. You pretend in your mind to see them and start counting—silently," he added, "until you just can't anymore, and it will put you to sleep."

"I'm a good counter," he boasted with pride.

"I know. See?" Ryan's lips raised to meet his cheeks— the plan seemed plausible. "It's perfect for you. We can't keep going on like this. You need your sleep."

"What do I get if I do it?"

"What do you get?" Ryan's voice sounded as taken aback as his head went.

"Yeah."

Ryan rolled his eyes at his son's confirmation. He wasn't one for bribing his kids. But I could see by the way his shoulders drooped slightly that his reservation was switching to resolve. The traumatic loss those little ones had been through and almost losing Joel himself, I am sure had a little something to do with that.

"I don't know. What are you thinking?" he carefully questioned.

"A puppy!" Joel hugged Lyric, who was sitting right beside him.

Ryan's exasperating release of breath was put to an abrupt halt when Sallie rejoined the conversation, desiring her fair share. "I want a phone."

"We already talked about that … no."

"Then makeup."

"What?" Ryan shook his head.

"Yeah, like Willow did for me." Sallie looked at me like I was going to be her backup since Willow was my friend.

"What! No! No, makeup," Ryan exclaimed.

"I sleep good," she whined.

"That's great. Thank you," he acknowledged his daughter.

"She wants it for her boyfriend."

"Her what?" an astonished Ryan started to question his son.

But as Joel started saying the young lad's name, Sallie practically tackled him. "Joel, he is not my boyfriend!"

"You always play with him." Joel's smile was full brotherly sneer.

"Uh … who …?"

Poor Ryan. The Thompson children were definitely getting the lead in what should have been a very simple agreement. In his job, Ryan was used to tough negotiations but was always prepared. Those two were throwing things at him without any prior knowledge.

"It's okay for girls to have boys who are friends," I jumped in, hopefully to aide Ryan and Sallie. "My best friend is a boy. And we play together."

When I winked at Ryan, Joel called out, "You mean Daddy!"

The soft smile on Ryan's face momentarily dissolved his exasperated expression. "Okay, okay, let's please get back to what we are talking about." The children sat a little more still as Ryan continued. "First of all, I don't think you should get anything—either of you—for doing something that is expected. But another puppy is out of the question."

Ryan looked at me, knowingly. We had talked about how the fundraiser would, no doubt, spur another pet request from the kids. We didn't expect it before then, though.

"Why?" Joel partially whined.

"Because, I don't think I have to explain, but adopting a dog is a huge responsibility." Ryan tilted his head Joel's way. "And what happens if you don't live up to your end of our deal?"

"I will," the youngest Thompson begged.

"You can't guarantee that," Ryan challenged, and I knew he was refraining from mentioning Lyric's health scare in order to stay focused.

"Then we give the puppy back. We only adopted him."

That time when I stepped into the conversation, I didn't do it with as much levity. "Joel, do you know what adopting means?" Before the dog-lover could respond, I continued, "Adopting means they are a part of your family forever. They are in your heart. They are yours to care for. There are no givebacks. It means a lot. It's a big deal and a wonderful thing."

Ryan seemed to be listening as much as the kids to my little soliloquy. When I finished, he reiterated in his TV judge voice, "It's a no to the dog ... and to the makeup. Goodness." On their obviously disappointed faces, he made a suggestion of his own. "How about if I take you both into work with me one day?"

"Yes!" Sallie spilled out instantly.

Joel was only a second behind. "Can I sit at your desk? Can I record at the studio? Can I—"

"You need to sleep first and then we can see what you can do at the office." I think Ryan was already regretting his offer, but I had to admit it was a great one—a chance to spend time with their dad at a place they didn't usually go was more valuable than anything.

Hands were shook. Because, why not? Ryan Thompson was a negotiating businessman, after all. And the sleeping contract was a deal we both wanted closed. Not only were Joel's sleeping issues interfering with the little boy's behavior and ultimately health, it was altering ours. Ryan and I weren't getting uninterrupted sleep or "play" time, either.

"What do you think?" he asked me later, after the kids were both tucked in. "Do you think we even get one night?"

"I think your bribe ..." I fake coughed. "I mean, offer, is very worthy of him achieving the goal."

"I had to try something. But another dog? Really?"

"He learned from the best. He shot for the stars and had you negotiate to a middle ground."

Ryan laughed. "True enough." He paused for the slightest of seconds. "You were very passionate about your stance on the dog issue."

I breathed in and out again. "It wasn't so much about the dog."

"About adoption, though, right?' His perception was straight on.

"Yes," I confirmed.

"Any particular reason? Not that I didn't appreciate it and agree wholeheartedly."

It was something I had never spoken with him about. But not telling him right then would have been like a lie. And I was not brought up a liar. Just pretending not to be in love with Ryan in the beginning of our relationship had nearly given me an ulcer.

"Garrett is adopted."

My fiancé's mouth dropped open slightly and then opened a little bit more before closing again. I let him do his processing. I knew there would be some kind of question. So I waited.

"He's ... he's adopted. Huh," was what first came out. "He looks like the rest of you."

I smiled. "He does. Pure coincidence. We all have dark brown hair and brown eyes. And, yes, Ella and I are biological sisters and of my mom and dad."

"How come you never told me?"

"Because, Ryan, it's exactly what I was explaining to Joel. Garrett is my brother just like Ella is my sister, or Sallie and Joel are siblings, or you are with your brother and sisters. We fight as siblings and we love each other as family. There is no difference. He is family. I don't even think of it. And no one else does, either. It's like, I don't know ... like you telling me one of your sisters has a birthmark on her back or something. I don't need to know that. And you don't need to know that Garrett's chromosomes or whatever are different."

"I get that. I hope you know, though, you could tell

me."

"Of course I know. And"—I tilted my head a smidge closer to his—"I know I can trust you not to say anything." I then answered his silent, inquisitive look. "Garrett doesn't know."

"He doesn't?" Another shock.

"So ... no."

"But you do?"

"Well, I was seven almost eight when he came along. I kind of knew the difference of a mom being pregnant versus a newborn baby just appearing from out of nowhere."

"Hmmm, yeah."

"But my parents never said anything. So it was always pretty much a guess or assumption. Ella was a little younger, so she either was too preoccupied with her own stuff or wasn't mature enough to put it together. But when the whole bone marrow issue thing came up and Ella and I weren't a match, we talked with my parents privately, and they didn't deny it. They were prepared to tell Garrett, but he was already going through so much. He didn't need stress on top of fighting a deadly illness. And ... they think the same way I do about it not mattering. He is one of us. We are a family."

"Why did they adopt?" He was very mellow and obviously invested and wanting to know.

"Get this ..." I almost chuckled. "They waited until they were settled to start their family but knew they wanted at least three kids. So, they had me and shortly after had Ella. Ella was just a baby—only around six months old—when they discovered my severe allergies. Well, you already know how crazy spastic my mom is with that. She was so afraid all of their kids would have the same thing. And, yes, they knew any child was a blessing from God. But with my mom—her anxiety—they decided to adopt. The whole process took a while—as it usually does, especially with newborns. But they got Garrett. And, well ... then look what happened with his health."

"The cancer."

"Yep." I closed my eyes in a prayer of thanks, as I always did when talking about my brother's remission a few years before. "And Ella doesn't have any allergies."

"Life is certainly unpredictable," Ryan noted.

"But sometimes in wonderful ways … like finding you, boyfriend." I wrinkled my nose and poked him in the side.

"Oh, geez, boyfriend talk. I'm not ready for that."

"Neither is Sallie," I reassured.

"You know how you told the kids we play together?"

"Yeah." I chuckled.

"I'm pretty sure I know what you meant." He winked. "But you know what I'd love to do with you right now?" He continued before I had a chance to come up with any options. "Grab the guitars and write some songs."

"Oh, my goodness, Ryan. There is nothing that would make me happier."

Yes, we had been thrown quite a loop with Kari's passing. But I would have never predicted life to had led me to be with him in the first place. Being us was absolutely worth all the detours and false starts and kids crying out in their sleep.

# CHAPTER FOURTEEN

The sense of peace which Ryan spoke of really did seem to find all four of us over those next few days or so. The kids had a good session with the psychologist and talked about Kari a little more in the past tense. Ryan's mom's recovery was going smoothly. And with the Fourth of July at our doorstep, we were even going to have a legitimate reason to celebrate. We were truly beginning to settle into our new normal. And it felt good.

The kids didn't notice Ryan's car was in the garage when we pulled in after camp the day before the holiday. They were too excited seeing the inflatable basketball hoops and giant run-through maze in the side yard of our next-door neighbor. Bouncing as if he was already in the fun structures, Joel started immediately toward the Radcliffes as soon as the car was in park.

"Sorry," I lightheartedly said to Rebecca, who was watching her own children play. "You didn't really expect them to pass that up." I watched as Sallie, who had been more subdued than usual in the car, followed her brother.

"Ha! No. The kids are who it's there for. Let them stay and do a test run for tomorrow," she spoke of the Fourth of July festivities. "Go do whatever you need." She nodded at the tray of goodies in my hands that I had brought from the coffee shop. "I'll watch them."

"You sure? Ryan's home, and I wasn't expecting him this early from work. I want to see what's up."

"Yeah. Go. I'll walk them over when they exhaust themselves."

"Perfect!" I smiled and joked. "So, you'll keep Joel for a few days then."

"Yeah, right." Her answer was as equally sarcastic.

"Thanks." I waved at the kids and entered the house.

It was hours before Ryan normally got home, and the kids and I were back even earlier than usual. First entering the breezeway, I called out for him but got no response. I petted Lyric, set the treats in the kitchen, and continued my search, finally discovering Ryan on the back patio. Before I could say anything, someone else did. It wasn't him. He hadn't seen me approach at all. It was Kari's voice … from beyond the grave.

"This man … this man right here," she said slowly. "He is a savior."

I looked at the tablet in Ryan's hands. The screen showed Kari wearing form-fitting, torn jeans and a racy, crocheted top. Holding on to a bald, tattooed, fit man, it was obvious they were both drunk. By the crowd and the classic wood ledge stretched out behind them, they were in the perfect place for it—a bar.

"Yeah?" The guy laughed while trying to stay in the video shot someone had obviously been filming of the duo.

Kari stuck her index finger toward the man and, with a slur, said his name, "Olsen Lasker." She planted a sloppy, quick kiss on his cheek. "Thanks for distracting me from thinking about how happy they are and how I gave it all away."

"Better off."

"Better …" She brought a bottle momentarily up to her lips. "Off."

"That's him?" I asked as the video ended. "When was that?"

"Sheez!" Ryan swirled around on my voice and put the tablet down. "I didn't know you were here."

"Ry?"

It was hard to exactly pinpoint his disposition. He seemed slightly jittery—no, distracted—as he stood. "Where are the kids?" he asked, and I realized his fear of them seeing what I had.

"Rebecca has them for a bit." When he breathed out a small pant of air, I asked another question, "Is that online? What is it?"

"It's cell phone video of her last night alive."

"Oh." Oh. Oh. Oh, wow. Oh, dang.

"Someone just posted it today. There were calls coming into the office. I decided to leave for the weekend. I ... geez. Really? There's already tons of hits." He partially grumbled.

"Why now? Why didn't whoever filmed that post it before? I mean ... right when she died?"

"Probably thought they would get more coverage now when there isn't so much stuff out there flooding the sites." Ryan really did think like a manager. "And it's her birthday and a month to the day since they found her ... since she died."

"Oh," I practically whispered again.

I hadn't realized either of those facts. It wasn't like I was counting days ... not when we were simply trying to get through and find some kind of normalcy. But when I mentally backtracked, I realized it was, indeed, exactly a month since our world went from white lace and promises to a black Cadillac hearse. And it would have been Kari's birthday? Figures. The double whammy.

"I didn't know that," I admitted. "Do the kids?"

He sighed. "No. I'm sure they don't. Kari didn't like to celebrate or even acknowledge her birthday. She hated getting older. She was even pissed that Wikipedia had her birthdate listed." Did he notice how hard I was trying not to roll my eyes? "And she was usually away this week, singing somewhere for the Fourth. You remember last year."

I did. Ryan and I had the kids for the neighborhood party then, too. So, at least Sallie and Joel wouldn't have an association with their mother for the holiday. They could hopefully enjoy the fireworks and picnic the way it was supposed to be.

"They can't be anywhere near press for the next couple of days." Not like Ryan wanted them ever to be. "Bethany, I … geez, he was telling me the truth when I saw him. She was really upset about us getting married."

"Ryan!" I couldn't help but yell. "We were—are— allowed to be happy. She never said anything to the contrary. We coexisted well this past year. Please, please don't take this on. This isn't your—"

"All right," he abruptly shut me down, and then a tad bit softer, but still distant, said, "Let's see what we need to do to get ready for tonight. It's the worst timing."

"Yeah." I sighed.

***

Although the timing could have been better, meeting with a few television network executives wasn't altogether awful. For one thing, it was taking place at the house. Therefore, Ryan wouldn't have to be in public and have the potential of someone—good intentions or not— approaching him regarding the latest Kari commotion. There were times when he was recognized for his onscreen judge role and his place in the media world and he didn't mind. He was usually brief but gracious. But I knew it wouldn't have been the case that day. Our home could at least bring him a certain comfort level. And, because of the timing, it would actually help keep his mind focused on something other than Kari, her birthday, and her last night alive.

The reason for the gathering was because one of the big execs was in from New York and wanted to meet with the talent in person, since all three were once again signing on for another year of *Singer Spotlight*. The show was a double-edged sword for Ryan. He didn't like the fanfare, but it gave him a chance to really enjoy the artistry and creative side of music, rather than just simply the business. And, it was how we met … so it definitely had good vibes.

The two other judges—pop artist Jorja and rocker Calvin—joined the three executives and Ryan in the living room. I talked with them for a bit as they arrived and then went about the task of cutting and serving an array of desserts, including my chocolate wafer recipe and the delicacies from the coffee shop. Besides drinks, that was all we served since the meeting was later in the evening. Once everyone seemed content and business talk commenced, I excused myself to check on the kids, who had done as they were told—gone to sleep after one more chapter for Sallie and ten more game points for Joel. I then browsed my social media accounts and went into the kitchen to start brewing coffee.

When I reentered the living room, the New York gentleman was speaking. "I never had a chance to send my condolences about your wife."

"Thanks, Sonny," Ryan dutifully acknowledged as he stood to grasp my hand. "But this beautiful woman here is who I consider my wife."

I met his eyes for a splinter of a second and did the tiniest of smiles. While I knew he said those words to drive a point to the exec, I also believed he meant them. And that was the sweet sentiment I held close.

"Of course." Sonny smiled at me. "No disrespect. I meant Kari."

Ryan nodded, let go of my hand, and repeated, "Thanks."

"Bethany is one of our great success stories," Cord, the

executive producer of *Singer Spotlight*, broke the tension by singing my praises. "It's nice how much you're accomplishing with your songwriting."

"This is just the beginning." Ryan beamed at me and then turned to Cord. "And don't try claiming stakes on my discovery." He was teasing but also accurate. Ryan had brought me to his agency separately.

"*Your* discovery?" Jorja laughed. "You were the first one to tell her no on the show."

"Yeah, Ryan," I played along, knowing we could and had joked about it in the past.

"I never live it down, believe me," Ryan mockingly complained.

"All right, before we start a lovers' quarrel, can we agree that Bethany—well, the two of you—provided us with one of our most-watched shows?"

I knew Cord was talking about the time I—at the last minute and with his encouragement—surprised not only the audience but Ryan and myself by going on stage and singing at the end of the show. It was immediately after Ryan confessed to the world that he and Kari were divorced and he loved me. Neither of us had certainly done either of those things for ratings but, at the same account, had no regrets, for it led to us finally, truly being together. And any blowback turned positive for all parties involved—Kari had gained the sympathetic vote while Ryan and I got the hopeless romantics.

"She's a showstopper." Ryan smiled in my direction.

He was saying all the right things. But I knew part of it was his businessman persona. I knew the difference. While things in general had started to improve, he most definitely seemed distracted after watching the video on the patio and maybe, when I thought of it, the day before, too.

"Anyway, I didn't mean to interrupt." I steered the conversation back to where I meant it to be originally. "I wanted to find out if anyone needed anything. Coffee? Something else?"

As everyone declined, insisting they were fine and that everything was so nice, Ryan said to me, "You should stay."

I didn't completely know my part in the evening. We hadn't specifically talked about it. But I wanted to respect his work, and it really wasn't a part of me.

"Yes, yes, please," Sonny chimed in. "This is just a get-together, really. Wanted to meet up … touch base. It's lovely getting to know you." He nodded at me. "I'm sorry my wife couldn't make it this trip."

"Well, *I* only came because I thought the neighborhood bouncy house was included," Calvin razzed.

On everyone's collective laughter, Ryan tossed in, "We should see if we can negotiate that into our contract."

"Thompson, I think you could successfully negotiate anything."

Before Ryan could reply to Calvin, we heard a "Daddy?"

Ryan slightly shook his head at Joel's voice and joked with everyone in the room. "Well, except with a five-year-old. I don't seem to have any leverage in getting the staying-asleep-for-the-night deal closed." He looked at me. "You would have thought all the activities next door would have tired him out."

"Probably overstimulated," I suggested since Joel had worked really hard at trying to stick with the sleeping contract. "I'll check on him."

"It's fine. I'll go." He left so quickly it made me wonder if he chose the task because it was his name Joel had called out or if it was just to give himself a break from the room.

"Bethany, so … what's new for you?" broad-chested Sonny asked. "Anything on the horizon? Writing the next chart-topper?"

I looked at the collective bunch. Even though I wasn't prepared to talk about myself that evening, I wasn't nervous in front of the group. After all, I knew most of them casually through Ryan. And when I talked about lyrics and symbolism and harmonies, it got me energized. "I'm always writing, even if the words don't make it to paper. I feel like every person … every moment has a story to tell. And the ones I hear over and over again with chords and instruments behind them, I make sure to get them down." When the musician in Jorja seemed to happily sigh, I added a little lightness to my answer, "And, I write because I like to keep my manager happy."

"Are we starting to see his beard again? Is Ryan going back to that?"

I turned to the *Spotlight* producer who had raised the question. "Wha …?"

"I mean, it's been a whole season with the clean-shaven look."

"Uh … yeah. Right," I verbally stumbled and bumbled around with my words.

Ryan's face had been smooth and free of hair … yeah, at least a couple days before. But when I thought of it, he probably did have some dark shadow. It was one of those things that subtly started appearing and you could miss noticing when you saw a person every day. It hadn't been like that for over a year. He had shaved the beard off. The show had wanted him to keep it since it was his signature look. But he didn't care for it and, most importantly, he did it for me, knowing it reminded me of how he looked when he had rejected me on the show. And he hadn't gone back. Besides, he told me he had only initially grown the beard because he was depressed over his divorce and didn't put any extra effort into anything. It was before we were a couple. It was his "Under the Bridge" days.

"Hey." Ryan's voice broke into my concerned internal thoughts as he reentered the room. "What's going on in here? Anyone need anything?"

"Is your son okay?" Jorja, a mother herself, questioned.

"Well, get this …" Ryan swiveled in my direction. "He lost his first tooth."

"Hmmm." We knew it was going to happen soon …

the tooth had been getting more and more wiggly. And I'm glad it happened when Ryan was around, since I didn't necessarily want to pull or yank or see any blood. "How did he know if he was asleep?"

Ryan rolled his eyes. "A little glow of his tablet under the sheets tells me he probably wasn't." When I let out a click of my tongue for being fooled earlier by the little boy, Ryan turned to our guests. "So, I think I might need to renegotiate the contract. Tooth Fairy money needs to be factored in."

And there he was, joking and playing Mr. Personality again. Was it all an act? Temporarily out of the conversation, I looked more closely at him. Although in the beginning stages, I feared the beard *was* on its way back. And I worried that some of the feelings he associated with it were, too. But, why? Why right then? The past four weeks had been hard, but recently there seemed to have been a light … a brightness … hope. What was he feeling and why?

\*\*\*

"He's really asleep this time." Ryan reentered the living room after saying goodnight to his *Spotlight* coworkers and then making his son's monetary Tooth Fairy delivery.

"Good."

"Come on." He nodded toward the hallway. "It's late. We'll get anything else in the morning."

I looked around the room. There really were only a couple of napkins and baskets with mints, which I put in the end table's drawer. The candles had been blown out. The dishes were rinsed and either in the sink or dishwasher and the food was packed away.

I was the more orderly of the two of us, not that Ryan didn't like things structured. He blamed it on me being a firstborn child, as if it was a fault. I think I was just used to living in a very confined space before moving in with him.

My living area in my apartment had only housed a twin bed, desk, chair, dresser, and closet. The bathroom was shared and the dining area was communal on the first floor. I had learned to have everything have its own spot. Ryan's home was not only ginormous, but it had two active children living in it.

It wasn't the tidiness factor that made me pause, though. I couldn't get my concern for Ryan out of my mind. But it *was* late, and I didn't know if I wanted to get into it with him right then.

Instead, I looked for a middle ground. "I think tonight went well."

He tilted his head toward mine. "Yeah. I'm glad you joined us."

I appreciated his thought, but part of me wondered how much he was glad because I was his fiancée versus if he just didn't want to be the only host taking on the pleasantries. Ever since the Kari video and then the beard revelation, I was scrutinizing everything. In the end, though, it didn't matter. I wanted to be there for him no matter what.

Wrapping my arms around his back, I rested my head on his chest, covered only with a partially opened white button-down. I squeezed extra securely. "I love you, Ryan."

He pulled me far enough away so we could see each other, and I placed my hands up to those disheartening whiskers and kissed him. When he kissed me back, it was with a bit of greed. I let my mouth match his, needing him to know it was mutual. His hands found the tie around the waist of my gray dress, and he expertly unwrapped it. I snuggled in closer, wanting his body close to mine ... to feel us together and connected.

"Hmmm," his moan came as I started on his black trousers. And then he slowed and put his hands on *my* face, releasing our lips. "No, it wouldn't be ... I've had ... too much."

I knew he wasn't talking about alcohol. He had been drinking but respectfully. It was something else. Trying to keep the tears behind them, I closed my eyes, regulated my breath, and took a mini step away.

"Okay." I pulsed more than nodded my head.

"Bethany?"

"It's okay," I repeated, wanting to believe it myself but failing miserably, both internally and, I guess, externally, judging by his reaction.

His voice rose. "No, it's not. It's not okay. Nothing is okay."

On the reality of his words, I felt the tears silently rolling down my face. I had really wanted to keep them at bay, but I couldn't. His face, his disposition, his words, his rejection all saddened and worried me.

"Dang it!" That wasn't helping my fears.

"Ryan …"

"I'm sorry. I'm tired, and it's been a day, and … Bethany, I can't right now. I can't … I can't … anything."

I stared at him. He can't anything? He can't love me? Right then, he couldn't even look at me. Yet, despite the sting and the hurt, I wanted to help him. But I didn't know how.

"Okay."

"Don't say that." He admonished the only word I seemed to know right then.

"I don't know what else to say," I burst out my own frustration. "You said you can't. I'm trying to understand. But—"

"I know." He exhaled long. "I need to have this day be done. I need to sleep. And I would still like to do that with you in my arms, but if y—"

"Okay." I cringed on the word and then purposefully slightly changed it. "*Yes.* Let's stay right here, all right? Can we just sleep on the sofa tonight?"

As it popped out of my mouth, I wondered why I had made the instant request. But when he brought me immediately into his arms and chest, I knew. He was telling me his honest truth and giving me all he could at the moment. And since it included me ... wanting to hold me ... I didn't want to detach our bodies or thoughts from that idea, even if to just climb the stairs to our bedroom. I needed the day to be done, too. And even though it had brought additional concerns, at least we were together. As we made our way to the nearby sofa, it turned out I was glad that not all of the napkins were put away because I needed to discretely dry my eyes while hoping for a better tomorrow.

# CHAPTER FIFTEEN

Upon waking, we didn't mention the night before, but our location was a direct reminder. It was one of those times when things were a little too raw to get into right away. And, besides, it was the holiday and a very, very busy one at that. We started the Fourth of July with red, white, and blue pancakes—which Joel helped me make with red food dye, blueberries, and whipped cream. Sallie, who was usually my sous-chef, uncharacteristically decided to skip the culinary fun and do some writing. And, unfortunately, Ryan did not help, either. He was busy catching up on the fallout of Kari's last-day video. But he promised after to leave it all be—going as far as ignoring his phone, except for emergencies, for the remainder of the day. I tried to negotiate the entire extended weekend, but I didn't seem to be as good at dealmaking as Joel.

Midday was the picnic, worthy of the elite people who lived in the neighborhood—renowned doctors, a lawyer to the stars, news anchors, a chain bakery founder, a multi-award-winning restaurant owner, a professional football player, and the home builder himself. At first, they had all been a little intimidating to me, but the more I got to know them over that previous year, the more—for the most part—normal they seemed. But, why shouldn't they be? Just because Ryan made a good amount of money didn't alter the genuine human being he was. And they weren't any different.

Besides the inflatables for the kids, there was a baseball game for all ages, complete with custom-made team T-shirts. Ryan put on a clinic for our team, smacking the ball so far it should have counted double for his three home runs. But despite his constant coaching, I only managed to get in one hit at my turns at bat. Even Joel did better.

"Do I need to trade you?" my fiancé teased.

"Should have dated my sister," I claimed. "She got the athletic genes."

"We fall behind, and I'm calling her up." He was joking, but I knew the competitive side of him would have thrown me under the bus had we not been ahead.

"Go for it," I played along, using *his* sibling as banter. "I'd be very happy sipping wine with Dylan."

He squinted his eyes very quickly at me and ended with mockery. "Firstborn fun."

"I tend to remember having the best weekend at the winery with *you*," I offered because I then understood the narrowing of his eyes.

Kari's betrayal of their marriage had left Ryan a little protective of his heart when it came to jealousy. He should have known he didn't have to worry about that with me. But everything that had been starting to go positively back up seemed to suddenly and sadly be finding its way back down.

I wouldn't know if he was going to say something sentimental, romantic, or otherwise, because Sallie—who was not playing but coloring some pictures—came up to us. "Daddy, I need to go to the bathroom."

"Okay, baby. You know where the bathroom is in Mr. and Mrs. Radcliffe's house. Go ahead."

The ballgame was being held next to their home in the two empty lots that were yet to be developed. The homeowners in the neighborhood hoped they never would be. It provided a great spot for things just like that game.

"I don't want to go by myself," she partially whined. "And I want to go home because I need more of my special coloring paper."

Ryan cringed at the other team catching a ball that surely otherwise would have led to a run for our team. He looked back at Sallie and then at me. "Can Bethany take you? She's ... benched."

My mouth shot open as much as my eyelids. But I actually didn't mind. Baseball was not my game.

"Come on, Sals, girl power." I wrinkled my nose and teased Ryan. "Some people don't know talent when they first see it."

"Never. Live. It. Down," he grumbled.

I started to walk. But Sallie didn't follow. She was still at her dad's side and looking at me with a face I couldn't decipher. It wasn't quite apprehension. It wasn't quite bewilderment. It was a standstill ... almost like when she didn't want to walk up to her mother's coffin. Only, it was kind of the opposite. She didn't seem to want to be with me, and she wouldn't take my hand.

"Dang it! We're on the field." Ryan scowled and looked to Sallie again, astonished we hadn't left. "Sallie, go with Bethany."

"I can hold it in," the little girl offered.

"All right. Your call." He then directed me. "Outfield near Kingston. Let him get anything that comes near."

"I thought I was benched," I complained.

"All hands on deck." He played coach and then, before turning away, added with a serious and slightly sad tone, "Besides, I couldn't live with knowing I told you no about one more thing." We had always been able to tease about him not moving me on to the next round of *Singer Spotlight*. Why was he so serious?

"Sallie, you sure? You all right?" I refocused once again on the little girl, wondering how many Thompsons I could be worried about at once.

As she shrugged and resumed her seat on the grass, I heard Joel. "Daddy-O! We've got this. Three strikes and they're out of there. Three strikes and out." He was high-fiving Ryan on the pitcher's mound ... at least I could count on Joel.

***

When the game ended, everyone was ready to begin munching on burgers, steaks, hotdogs, chicken, corn, potatoes, Caesar salad, and more. I excused myself and went back to the house to get our contribution to the annual dessert contest. I had made barbecue chocolate cupcakes midmorning. It was my first attempt and, admittedly, I thought a pretty good one. All they needed was the finishing touch of icing.

While I went about my task, I was also mentally retracing the details of the day before and the holiday itself. On top of Ryan's comment about saying no to me, I noticed how he seemed withdrawn or removed in general throughout the day. We were speaking, but it was only in the company of others—not that there was much of an opportunity to be alone. And the talk was idle chitchat and nothing deep. My confusion and concern were only escalating that he—or we—were somehow backsliding ... just when I had thought things were beginning to look up.

I sat more affirmatively on one of the tall kitchen stools and allowed myself a moment. It kind of surprised me that it was accompanied by a silent display of tears. But I figured if they were needed, it was best I did it in the rare privacy of an empty house.

But it wasn't empty. I wasn't alone. As I was sucking on my lips, wet from fresh tears, and brushing my hand to my cheek, Joel's little sneakered shoes came to a screeching halt as he was suddenly in front of me. He looked a little frightened—but mostly concerned— at the sight of my appearance.

"Why are you crying, Bethany?" he asked softly and pitter-pattered a little closer to me. "Bethany, don't cry."

I rubbed at my tears with a little more determination. The last thing I wanted was for the kids to feel any more stress in their lives. Especially on what was supposed to be a celebratory day.

He was then up against my knees looking directly at me. "Don't cry," he said, that time as if it scared him.

"Oh, sweetie," I tried, now with a dry, yet surely distressed, face. "There's ... You know how I get when I'm cutting onions?" I got down from the stool.

He squished his lips together and toward the right side of his face. "Yeah?"

"It's like that. That's all."

"Really?"

"Yep." I attempted a smile and crouched to his level.

"I don't like onions."

"Well, I don't like cutting them."

Joel wrapped his arms around me with all the might of a five-year-old who wanted to believe, and I held on almost as equally tight. I wanted to believe, too. I wanted to believe it was that simple—nonexistent onions and comforting hugs. I, unfortunately, knew better.

I think we both heard Sallie and Ryan at the same time. They had, of course, been behind the speediest boy in the land. And by the sound of their voices, they were then only a few steps away.

Joel released his embrace. "I get the bathroom!" he yelled out as Ryan and Sallie entered the kitchen.

"Joel! That's not fair! We were coming home because I said I had to go!" Sallie pouted but had clearly lost out to her little brother, who was already feet away scrambling to the powder room.

As Sallie took off, too, Ryan turned to me. "It's not like we only have one bathroom in the house. Geez!"

I tried to nonchalantly dab at my cheeks and right

below my eyes. My face felt drained from crying. And I was pretty sure it looked the same.

But Ryan didn't seem to notice, and that made me both glad and disappointed. "How did the cupcakes turn out?" he asked. "They look good."

"I think pretty good." I looked at my culinary creation and then back at him. "I guess we'll find out once everyone votes. But, you know, I don't have a good track record in competitions," I sassed. "At least we'll be gone before the contest, so you can't be a judge."

His eyes shifted as if he were examining different parts of my face, but most likely was formulating how to respond. His verbal hesitation matched his expression. "Bethany …"

To not let things get awkward, I continued, "Plus, I am going against a baker and a restaurant owner."

"You know—"

"I'm ready!" Joel announced, interrupting whatever Ryan was going to say.

Ryan took another second to look at me and then turned to his son. "All right. We're going to get some of those burgers. But first we need to make sure we have everything packed in the car for our campout. You wanna help me?"

"Yeah!" The little boy's full grin showed off his missing tooth.

"Where is your sister? Maybe she can help Bethany with the cupcakes and the food at the picnic."

"I wanna help you, too, Daddy." Sallie made her presence known by first looking at Ryan and then shyly at me.

I could feel my eyebrows automatically furl. Something was definitely up with Sallie. And I was pretty sure it had to do with me. I understood that both kids were a little clingy with Ryan since Kari's death. They needed to see him and be with him as much as they could. But with Sallie, it all of a sudden seemed to also mean some kind of insecurity with me. Gosh, just when I thought we could have a normal—or even semi-normal—day.

"Go ahead," I offered. "I'm good with the food."

"What about your things for tonight?" Ryan asked me.

"I put them in the backpack with yours."

"Everything?" He seemed surprised.

"It's an overnight in a tent. What all do I need?" I secured the lid on the cupcake box—my job was already half done.

"Nothing. No. Perfect. A woman with priorities straight."

I'm pretty sure he was thinking of Kari and the entourage she would have traveled with just to get the mail, but I again took the lighthearted road. We needed it. "Yep. See? I got the food." My lips lifted in a smile as I lifted the box. "I'll meet you three at the picnic."

"And then we're off for the fireworks and camping!" Joel exclaimed.

"We are." Ryan ruffled his son's hair before we all went on our missions.

*** 

Camping at the beach that evening had been Ryan's idea. He was truly an outdoor boy caught in a busy, city world. He wanted a break from the constant commotion his life entailed. I didn't blame him. I appreciated it, too … and I certainly didn't have to deal with the press like he did. My biggest hope was that he got a chance to relax and relish the joy of just the four of us.

We set up the tent in a secluded spot and had a little bit of time to enjoy the nearby water. Even though it was calm, there wasn't a second that if the kids were in the water, Ryan wasn't right at their sides. It was going to take a while—if ever—for him to stop imagining his little boy struggling in the pool and nearly not making it. I also noted that Joel, while not afraid of the water, was a lot more attentive to the rules when around it.

Afterward, as the sun set, the kids got a chance to use some handheld sparklers. They twirled around and tried to write out their name before the fire completely fizzled. Sallie, of course, had hers as far out from her face as possible. But we had to keep reminding Joel to try to do the same.

And then, sitting on the beachy area outside of our tent, it was time for the main event. I leaned my head against Ryan's shoulder and watched as the fireworks erupted in the sky. I thought they were especially beautiful over the water. I had always loved the Fourth of July growing up, but the California displays far outranked those in my hometown.

Uncharacteristically, Joel decided the excitement of the noise and lights was a time to calm down. And he chose to do it on my lap. Ryan touched his son's shoulder as Joel leaned against my chest, and we both looked once more to the sky.

"Sallie, look at that one!" the little boy cried out, amazed at the latest bloom.

When I glanced over at Sallie, who was sitting on the other side of Ryan, she wasn't looking at the sky. She was looking at me. And she had her same look from the baseball game. I gave her a soft smile, and she buried her head under her dad's arm. Or course, Ryan, with his face of ever-growing whiskers, didn't notice and was looking upward.

I realized a moment alone with Ryan to talk was simply not going to happen. The kids were sleeping in the same tent as us. And even though it was supposed to be made for six people, we were a foot or two away from being human sardines. We all snuggled into our individual sleeping bags—Sallie's with an assortment of princesses on it, Joel's looking like a pair of jeans, Ryan's camo, and mine—bought just for the occasion—was half blue and half yellow. We told stories, shone the flashlight around our faces and hands, and then the kids, thankfully, tuckered out. It had been a long, excitement-filled day, after all.

"Go outside with me for a minute or two?" I whispered to Ryan in the complete darkness.

He met his hand with mine. "Okay. Careful," he noted the kids sleeping the opposite direction at our feet.

We ducked out of the tent and walked a few steps or so away. The stillness was so peaceful. There was only enough light so I could see his face—that gorgeous face with the deep blue eyes. I loved him so much. I knew we were going to be okay. We simply needed more moments like the one we were in.

"Ryan, you know I was teasing you earlier about the not-knowing-talent thing and the judging, right?"

"Well, I wasn't exactly teasing you about your baseball skills." He bumped his hip jovially onto mine, and I was glad to find that teensiest bit of Ryan and Bethany again.

"You *totally* have a right to do that," I joshed back. After another moment of just looking out to the water, I said, "Are you all right? Is everything—"

"We need another—Oh, oh, crud!"

All of a sudden, the skies let loose. But it wasn't with leftover fireworks. It was with buckets and buckets of rain, as if God had been holding on to his tears alongside us those past few weeks. And the "expert" weather forecasters hadn't predicted it at all.

Ryan dipped me under his arm and onto his chest the best he could, and we scurried back into the tent. I wanted to shake off but really couldn't in the limited space. Instead, I drip-dried a little as Ryan and I both looked at each other.

"What's going on?" Sallie had awoken.

"Just rain, baby," Ryan whispered back, crouching next to her as I made my way into the comfy snugness of my sleeping bag, which was acting like part towel.

"No thunder or lightning?" she questioned with

obvious concern.

"No. Go back to sleep. We don't want to wake your brother."

Sallie looked at her dad with a head shake. "No. We don't!"

Ryan kissed her blonde head and elongated his body into his own sleeping bag. He turned to me. "You good?"

Yes. No. I wanted to talk. I wanted to understand him and whatever was going on.

Sallie was lying in her sleeping bag, looking at us. Joel, with Eli tucked in next to him, was starting to stir. I wasn't going to get any answers that night. And I knew I couldn't reply to Ryan without lying or expanding the conversation. With the zippered cocoons around our individual bodies and the kids next to us, we were even farther apart than the night before lying on the living room sofa. I scooted closer to him so I could at least feel his body through the quilted fabric between us. I closed my eyes and didn't look up when his lips rested on top of my head. And that was how it was going to have to be … to end—another day done.

# CHAPTER SIXTEEN

Since the following day was Friday, most of the country had taken the additional day off, too. That included Ryan and myself. And the kids didn't go to their summer day camp. So, after a lazy wakeup from our tent and some more time in the water, we stopped for something to eat at a quaint country restaurant, which reminded both Ryan and me of our hometowns. It was the kind where the waitresses wore checkered aprons, a bell was rung when a meal was ready, and everything seemed to be served ala mode.

When we returned home, Ryan went to pick up Lyric—who the Radcliffes took in for the night. In the meantime, the kids and I made our way to the game room to figure out what our afternoon plan was. The unusual weather pattern persisted on being drizzly to overcast. So, we had to do something indoors. The kids had paper, markers, and a word game that was sort of like the classic Pictionary, but you could use charades, words, or pictures to have your partner guess. Sallie instantly picked the teams—Joel and I versus Ryan and her. I knew I was at a disadvantage since Joel was known to blurt out the actual word more than anything. But I feared Sallie would have it no other way since her puzzling attitude toward me had not faltered. And without her, there wasn't a game. I just couldn't understand what was holding up her partner. I thought I had heard Ryan reenter the home, but he hadn't made his way down to us.

Even though we were in the same abode, I decided to text him. *What's up? Where are you?*

*B there in a min*, was his reply after a couple.

And then I realized if Ryan had a moment to himself, I knew what he was doing. He was checking in with someone or something. He had been disconnected from his electronics for a whole day plus, which was almost a minor miracle.

I wanted him removed from it all. I think he needed it … we all did. So, I devised my plan.

When I dialed his number via video chat, he replied with a close-up shot of his face. "Bethany, what are you doing? I'm in the house."

"Daddy, it's game time!" Joel interrupted, bellowing into the phone's camera.

"You are my partner," Sallie tagged on, while smushed cheek-to-cheek with her brother so they were both in the frame. "Joel and Bethany are already teaming up on me. I need you."

"No more work!" Joel admonished his father and looked at me.

I hadn't wanted the five-year-old to say that and hoped the phone didn't capture my image right then. But it was true. I had the kids make the plea since I recognized the last thing Ryan needed was an "almost" nagging wife.

"No more work!" Sallie repeated.

"Don't worry, Sals. We got the schemers. They'll try every trick." And all of a sudden, I heard his voice double-time because he had entered the room. He ended the video chat on his end, and I went to my phone to make sure mine was disconnected, too. "Sorry?" he offered, knowing I had pegged him dead-on.

"If only," I lamented.

"I put it aside," he reassured, although seemingly a little bothered by it. He caught my eyes, as if he thought I was going to debate. "I needed to check on things, and I'm done."

"Good." I breathed in a little easier.

"So, what are we playing?"

\*\*\*

Ryan and Sallie were creaming us. Even though Ryan wasn't at his baseball level of competitiveness, there simply wasn't any mercy. It wasn't going to be a throw-the-game Frisbee event. But, despite our record, I do think Joel and I had more giggles with our interpretations of the words than the father-daughter team.

After another epic fail for Joel and me, Ryan noticed that I was rubbing my upper chest and squinting my eyes. "Hey ..." He reached his arm over and touched my hand. "What—"

"I'm all right. Probably ate too much of the delicious apple turnover at the restaurant." But as I tried a smile, my headache seemed to get worse.

"You sure? It's not an allergy thing, is it?" Ryan was on alert and starting up off the floor where we were all sitting.

"No. No. You would be jabbing into my thigh by now." I meant the epinephrine pen, but as soon as I finished the sentence, I realized the sexual way it could be interpreted. I started to chuckle but realized Ryan wasn't, as he normally would have been. Hoping it was solely due to concern, I reassured, "I'm just tired. Don't want to get sick. Sorry, Joel. But I think they got us. We'll get them another time. I think I'm going to get a little sleep."

"Like a nap," Sallie suggested, I'm sure thinking it odd that adults sometimes needed those, too.

"No!" Joel bounded up and practically bowled me over to hold on to me.

"Joel ..." Ryan sounded as surprised as I was.

"Hey," I said to the five-year-old. "I'm sorry. It wasn't our game. I seem to be striking out this weekend." I looked at Ryan in reference to the baseball game but internally thought of our failed attempt at making love, too. "Let me get some sleep, okay, so I can feel better. Sorry to let you down, mate."

Joel continued to hug me. "You'll get better?"

"That's the plan."

Ryan stuck out his hand to help me up, kind of forcing Joel to let go. "Joe, it's your turn to pick the movie. Go see what you want, and Sallie can help. But don't argue. It's his turn." As the kids went toward the television, Ryan asked me, "You sure you're okay?"

"Yeah," I reiterated and spoke the truth. "I've just been going nonstop. I want to give my eyes a rest before going out with Willow tonight."

"Maybe you shouldn't."

"If I still have my headache after my nap, I'll cancel, okay?" I offered, but, in truth, I was really looking forward to an adult girls' night out with my best friend.

***

I was back awake, dressed, and ending my phone conversation when Ryan entered the master bedroom. "Hey," I said, placing the phone on the nightstand.

"Who were you talking with?"

"My mom. She wants to know when we are rescheduling the wedding."

And, of course, she had cautioned me again about taking care of myself. Unless I was in the emergency room with an allergic reaction, though, I pretty much stayed healthy. A cold or virus were mild once-in-a-few-years-or-so occurrences, and I was, oddly, proud of that. So, I most certainly didn't want to admit to her or myself that I might be rundown as she had predicted. But taking a nap was far from my norm.

Ryan blew out a gust of air. "Like the wedding is the top thing to be concerned about."

Of course I knew there were still a lot of concerns hanging over us like the dense clouds that day, but I didn't like his immediate blowoff of something that only a month before we were both looking forward to more than anything. "Is it at least in the top ten, Ryan? Or even one hundred?" I questioned, with, yes, a bit of bitterness.

We hadn't really talked about the specifics of rescheduling with everything else going on, but it was time to at least have some kind of idea, wasn't it? It was beginning to feel like when I had been awaiting his and Kari's divorce announcement … and I didn't want to feel that way. This was different and it involved the kids, but I was wearing out emotionally and, I guess, physically, too.

"Geez, of course." He exhaled again. "It's trying to refigure getting to Carolina in the midst of everything else that is hard." He dipped his head slightly as if wanting to know if I could understand, let it go for right then, or both. When I answered with a slow blink, he tried another question. "How are you feeling?" And I knew he wasn't simply changing the subject—it was out of genuine concern.

"Better," I answered with a twinge of deception. "Getting there. How's Joel?"

"Joel?" His face scrunched back a tad. "He's fine. Why?"

While I was getting ready, I had thought about his son's reaction and how it might have had to do with more than losing a game. "Ry, I think maybe he was scared of something earlier … before I went to sleep."

"No. No." His eyes squinted. "He's fine."

"Really? He—"

"Yeah. They're both watching the movie, and I was, too. No work or anything else, by the way."

I smiled appreciatively. "Good. Okay, if you say so.

You know, I wanted a minute to talk with you about Sallie, too. Have you noticed how she's been acting around me?"

"What? Do you think she's scared, too? You really are tired."

I plunged on. "Ryan, she's been really distant with me the past couple of days—not wanting to do things with me, shying away from me, not letting me help her, and, I don't know … kind of looking at me funny. And her artwork—it's not precision, immaculate Sallie. She's putting a lot of force on the crayons and—"

"Geez, first of all, I didn't take you as an always-draw-in-the-lines kind of gal."

"I'm—"

"And, she seems to be acting the same to me. I mean, she had a traumatic thing happen to her, Bethany. She—" Why wasn't he listening to me at all?

"I know." Noting my voice escalating, I took a mini breath, trying to concentrate on the fact that I wanted to help, not bother. My dad had said just me being me helped, but I wasn't quite sure at the moment. "Look, I'm not their counselor. I'm just saying—"

"She's fine. They're both fine." His uncommon frustration rose. "And no, you're not a counselor or a parent. I think I know my own kids."

If his opening statement about rescheduling our wedding didn't tick me off, the one about me not being a parent sure the heck did. "Fine. Okay. I'll let it go. I won't mention it again," I spit out and added with even more venom, "I should know my place. Everyone seems to keep telling me—the hospital, Irene … I'm simply the whore babysitter … someone who manipulated my way into your life for your money." I had put up with those rumors in the beginning of our relationship from irate Kari fans, too. "Maybe I should sleep in the guest room when I get home tonight."

"No," he immediately refuted in an even more agitated way. "Don't make this into something it's not."

His insistence and tone made me even angrier. Normally, I would have given more back. But surprising even myself, my body said otherwise. I started to cry ... and not a few tears I could swipe at like the day before in the kitchen. I sobbed.

"Oh, man." He closed and reopened his eyes.

Ryan was not used to me crying like that. I could either give as good as I could take. Or, I would remove myself from the situation altogether.

"Bethany ..." He took a deep breath and seemed to reboot with concern. "What's going on? Joel just told me you were crying yesterday, too. And don't tell me it was onions. There aren't any onions in cupcakes. I know—"

Like the tears, my words seemingly came out of nowhere, but yet were obviously just holding on to the edge of my truth. Maybe I was having my own grief burst, but my loss was a different kind. "I'm not losing you, am I?"

"What?" he asked immediately and then repeated with even more surprise in his voice. "What?" followed by a very insistent, "No. What are you talking about?"

Didn't he see? Couldn't he feel what it had been like those past couple of days? How he was acting? How it was almost as if he was distancing himself from me ... at least emotionally. And the growing beard.

"Bethany?" The concern in his voice hit a whole new level when I didn't answer him.

"That, for one thing."

"What? What thing?" His eyes swung back and forth at me, as if they were searching for something he couldn't find.

"Calling me ..." I sighed.

Bethany, after all, was my name. And it wasn't that he never used it, but it was mostly during serious times. Things had been far too serious.

I reached up for his face, softly rubbing the physical concern. "And this for another." I brought my hands back down, feeling a few straggling tears reach my cheeks, probably right where my line of freckles resided. "I'm worried about you … and about the kids—both Sallie and Joel. I'm worried about us." I looked away because I was becoming even more emotional, plus my phone was singing out. "I gotta go," I said, noting the phone's message that the Uber was waiting outside our front door.

"Sheez!" He wrung his hands through his hair.

"Ryan …"

"We need to talk about all of this." He watched as I placed my phone in my purse. "I'm just overextended."

I wiped desperately under my eyes, hoping the brown waterproof mascara, which matched my eyes, didn't smudge. "Uh-huh."

He placed his hands tentatively and then a little more confidently on my shoulders so our eye-to-eye contact couldn't be denied. "You are *not* the babysitter or any of those names that nasty woman called you. I know why we're together. I know the real you—the woman I want nothing more than to be my wife." My movement away from him seemed to allow his already high-tilt emotions to run even deeper. "Geez, Bethany, come on. At least promise me … not the guest room."

I knew the guest room amendment would bother him. Even though it was the first place we had ever made love—a time I would always cherish and never regret—it also had a significance. He never wanted me to feel like I was a guest in the home, and he had made a point of that after our first time. And for me to sleep in there alone? Well, that would be the ultimate heart dagger.

I turned to him once more, nodded my agreeance, and, before the waterworks started again, walked away. Just like he seemed to have reached his breaking point, so had I. Whether my emotional state had caused whatever physical ailment I seemed to be fighting or vice versa, I had, indeed, hit a wall. And I knew it wasn't a good thing that we both were at that horrible spot on the emotional map at the same time. But it was what it was. Maybe a night out and apart was what we needed. Because the current road stretched out before us suddenly seemed darker and longer than ever before.

\*\*\*

After my blowup with Ryan, I even more so appreciated Willow's suggestion to go "old school" and get a car service for our girls' night out ... just as I had when not having a car. I was in no state to drive. My tearing eyes needed their own windshield, nonetheless trying to look out a moving vehicle's. In addition, I wanted to drink. I wanted to let go for the night. It was something I rarely did because, honestly, I didn't feel a need to. And bad things usually happened when I went too far. But, then again, I had been swallowed up in bad things for a month already.

The funny/not funny part was, we were going out to console Willow. She was the one who originally needed the night out, and it was because of a man, too. She and her boyfriend of nearly two years were splitting up. It wasn't that they didn't care for each other, and no one was cheating. Tilman wanted to follow the Red Cross, where he worked, to South Africa. It was something he was personally and professionally super excited about. However, it was quite the opposite of Willow's sparkly, fashion aspirations. Her administrative assistant job at the fashion magazine was only the start. She wasn't about to leave ... and he wasn't about to stay. And the more they talked, the more they realized what different lives they ultimately wanted to lead. It was sad. They were both good people but, in the long run, not meant to be.

"The worst thing is," Willow said, "we connected in so many other ways."

"He was fun and spontaneous and into you and—"

"Ah, man, Bethany, you're supposed to be helping,"

she whined.

"He was perfect for a period of time."

"Yeah." She downed the rest of her drink and flagged the bartender. "I just wish I would have seen it coming."

"Don't we all." I griped and nodded to my empty glass. "Hit me up another, too."

"You go, girl." As she stuck up her fingers for two, I wondered what was helping me more—talking with my best friend or the harshness of the liquor going down. Willow went right back to topic-Til. "I mean, geez, I was even starting to think I was getting a ring soon. And if you and Mr. Mean took any longer with the wedding delay, we could have had a double ceremony."

My drink arrived in perfect time. I practically swiped it from the bartender's hands and gulped down a mighty swig. That one seemed even more potent.

"When *are* the two of you getting hitched?" She put her own glass up to her lips.

"I don't know." I tried not to sigh, but I'm afraid, especially with the aid of the alcohol, I did. "It was one of the things we argued about before I came to meet you."

Her head shot back a little and her eyelids lifted. "You two never fight, and you are telling me it was about more than one thing?" She was starting to sound drunk, and I was amused and a little envious.

"Yes, we do. We disagree about things for sure, but, yeah, this one was a doozy," I admitted. "You know, funny thing how you and a bar seem to be an end result of Ryan and I arguing."

"Oh, yikes! It's not as bad as that, is it?" A best friend doesn't forget your ups or downs, and the time just over a year before when we were sitting in a similar bar because I didn't know if Ryan and I were going to make it, definitely qualified as a down.

"I ... no. I hope not." At least I wasn't leaving town for a few days and not answering his calls. "It's ... everything has been such a mess since ... since Kari. I thought things might be getting better, but he's … and the kids …"

"Man, those kids." Willow was definitely drunk, but it didn't take much with her way-too-slender model body.

"Yeah." I took another swig. "And, I feel guilty for wondering even for a moment why it can't be about me … me and him. I know that's not fair."

"Girl, we're all human." She tapped my hand and then became serious … well, as serious as she could be at the moment. "You need to set a new wedding date at least. Some of us are really looking forward to it. Because, you know, weddings have nothing to do with the bride and groom. It's all about the guests."

I laughed because it did seem some weddings were like that. But Ryan and I had been blessed. Neither of our families interfered. And it helped that we kept the guest list low with only family and very close friends invited, i.e.: no business or media. It was also nice that Ryan was actually interested in helping plan the nuptials. For even though ours was to be his second marriage, it was his first wedding. He and Kari had eloped in the spontaneous way that two young people do when they found themselves in Vegas and didn't want to be bothered with any outside forces. Knowing Kari's mother, I couldn't really blame them.

"Refuse to have sex with him!" Willow suddenly shouted out, breaking into my thoughts of our day not-to-be.

"Willow!" I looked around to see if anyone else had heard her, but either the bar was too loud or, if they did, they didn't care.

"Yeah," she continued as if she was plotting to sneak backstage at Fashion Week, "just until you have a day picked out. I know that would be bad for you, too. I'm sure …" She paused to lift her eyebrows a couple times. "I'm sure he's good in bed." When I didn't answer her, but the heat in my cheeks surely did, she smiled. "But you can hold out, right? Play the headache card."

"Ha!" I pointed my finger at my friend, maybe feeling a twinge tipsy. "I wouldn't need to."

"Why?"

"I had a legit, good one today."

"Feeling better now, I guess." She chuckled, looking at the glass wrapped around my hand.

"Yeah. Haven't been up to code. My stomach was acidy and I was tired ... beat."

"You're not pregnant, are you?"

I was thankful the liquid sprayed out of my mouth and not my nose ... and I hadn't had a lot of beverage in my mouth to start with. "Geez! No. Oh, my stars, that is all we would need."

I reclaimed my drink and sipped with a little more determination. Then, slowly, I started placing the glass back down. My world was beginning to swirl and only part of it was due to the alcohol.

"Willow?"

"Yeah?" At least she was a happy drunk.

"Oh, man, Willow, can I be pregnant?" The last part came out so slow, I think each word was its own sentence.

"You need me to explain how you get pregnant, preacher's daughter?"

I playfully smacked her and her humor. "No!"

"Why? You think you might be? I was just kidding." Her eyes seemed to glisten with the possibility.

Whereas mine, I am sure, were dipping darker. "I ... I don't know. I know I am super emotional right now, but with everything—"

"Oh, boy."

"Shit."

"Preacher's daughter *mouth,*" she exclaimed.

"Ha! Ha!" I bounced back. But if Ryan hardly ever swore, I *never* swore. Unless ... "Drunk mouth."

"Let's go find out." She suddenly was off her tall wooden stool.

"What?"

"Let's find out!" she reiterated, clearly excited, and then called out for the bartender to close our tab.

"What? How are we going to find out?"

I was still trying to even process the idea that I might be … Could I be pregnant? Oh, the alcohol swishing in my brain didn't help comprehension.

"Geesh, I *do* have to explain everything," she mocked. "We go to a drug store, get a little white stick, and you pee on it. *Voila!*" She put her hands up dramatically like she was the magician of pregnancy reveals.

"Now?"

"Uh, yeah. Girls' night extreme. I love it. Thanks for taking my mind off of … what's his name?" she joked.

And, before I knew it, we had made our way to a convenience store. The fluorescent lighting was especially obnoxiously bright as we giggled and swayed our way through the aisles. Slightly balancing onto each other, I tried not to laugh. The situation was not funny—I couldn't be pregnant. But laughing was better than crying. I was glad Willow was there for all sorts of reasons but mostly because I had no idea how to even go about choosing a test. Who knew there were so many? And I'm sure the clerk at the counter was not impressed at all by our behavior, especially combined with our purchase.

As I finished paying with crinkled bills, a text came in from Ryan. *I know to let U B right now. Left light on.*

*Thanks.* I managed to get the word spelled correctly after only three tries. But I wanted to make sure to say it because he was not only respecting my need to be alone but was trusting that I would come back and to our room.

Luckily, the Uber driver had waited, and we slid haphazardly once again into the back seat. And then we were off to Willow's apartment. It was the same place I had lived at before moving in with Ryan. Some things had changed since then … some had not. And after a few minutes in the bathroom, I would know if the biggest change in my life was about to happen.

\*\*\*

I shed my bra from underneath my shirt and stripped off my jeans, all of which smelled of the establishment I had been in for most of the night. And then I quietly lifted the sheet so I could slip into bed. I couldn't see much of anything since turning off the hall light. It was the one Ryan's text had been referring to and what I usually did for him when he had a late business night.

"Good night, Mr. Mean." Since he was sleeping on his belly, I kissed the back of his bare shoulder and then turned over to snuggle tightly with my pillow.

"Hmmm," he partially murmured and then a little more awake asked, "Are you drunk?"

"Mmmm-hmmm," I answered, trying not to resuscitate my giggling with Willow from before.

"You all right?" I could tell he turned because of the sound of his voice. "Not bad decisions drunk?"

"Uh," I said, feeling every bit the next words I would say. "Tired drunk."

"All right. I'm glad you're home ... in our bed." I felt his hand softly stroke the back of my head. "Good night."

"Uh-huh. Tomorrow."

Tomorrow we would have to face each other. Tomorrow we would have to talk. But at least in that tiny moment, with his hand caressing my brunette locks, I thought everything was all right.

# CHAPTER SEVENTEEN

Somehow, despite taking a nap the day before, I was the last one up the next morning. Well, okay, not *somehow*. I'm pretty sure the night filled with drama and alcohol aided in me crashing soundly.

After putting on my pair of loose, gray sweats and a similarly hued graphic tee, I let my nose and slightly hungover disposition lead me directly to the kitchen where the coffee pot was nearly full and hot. I took out one of the larger mugs and poured, skipping any creamer or sugar. I needed it straight. And I wasn't quite ready for food.

I peeked into the family room. Sallie and Joel were on the floor, munching on some cereal and watching cartoons. When I didn't spot Ryan with them, I turned to look elsewhere.

"Hi, Bethany!" Shocked at whose voice it was, I swung around to see a jovial Sallie looking up at me.

"Morning, you two," I acknowledged, and the four-legged furball, who had been lying next to them, scuttled over to greet me.

"Are you going to have breakfast with us?" Joel asked.

"No. No breakfast. Need to just start with my wake-me-up coffee. And I should probably find your dad." I bent to give the dog a rub on his back. "Besides, it looks like Lyric is keeping you company."

"Oh. Okay. Yeah."

Because Sallie seemed disappointed, I added, "But we can make something special for lunch if you want."

Their joint smiles and bright eyes made me feel even better than the couple sips of coffee. As I left the room, I wondered if it *was* simply my hormones that had me question Sallie's previous behavior toward me. I had to set it aside, though, because it was her father's attitude and temperament that I was immediately concerned about. Even though our goodnight in bed was peaceful, I knew with all spoken prior, we definitely had some things to break through.

In just a few more steps, I found him in the living room. He was on the sofa. His own coffee and a few pieces of paper were stationed on the end table beside him. The way the furniture was positioned, he didn't know I had entered. I was only seeing the back of him and the pencil he was twirling in his right hand. I fondly recalled that was one of the very first things I had noticed and liked about Ryan—his simplicity and authenticity like using paper and pencil instead of all electronics.

"Morning," I greeted after a beat of praying we could get back to where we belonged. "Thanks for making the coffee."

"Probably not as good as the coffee expert in the house, but I figured you would need some," he spoke while putting his pencil down.

I'm not sure I heard everything he said, though, because as I made my way around the sofa to face him, I was taken aback. He was clean-shaven. There not a trace of a whisker on his face. I'm sure I was staring, and I'm pretty sure he knew why. That sight alone gave me the confidence to sit next to him.

"How you feeling?" He pulled one of my dark, out-of-place hairs away from my face.

"Not bad. Cold or whatever went away. Tequila helped." I noted his eye roll before I continued. "And coffee is helping the tequila." I took another sip and placed it on the table in front of us.

"Hmmm."

It was my turn to touch him, and, of course, it was the back of my hand softly caressing his smooth, handsome, bare cheek. "You didn't need to—" I offered, although I sure the heck liked it.

"I heard you yesterday." He looked me dead-on, and I couldn't help but do the same. "I heard what you were trying to tell me. I didn't want you to think I didn't."

I let my hand drop, knowing I was going to need complete concentration on his words. We needed to talk. We needed to listen. He knew it. I knew it. And it was starting.

"I'm sorry," he continued. "I was … I don't know … abrupt or defensive or …"

"Yeah, all those things." I didn't say it cruelly or harshly, but it was the truth.

And he double admitted it. "Yeah."

"It's not just the beard, Ry." Again, my words were soft but with a little bit of preach.

"No. No. I know." He brought his hand over to cover mine resting on the sofa seat. Again, he made sure to meet my eyes. "I talked with the kids. We had root beer floats after you left. Well," he admitted and let his eyelids dip for a moment, "after I calmed down."

My eyes blinked a couple times on his admission. We had both been so upset. Was it strange, sad, or wrong of me that I was glad he had been, too? He totally won in the control part, though. Root beer and ice cream were a far better choice than tequila and, well, more tequila.

I squeezed his hand a bit as he continued. "We sat and talked. Really talked. And you were right."

"About?"

"I just didn't want to see it, I guess. I wanted

everything to be fine. But you were right—something was bothering Sallie."

"Yeah," I agreed in an even tone, thinking the drunk me from the night before would have yelled out an I-told-you-so. "Did she tell you?" I asked instead.

He squeezed his lips together, nodded, and said, "It's you."

"Oh, no." Not only did I release my hand from his, but I squirmed a little in my seat. "What? What's wrong? I thought so, but that makes me so sad."

"Listen, okay?" When I nodded, he pushed forward. "She loves you. Both the kids do. You mean a lot to them." I knew his words should have reassured me, but why then ... what was the "but"? "Sallie? She called you mommy the other day at camp. And it confused the other kids, and it confused her. She feels guilty ... like she is being mean to Kari or forgetting her or both."

"Oh."

That was all I could say. In only a couple of sentences, he had told me so much. It made my heart both bloom with love and hurt with sympathy. And I didn't know how to react to it or, most certainly, what I would have said if I had been the one Sallie had divulged those feelings to.

"I explained to her that no one will ever replace her mom. She will always have her in her heart, but her heart is big and she is so loved that she can have more than one mom. She can share that love and can call you whatever she wants. Is that okay with you?"

Well, that was why Ryan was such a good dad. He knew what to do and say. If Sallie's words didn't melt my heart, Ryan's sure did. The fact that he embraced me in that role in Sallie—and Joel's—life, left me almost speechless, especially after the "parent" comment the night before. I knew to and could definitely let that go. He had more than apologized with his story about Sallie. And I suspect he hadn't really meant it to begin with, just like Joel and his meanest-daddy comment. We all say things in anger and regret them.

"Yes." I pressed below my eyes. "Of course."

His closed smile lit up his dark blue eyes. "She seemed so relieved. You'll see."

"I think maybe I already did." I internally smiled, replaying in my mind my interaction with Sallie in the family room.

"Good. Good. You know, I think it would have happened even if Kari hadn't died. She looks up to you a lot."

"And she needed you to tell her it was okay." I reinforced the conversations Ryan and I had previously had. "She seeks your approval."

"I know." He sighed. "I know." He then went on to his other child. "So ... Joel ..."

"Yeah?"

"I think he's always going to have some kind of issue with sleeping because, God help us, he is such an active little boy."

"He is." I resisted saying the word "understatement."

"You know, since he was really little, he fought sleep. And I get the nightmare thing. It's to be expected with what they are dealing with. Plus, we all have those every so often." Ryan was known to toss and turn himself. "But now ... the middle-of-the-night stuff again? And, yeah, with how he reacted with you yesterday? I shouldn't have blown all of that off."

"Ryan, you haven't. You go to him. You're trying to reward him."

"But I didn't listen to you or him, really." He plowed forward, "I did last night." On my nod, he explained, "I guess he's worried because I said Kari was tired and sick and then she died. So, he's afraid something like that will happen to him when he's sleeping. And you? On top of being tired in the middle of the day, you mentioned being sick. He was afraid that you were going to ... to be next."

"Oh, man."

"Yeah, right?" He shook his head. "He can't remember to bring his jacket home, but he remembers something I said—"

"Did you explain it to him?"

"I tried. But there's such a fine line. I'm gonna talk with their psychologist, too. I just want them to be okay, you know? I know they'll never be the same. I know. But I want them to be okay. And I've got to understand it will take time, and there will be little things like a slip of the tongue or an illness or ... a special day or video that smacks them without warning." The way he looked down and then back up at me, portrayed his sense of guilt for also being susceptible to the grieving process. He was the one—not the kids—who knew of the days and video. Before I could tell him I truly understood, even regarding his own feelings over the loss of Kari, he spoke again. "So, I sat up and wrote for a little while last night ... everything that was compiling. It helped."

"I know how that is," I agreed with the having-things-pressing-down-on-your-life issue *and* how lyrics seem to ease some of it. Right then, though, I was really beginning to feel the opposite. I had been dreading our talk because I was afraid nothing had changed. But from his fresh, clean face to his conversation with the kids, I knew it was the opposite. So, I decided it was my turn. "Well, there's one thing you won't have to worry about."

"What?"

"You're not going to be a dad again."

"I'm not gonna what?" I'm pretty sure his shocked face mirrored mine from the night before when Willow had initially suggested the pregnancy prospect.

"I think you heard me."

"I did." He spoke a little slower, while carefully watching me. "What does that mean?"

"I wasn't feeling well and was emotional ... so, I took a test when Willow and I were out," I explained our unexpected detour of girls' night.

"A pregnancy test?"

I might have laughed and been sarcastic—no, a spelling test, Ryan—had he not been so taken aback and focused. "Yeah," I answered quietly, realizing maybe that had been my bad-decisions-drunk part of the night. I probably shouldn't have done something personal like a pregnancy test with Willow. I should have waited for him.

But that didn't seem to be his concern. "I thought we were good. You're on the pill."

"Yeah, I am," I reassured. "But you never know. There is still that one percent."

"Bethany, back up." He was definitely getting antsy in his seat, and I felt bad—my news was supposed to be a good thing. "Are you pregnant or not?"

"Not," I reiterated. "You're in the clear. With everything going on, I'm probably a little screwed up."

"What makes you think that would make me happy— you not being pregnant? I mean, I know it wouldn't have been exactly planned, but ..." Wow, he was so serious.

"You have your kids," I spoke honestly.

"I do, and I love being a dad. It's my number one job. Why wouldn't I want to share that with you?"

"I ... I ..."

I guess I always just assumed he was happy/content with two. We even had that talk about being overwhelmed by more. But we had never directly spoken about it.

"Of course I would have another if that's what you wanted. I thought we would do it proper and wait to get married first, though."

"Really?"

"Is that what you want?"

Well, that part of our talk was ending up being the same as the whole beginning part of the conversation— nothing was what I expected. I knew my mouth was a little agape as I tried to prewrite in my mind what I wanted to say. It shouldn't have been hard. It was the simplest of truths, really.

"I want to be happy with you," I said, feeling a little teary-eyed. "Whatever road that leads to. Our conversation got cut off last night. So, let me finish it. I'm really looking forward to being your wife, too."

"Good." He smiled a legitimate smile. "Because you not only mean a lot to the kids, you mean more than a lot to me. For real."

Oh … swoosh. For real. For real. I hadn't felt 'for real' in a while.

I was so much more at peace, but it seemed Ryan had one more thing to unburden. "I'm sorry. I know I checked out on you for the last few days. I … Guess what?"

"What?"

"I talked with your dad last night."

I think five different reactions scrambled around in my mind before I managed to speak. "You called him?"

"I did."

"Did you tell him we were arguing? How did that go? Did you say you'd like to have a little conversation about how to deal with his irrational daughter?" I only partially teased.

"No. Hardly." He shook his head in denial. "I didn't think you would want me to invade your privacy like that."

I loved my dad, but Ryan was right. I believed in honesty and truth, but there were things between any couple that should solely be theirs. "So?"

"He had texted me a couple pictures of some antique cars at a car show he had been at." Ryan had gained a bond with my father the instant he had shown him a photo of his very own classic red Mustang. "So, I took the opportunity to call him. You told me once that I could talk with him … that he'd help." As I recalled our conversation on the day Kari died, Ryan continued. "I think it shocked him a little. I knew it was late, but he had just texted, so …"

"He was probably up working on tomorrow's sermon and procrastinating online."

Ryan laughed but then admitted how he used my dad for guidance. "I should probably go to a counselor myself, but your dad ... he's a good listener."

"Better than his daughter." I looked down.

"No ... just outsider perspective. He helped me figure out why I kind of crashed emotionally. I thought things were getting better with the kids ... with everything. I had started to relax a little. And then I knew Kari's birthday was approaching and then the video. And I couldn't. I couldn't handle one more thing, especially when I thought things were turning around. It was like the whole one step forward, but not only two ... it was *ten* steps back. And, yes, I checked out a little. Subconsciously, I think I knew you were there to hold it all together. But I shouldn't have put that on you, and I most certainly didn't mean to hurt you in the process."

The gust of breath escaping my lungs was tense because listening to his personal unveiling saddened me. It was part of what I had been afraid of weeks before when he felt like he needed to be strong for everyone. Even though things were seemingly getting better, he had never let himself truly feel. And then came the straw on the camel's back—Kari's birthday and the video simultaneously.

"I should have understood." But, I hadn't. I hadn't seen past the masked outward messages he was giving to truly notice the internal struggles he was dealing with. I think maybe it was because I was trying to simply stay afloat and be brave myself. "I should have stepped up," I insisted.

He ignored my offering. "Bethany, you have no idea how sorry I am that we had to cancel the wedding. And the other night?" He bit his lower lip. "I knew if I made love with you, it wouldn't have been that. It would have been just sex because I was hurting and needed to feel. I didn't want that with you." And he knew I wouldn't have wanted it that way, either. "I know you didn't understand, but I was simply trying to put one foot in front of the other to keep it all together."

Ryan wasn't necessarily one to shy away from his feelings, but he was also a man's man and wanted to be strong. It was such an interesting mix—living with and loving every side of him. And the vulnerability he was putting on display right then was remarkable and worthy of not only my interest but my love.

"Is that what you meant at the baseball game about always saying no to me? It was about the wedding and the other night?" He shrugged sheepishly, and then I had an admission of my own. "I *was* confused and afraid, but mostly, Ryan, I was concerned because I love you." I claimed his hand in mine again.

"I know ... to both." He caressed our joined hands with his thumb. "Thanks for riding it out with me. But, mostly, thank you for giving me the swift kick you did last night to get me back to where I needed to be."

I wasn't sure I did that. I had just been letting my messed-up emotions out and telling him how I felt and what I feared. But I played along, wanting us to simply forgive each other and start moving on. "I may not be good at baseball, but don't underestimate my karate skills, Thompson," I teased.

"Oh, brother. I *do* love you." He leaned over and kissed me most beautifully.

"You must to kiss me with my hair looking like Lyric's when he needs a good doodle brush out!"

My teasing was for his benefit as well as mine. Saying something funny helped me from tearing up after the gamut of emotional content we had just been through. He ruffled his hand through my brown, more-wavy-than-usual hair. I'm sure it only made it worse, but it was worth it to see the ease in his face.

"So," he said after an almost magical, silent moment, "it can't be quite up to weekend winery standards, but how would you feel about a real date night?" He continued straight on, not waiting for my response. "I talked with Maks. He said the kids could stay at his place tonight. I don't know who will love the video and hide-n-seek games more—the single bachelor or the kids."

"Oh, you must have been pretty sure I was going to say 'yes' since you already involved Maks." I remained in my playful mood.

"Well, if not, I was most likely going to drink myself into oblivion, and the kids still shouldn't have been around."

Knowing that probably wasn't too far from the truth, I immediately let him off the hook. "Yes, Ryan. Absolutely. Yes." I pecked him on the lips for good measure. "What do you have in mind?"

He tapped his index finger on my lips. "Up to you. We can get dressed up and go to a hotel or just stay here. Whatever you want. I know Joel and Sallie are still a priority, but I can't neglect everything else—you, my face …" He did a half-smile. "We've waited a long time for a me-and-you night."

"Hmmm," I agreed.

"We'll figure out a wedding date, too."

I nodded. The wedding was the first thing that had started our arguing the night before. He hadn't forgotten. Whether it was his talk with my dad, his own reflection, or me walking away, I appreciated every bit of effort he had made in helping us get back to us.

"And maybe start off the night by practicing making some of those babies." With that comment, I knew he was completely back.

So, I was, too. "Nope."

"Nope? Nope to what?"

"No rolls in the hay."

"What?" I know he was trying not to be shocked or disappointed, but he was a man, and there was no denying it. "What do you mean?"

"I thought you would appreciate the euphemism, farm

boy."

"Uh, not so much. Are you serious?"

"Yep. Not until we set the wedding date." His eyebrows drew closer to each other, and my lips curled to a half-smirk/half-smile as I clarified, "Willow's rule."

He made a *tsking* sound before razzing my not-there-to-defend-herself friend. "Tell Willow she is no longer on the guest list."

"You should be thankful I have Willow. You and I could not have continued like we were last night. We actually needed the time apart."

His eyes closed for a second on my truth. "Agreed. Still ..." His sexy smile revved right back up. "I can make it so you change your mind." He rubbed my shirt right below my breasts and then made his way underneath as he started kissing me.

"No!" I couldn't help but laugh. When he continued his parade of exploration, I jumped off the sofa. "No!"

"Lenay ..."

"Oh, now you use that name." I was still chuckling.

"Uh-huh." And he was still amused and sexy. When he stood up and went to take both of my hands in his, I hesitated, still playing our teasing game. "We'll pick a date. I promise." He played with my fingers. "And not because I want to be in your pants ... which I do." He smiled, causing me to do the same. "But because I want to be always in your heart."

Ryan claimed I was the expert, brilliant songwriter. But not only was he guiding me business-wise on that career journey, he was also a master of words himself. And his skill set, in reality, meant so much more because his words were personal and counted when most needed.

# CHAPTER EIGHTEEN

"Uhhh," Ryan partially grunted. "There was a reason why the beginning of June had been so perfect."

That was true. *Singer Spotlight* had been done for the season, there weren't any family obligations, and the kids had just finished school. Best laid plans.

Finding another date for our wedding truly was going to be a challenge. But at least it was the only nuptial obstacle. After all, we already had everything else planned—the dresses, the vows, the best man and maid-of-honor, my dad's church, the limited guest list. Reordering magnolias and rebooking the hotel reception site wouldn't be as difficult as finding a date on the calendar.

Because we were sitting next to each other in the restaurant booth, I could place my right hand on the top of his thigh without being noticed. Softly tapping my fingers like a piano, I said, "I'm sure we can pick a date."

Those deep blue eyes blinked at me as if he was taking a sexy photo and, placing his left hand around my back, he tugged me in a little closer to his side. "Yes, I'm anxious for dessert."

While dinner at the hotel restaurant was scrumptious, I

knew food wasn't exactly on the menu for dessert. But we were sticking to our informal agreement and setting a wedding date first. And because it was hard for me, especially knowing how much we were again emotionally connected, I wasn't making it easy for him. I teased my mouth on his.

"It's already July," he said, after an exasperating, in more ways than one, breath. "And Joel's birthday and your birthday are both in August, plus the hospital benefit in between." When I let my hand move to rub his pant-covered inner thigh, he squirmed. "You know, this is defeating your purpose."

"Yeah? How is that?" I smirked and slipped my hand into the one side of my sleeveless dress to fiddle with my bra.

"The more you distract me, the more I can't concentrate to find a day."

I laughed—he had a point. "I should have gotten in on the deal with Joel and Sallie to go to your office, too."

"Huh?"

"Defeating my purpose," I quoted him and then explained, "The day after our first kiss. I asked to meet you at your office instead of your house. You said it was 'defeating my purpose' of *not* wanting to be alone with you because it was a Saturday and no one was at the office."

"Ha! Yeah."

"Funny, tonight's a Saturday, too. But this time, I *do* want to be alone with you."

I watched as his eyes squinted the tiniest of bits, his face tilted as if it helped him read my mind, and then he said it. "Geez, Lenay. The office, yeah?"

I hadn't been serious when I first brought up the idea. It was just a continuation of my tease that had come from his innocent "defeating" comment. But the seemingly brightened look in his eyes and the prevision of the two of us really alone in the place where we first essentially met? Gosh, I suddenly really wanted it to be a reality.

"September. September," he said in an even more hurried pace.

"September when?"

"Uh ..." He panned through his phone, which merged and detailed his many obligations. "We've gotta let the kids get situated in school ... but before any of the TV promos start. Mid or late September? The twenty-first?"

"What about your family? Is that good? I don't think it should be a problem on my family's end."

"Uh ... my mom's birthday is around then. But I'm sure she'll be thrilled to share it with us. And, you know what? Between the spouses and grandkids, something is always interfering—a birthday, anniversary, sporting event. Late September, early October for Dylan with the winery ..." He seemed to hesitate and then changed his mind. "Eh, it's our day. They will come."

Knowing we once again had a definite plan for making our union formal made me so happy ... so at ease. I had always believed in the sanctuary of marriage. But considering how our relationship started—with so many people thinking we were somehow wrong—it made me want to legitimatize our love that much more.

Ryan seemed to feel it, too. But he actually verbalized it. "You know when I told Sonny I consider you my wife?" He waited the second or two for me to nod. "I meant it, wholeheartedly. I've been through the paper stuff before, and I understand it's not what makes a marriage. Knowing we are going to declare everything we are in front of the people we love, that means so much to me."

I didn't want to cry, even though they would have been happy tears. It was the tiny part of me that was vain enough not to want a post-tear-stricken face when we made love. So, I pushed the potential tears aside and used my sass that had been part of our attraction from the beginning of our relationship. "You didn't need to say all that. September twenty-first was all." I scrunched my nose and raised the corners of my mouth a bit. "I told you we could have sex as soon as we picked a date."

"Lenay …" He cooed a *tsk*.

"Ryan, don't make me cry," I begged.

He kissed my nose and went along with my request and sarcasm. "Okay, then. Heads go upstairs to the hotel room … tails my office?"

The narrowest but longest of breaths pursed out of my lips at the prospect. I was back in the game. And I made an amendment to the rule.

"You mean which one *first?*"

His light laugh shook my nearby body, too. "Well, of course."

He took our special quarter out of his wallet, and I ground my teeth together. I was nervous. Well, not nervous. Anxious. It was an anticipatory, jittery feel. I suddenly felt more alive than I had since, gosh, the bridal shower.

When the coin flip result was revealed, Ryan partially groaned. I knew it wasn't because the venue didn't excite him as it did me. It was because it was just a little farther away.

"Okay. I'm going to track down the waiter and pay this bill. You go to the valet." He took the ticket out of his pant pocket and handed it to me. "Get the car so it's ready."

"Ryan!" I laughed. "We're not making a mad-dash getaway."

"The heck we're not." He pecked me quickly on the lips. "Go!"

I scooched out of the booth as gracefully as I could, tossed my purse over my shoulder, and shook my tailfeather a little, knowing Ryan was most definitely watching. Because it was raining ever so slightly and the valet insisted, I waited in the covered section, which connected the restaurant with the outdoors. I would have danced in the rain I felt so free and happy. A little water couldn't dampen my mood. But … something else suddenly had the potential.

"Did you have the couscous? You always liked that."

Swiveling around, I came face-to-face with the person who had spoken those words. "Andre." His name came out almost in a whisper.

It had been over a year since I had seen him and, honestly, wouldn't have cared if I ever did again. Looking cleaner or maybe healthier, he was dressed in black slacks and a white top, which I instantly recognized as part of the restaurant staff uniform. His occupation seemed about right, considering he had been a food server in the apartment building I used to live in.

"Bethany." He nodded with an unapologetic open gaze. "You're looking ... well, as fine as ever ... maybe a little flushed. But that's probably just our little, uh, attraction thing we got going on, huh?" He winked, using his charmer act that had worked in the past and probably still did with other unknowing women.

Very unchristian of me, I spurted out the words like they were fire. "You wish."

"Can't deny that." He did a one-sweep of me with his eyes. "Still with Mr. Music, huh?"

"Despite all efforts from outside forces," I sneered and squinted at him—definitely one of the main troublemaking culprits.

"Hey, so, I'm sorry about all that. I saw the two of you in there, and I wasn't going to say anything, but since you—"

"Then why did you? It would have been for the best."

"I needed to. I shouldn't have done what I did—sold out you and ... and ..."

"Ryan," I helped him with the name, simply to expedite whatever the apology or what-have-you was.

"Ryan, yeah. Ryan Thompson. I shouldn't have told the mags and media about your affair."

"It wasn't an affair!" I brought my voice down in enough time to not cause a scene.

"Well, no one knew that, and you sure acted like it was." What he said was true, but it had been my and Ryan's business—not the world's. What Andre had done to us came down to simply not having any kind of human decency. "You don't understand how much I needed the money and how desperate I was."

"You needed it because you were trying to stay out of jail." Again, I managed to barely keep my volume in check.

"I know." He took a breath. "Bethany, I've paid my debt off to the apartment for what I took from them. I only did it because they paid crap, it was easy, and I thought no one would notice a little here and there. And I wanted a better life."

Geez, I thought, doesn't everyone? He was the same age I was. He just had to give it a chance—not simply feel entitled to more and take without earning it.

"I'm trying to be the person my aunt raised me to be. Believe it or not, I truly regret the part I played in your scandal or whatever you want to call it."

Scandal was a good word. Divorce Gate was another I had secretly called it in my mind. But that wasn't the only thing I held against the man standing in front of me.

"I regret falling for your Casanova line that I was special."

Those words had gotten a vulnerable, drunk me to sleep with him. Bad. Decisions. Drunk. Like none other. Not only had it been completely one hundred percent out of my character, but it had been before knowing Ryan was going to enter my life and totally reform how a man should treat me.

"No line ... swear it."

"Andre, come on."

"Totally the truth and totally a hot damn night. Will never say I regret that."

"What?" On Ryan's exaggerated one word, I literally stuck my arm out to prevent a suddenly present him from lunging toward Andre.

"He's … No," I pleaded.

"I told you, if I ever laid eyes on him again, Bethany, I would—"

I didn't have to stop Ryan that time because the presence of the valet did. "Uh … uh … ma'am, your car is here."

"Go ahead." Ryan's head-tilt signaled that he wanted me to go with the bystander valet, who was holding an open umbrella for me. "I'll just be a minute."

I knew Ryan loved me and would defend me with everything in him. But he didn't need to. He didn't need to be that guy in the bar with Maks and Olsen. He didn't need to prove anything to me, because I knew his love. I knew *our* love. It was greater than all of that.

So, I threaded my right hand with Ryan's left and squeezed tight. "I hope you can be that person your aunt wanted you to be, Andre. I truly do. I think it's in you. I hope you can find happiness. I know I have." I looked at Ryan—who seemed a little shocked by my gesture—and gently, but with persistence, pulled him toward our waiting car.

After finding our way out of the parking lot, Ryan finally spoke. "What a jerk."

"You mean bastard." I tried a smile while using the name Ryan and I had more commonly used for Andre … if we spoke of him at all.

"Hmmmf," he mumbled, as if trying to stop himself from laughing and instead hold on to his pissed-off stance. "You're right. I mean bastard." He patted my leg and switched lanes. "You good?" He glanced over at me.

"Are we still going to your office?"

"Yeah?" he asked in a hopeful way.

"Then I'm more than good." I smiled.

"You don't want to talk about it?"

"What I want is *you*." My comment got another quick look from the driver. "He's not going to ruin tonight. He apologized and—"

"He did?" Ryan had obviously not heard much of my conversation with Andre up to his protective pounce.

"As much as I think he could. But that's more than I ever expected. So, not only is he not going to ruin tonight, I'm not even going to give him one more thought in my life at all, as long as you don't, either."

"Who?" he asked in jest, causing me a legitimate laugh.

"I meant what I said to him, you know."

"Yeah? About what?"

"Being happy."

"Me, too, Lenay." He patted my leg and then lightened the mood. "And I am particularly happy my office is so close by."

"Ryan!" I smacked his arm.

"What?" he mocked. "Okay, how about song for right now?"

"Hmmm …" I thought about the solid state we were in as a couple and how much I counted on him for being the brightest spot in my life. "'You Make Me Smile,'" I settled on.

"All right," he said in an even but agreeable tone.

"What? You always pull this when you have the most fantastic song in mind."

"You can always start the game." He was in as good as a mood as I was—bastard Andre was, indeed, once again in the past.

"Go ahead." I sighed, ready for him to up me with the best song for the moment.

"Do you know 'The Way' by Clay Aiken?"

"No. No. Dang it."

"Go ahead, look it up. Play it. We'll probably be able to finish it before getting to the office."

I already couldn't wait to make love with Ryan. But that song soaring through the speakers as we entered the indoor parking garage of his office's building, toppled me right over. He knew I was misty-eyed as he secured the car and we made our way to the elevator. Obviously vacant on a Saturday evening, we entered, and, as he pressed the button for his floor, I took a step toward him.

"Don't kiss me, Lenay," he warned, backing up.

"What? Why not?"

Of course I was going to. It had been our thing since nearly forever. When we were still incognito as a couple, the empty elevator was one of the only places we could sneak a kiss in.

"Between the pick-a-wedding-date tease, you not letting me defend you in the lobby ..."

"Thank you for wanting to and for still not," I said honestly.

"And the fact I love you so dang much," he continued with the lightest of audible groans. "You seriously need to keep all body parts off me so we actually make it to the office."

"Geez!" I laughed. "Okay. Okay." I threw my hands up in surrender mode and backed flat up against the opposite elevator wall. But my sexy stare? I may as well have had my hands entwined in his hair. He decided to deflect by looking at the electronic numbers counting in what seemed to be snail mode.

Finally, we reached his floor. He took my hand and guided me through the darkness. I saw the leather sofa I had sat on while awaiting my first appointment with the music manager, and I saw Anamaria's desk—always immaculately neat. And then ... the door to his inner sanctum. Ryan took the key from his pant pocket and unlocked it. The other building lights from downtown LA were the only illumination in the room, and that was just fine. In a weird way, it was terribly romantic.

"What about the security cameras?" The thought suddenly flashed into my mind.

"Uh ... I don't know." He looked toward the door. "It's not like I've done this before."

And that had been another of my thoughts after the sex-in-his-office idea kind of steamrolled at the restaurant.

Had he with Kari? I had decided I didn't want to know. But since the answer was what I actually desired, though, I was glad it came out.

"Here, I'll shut the door," he offered. "Cameras should only film the lobby area. I'll check later, though."

And as soon as the door was shut, Ryan started undoing his belt and simultaneously, haphazardly slapping things off his desk. I looked at the photos hanging on the walls of Ryan with famous musicians and other artists. The ones with Kari had been removed since the divorce revelation, and any personal photos of the kids and me were on his phone and used as his laptop screensaver.

"Come here," he beckoned with a sexy moan.

When I did, he stood behind me and tilted me slightly over so he could shimmy his way under my petal pink dress and snake my dark pink panties down my legs. I turned around and allowed him to hoist me on top of his nearly cleared-off, smooth desk so I was sitting and facing him. Seeing it was my turn, I partially tugged down his gray slacks and dark briefs. But no other clothes were removed. We just found and met each other repetitively. And it was undeniably sexy and as hot as Hades.

We held each other there for a few minutes after, touching each other's faces and breathing. And then we did a little giggling as we straightened up the office and made sure to lock up. I was allowed to kiss him that time on the elevator ride down, and it was very much reciprocated. And on our way back to the hotel, we called the kids to wish them a good night.

Making love in the hotel room was completely the opposite of our sex venture in Ryan's office, but it was not one ounce better or worse. Ryan was gentle as he completely shed me of my dress and nibbled on my shoulder and bra strap. We whispered the words "I love you" numerous times. And when we came together, baring our bodies and our souls, it was with the utmost tenderness, love, and appreciation.

***

"Hey, handsome," I answered my phone. Since our argument, talk after, and date night a few days or so before, things were so much more relaxed ... so much more us.

"That is no way to talk to your manager," he jostled back in good humor.

"My manager should use his work phone to call me then," I assessed.

"Okay, you got me there."

"Is this a manager call?" I passed over the espresso blend.

"It is ... Miss Opala."

"Mr. Thompson, sir." I saluted if not with my hands, then with my voice.

"Geez." I could picture his slow head shake. "Do you think you can come over here?"

"Your office?" I asked and then quickly added with an edge of sexiness, "But there's people around."

"Yes, Miss Opala. And why shouldn't there be?" He kept in character.

After a part sigh/part groan, I answered my manager correctly. "It's slow here. I can ask if they can cover the tail end of my shift." With no one in line at the coffee shop, I started wiping the counter. "Just so I have time to pick up the kids after."

"Yeah. It shouldn't take long."

"Good news?"

"It's not bad."

"All right. Let me ask. If it's a problem, I'll let you know. Otherwise, see you in a little bit. Mr. Thompson?" I tagged on at the end.

"Yes?" His voice sounded as equally relaxed as mine.

"Can you put Ryan on the phone, please?"

"Lenay ..." And, gosh, so sexy.

"I love you."

"I love you, too … so much."

***

I have a few stand-out times in Ryan's office. The first time there, for sure. Little did I know how sitting on that leather sofa, palms perspiring with anxiety over meeting such a big manager, would change my life professionally and personally. The time I did the recording for my songwriting demo was a first-time experience and exhilarating. And, of course, our sexy romp after hours. Then … then there was that afternoon in mid-July.

After saying hi to Anamaria in the reception area, I entered Ryan's office. I raised my eyebrows twice while looking at his desk, once again full of papers and electronics and such. He laughed as I purposefully leaned over and gave him a kiss.

"Having a hard time concentrating at work now," he admitted, looking at the desk himself.

And then, getting back to the business at hand, manager Thompson told me the most amazing news. While in the past, I had not been able to stand still when he related something career-changing, it was the opposite. I needed to sit and catch my breath. He sat in his regular chair across the desk from me and seemed almost perplexed at my reaction.

Ryan had presented a proposal from a television network. And it had nothing to do with him. It was for me. They wanted me to be one of the mentors on a new reality show where teams competed to build a star from the ground up—help them write their own original song, sing it, and market it. Winner chosen strictly by television audience.

"Wow!" I managed to breathe. "Did you know anything about this? I mean, before now?"

"No. No, not at all. It was a complete surprise. I know

… I had to present it to you, though."

"I mean, it's awesome. It would be so perfect for me. I love it."

"You want to do it?" His easygoing demeanor seemed to sink a notch.

"Yeah, of course."

What an opportunity! Was there even a debate? Songwriting? National recognition?

"Shouldn't you ask your fiancé first?" His eyes narrowed slightly.

Still overwhelmed by the offer, I looked at said fiancé. "What?"

"Talk with me?"

"Okay. What? No? You don't want me to take it?" I didn't understand … was that really what he was alluding to?

"Bethany, I thought you weren't into all of this. All you wanted to do was write."

"But that is what I will be doing." I was still pretty darn excited, but there was a little proverbial poke in my side that said something was going to change that.

And it was his serious and slow tone that was confirming my feeling. "With press and publicity in Nashville."

"Well, yeah. It will help get my name out there."

"First of all, your name is already out there. That's why they picked you."

I knew and relished the fact that what he said was true, but I also knew another little tidbit that made my name an option. "And because it is a brand-new show and not reputable yet." I had been around the business and, in particular, Ryan long enough to learn a few insider things. "The big writer names can't be bothered. They don't need it like I do."

He didn't seem to appreciate my take. In fact, he appeared to be getting more irritated. "*I* am getting your name out there."

"I know you are." I tried to soothe, knowing how much he did for me.

"Are you serious?" He stood up. "This is something you really want? I didn't think you would. I told them—"

I felt my eyes open wide as I stood, too. "You told them no?" A tingling sensation erupted over both of my arms. "Ryan? You told them no?" I swear I lost vision momentarily with my mix of fury and disbelief. "How could you do that?" I tilted my head and gave him one more chance. "Really?" The sound leaving my lungs was like a wounded, starving animal. "I can't even ..." I sucked my lips in together and looked at him while I still could. "I ... I've gotta get the kids," even though it was a bit early.

"You're gonna leave? Not listen?"

"You're not saying anything I want to hear."

And retreating was the better solution than a full-blown scene in his place of business. Plus, since it was supposed to be a professional meeting, I would never shout at my manager. But, of course, I probably wouldn't have walked out like I did, either.

# CHAPTER NINETEEN

Ryan was late coming home from work that night. He had been plenty of times before. But it didn't take a genius to understand the reason he was on that particular day. He was avoiding me and the sure-fire part two scene that was going to take place. We hadn't talked or even tried to communicate since I left his office. And even though it had only been a few hours, every minute seemed to escalate the issue like a soaring mountain, where the higher you'd climb, the harder it was to breathe.

Sallie, Joel, and I had waited a little while before eating and then eventually did so without him. He arrived not only after we were done but just as we were about finished cleaning up. The kids were wiping the table, and I was loading the last item into the dishwasher. Entering the room, Ryan kissed the top of Sallie's head and fluffed Joel's hair.

"Can you two show your dad the food in the fridge and sit with him?"

I didn't wait for an answer. I knew Sallie and Joel would soak up any time with Ryan. And I didn't give him time to say anything, either. Because even if it had been kind, I wasn't at the point of feeling it back. Disbelief had set in for a while, and being with the kids had distracted me somewhat. But him in that room—the two of us together in front of the kids—was not going to work. We would not be able to pull off a positive, everything-is-all-right scene, and that was important for Sallie and Joel. So, I promptly walked out again.

It was a little while later when he found me in the game room. I figured it was long enough for him to have eaten and talked with the kids. It *wasn't* long enough, though, for me to cool down from the hurt boiling inside of me.

I started in right where we had left off in his office. "Ryan, that offer was a huge deal to me. You know that, right? And you just blew it off. You couldn't even ask what I thought or at least be happy for me?"

And he didn't miss a beat reciprocating. "For goodness sake, Bethany! I'm thrilled for you. I am."

The way his voice seemed to ache, let me believe at least that much. Yet, it didn't explain everything else. It didn't explain why he made that decision for me.

"But ..." I led.

"But nothing. I am."

That didn't help. I wasn't sure if he was saying very little because he thought it was all that needed to be said or because he knew anything additional would lead to more turmoil. But turmoil was what he was going to get because I definitely needed more explanation.

"No. Not nothing. 'But' something." My voice rose and his stayed mute. I tried again. "This is what you worried about, right? When you first agreed to be my manager and we started seeing each other—the personal versus professional line," I offered, having at least rationally thought of that over our time apart. "The emotions and negotiations."

"I ... maybe." He exhaled and sent his neck to one side to crack. "It's definitely not helping right now."

"You told me at the office I should ask you—my fiancé—for your opinion. But that's what I don't get.

Why? Why, if you are thrilled for me"—I threw his words right back at him—"don't you want me to take this? Because I know it's not Ryan the manager saying it. Right? Am I right?"

There was the sad sigh again. "No. As a manager, I would tell you it is a fabulous opportunity."

"Okay," I replied a little more calmly. "Then why did you shoot it down?"

"First of all, I didn't completely shoot it down. It can still be on the table. I—" He stopped midsentence and refocused on his justification. "I didn't think you wanted all the glitz and glamor. You said. We've talked about it ... even before ... when I knew I was starting to fall in love with you. I worried—"

Yes, our life goals and other talks ... and things hadn't changed. "I still don't want all of that."

"It's a big move—career-wise and physically," was his next counterpoint.

"Career-wise? Big is a good thing, especially when I am just starting out." I didn't need to tell him that, he knew. "And, yeah, I know filming is in Nashville."

That seemed to amp up his emotions-meter another notch and not in a good way. "So, how do you think it's going to work with you ... us ... the kids? We have a life here. If we're engaged or married ... God, Bethany, if we're in love, we can't live apart. It ... doesn't ... work." He spat out the last words like he was a dramatic military sergeant determined to get his command followed.

I heard everything he was saying and knew it was said not only with frustration but with love. But, yet, I didn't understand. I didn't understand what was making his stance so adamant. Ryan was one of the most even-tempered people I knew, even with all the pressures of his world. It didn't make sense.

I tried to keep as calm as I could, all the while still upset with his one-sided decision on the job proposal. "I don't know how it's gonna work. I didn't think about it. I was simply excited. And then I was upset, and I still haven't thought about it." Honesty.

"Well, I have. That's what being an adult is about." It was like he was saying I wasn't a parent all over again.

"What? What!" I don't know if I took a step forward or back or if I stomped ... the latter was probably most likely. "You don't think I'm an adult? I don't earn my own keep? Take care of you and the kids? Just because you're older doesn't mean—"

"Crap. No. That came out wrong."

"You better hope it did." I would have laughed at the irony of my words—sounding both adult and parent-like—but I didn't because I was once again as upset as I had been when I left his office. "Being an adult doesn't mean you stop being excited about things or hurt when someone dashes them away as quickly as a falling star."

Spite. Pure spite. And I meant every stinking word of it.

"Stop! I'm not dashing your—"

"You're saying 'no' to me again." I was on a roll, using my superb word memory skills to his disadvantage.

He made a low sound, closed his eyes, breathed in through his nose twice, and then looked at me once more. That time, he spoke slower and with more vulnerability than anger. And he did it with a recollection of his own. "You told me I should let you see me sad or scared. I am. I'm scared, okay?"

"What? What can you be scared of?" It seemed so implausible to me. "You're scared of me being successful?"

"No. Of course I want that for you," he said right away. "And, by the way, I already think you are." He paused for a second or two. "I'm scared of you leaving or changing or moving on ... or ... or all of it."

"What?" It was as if we were having a staring contest like the kids sometimes did.

"It happens. I'm afraid that world will eat you up ... all

that is good in you—"

There it was again—I wasn't strong enough or special enough or good enough. I had heard those words many times in my life, both from the music industry and others. And ... from him. The very first words he had ever said to me about others being way ahead of me reared their ugly head in my memory bank. I knew deep down it was unfair to think of that. But everything seemed so wrong. And because it was something I had been fighting my entire life, I didn't want to hear it one more time. I didn't want to hear it from the person I trusted and loved more than anyone in the world. I couldn't. I just couldn't.

"Don't patronize me, Ryan." I sucked back onto the adult comment and more. "I am not some young and innocent porcelain doll. I am not going to break. I have fought hard to live my life on my own terms and keep my integrity. I am also not solely a good girl, preacher's daughter. I have impure thoughts. I've done bad things. I've wished ill—"

In a way I was glad Sallie was suddenly standing in front of us. I was on a rant, and it was leading nowhere good. Ryan knew of my impure thoughts and some of the bad things I did—which in no way compared to a lot of people in the world. But had I continued talking, I would have mentioned Kari and how, God help me, I had at times wished she would have gone away. The guilt that she had done so permanently was something that would probably always eat at my soul. Mentioning Kari at that particular moment would not have been good. And even if I had managed to muffle those thoughts, I knew other can't-take-back-things, which probably had no merit besides simply for the sake of arguing, would have likely taken their place.

I was not, however, glad that Sallie was in front of us because it was obvious our demeanor concerned her. Her light blue eyes shifted from me to her father. And her fingers fidgeted in front of her blue floral tank top.

"Why are you fighting?" were her words.

Ryan hadn't seen Sallie as quickly as I had. He had just noticed that I suddenly stopped my mad monologue. He looked at his daughter. "We're not," he denied.

"We're having an *adult* conversation." It came to me, and I couldn't resist. I knew Sallie didn't get my double meaning, but Ryan's closed eyes and tension-filled face told me *he* did. My statement didn't necessarily pacify the sweet, little blonde, though.

She grabbed our hands in her own and started to tug us out of the room. "I need a snack for the show tomorrow."

"What?" I stopped walking, causing our human train to halt, too. "I asked you if there was anything you needed."

"I forgot." She looked down.

"Sallie ..." There was a smidge of warning mixed with exasperation in Ryan's voice as he dropped his hand, therefore disconnecting the three of us.

"I'm sorry, Daddy," she said as my hand dropped, too.

"All right." He sighed but appeased, probably knowing, as I did, that it wasn't like his daughter to be forgetful, but then again, she had a lot on her mind.

Ryan's readiness to forgive made me wonder why it couldn't just be that easy for the two of us to say "I'm sorry" and things to magically be all right again. Being an adult struck again. It certainly wasn't all it was cracked up to be.

"We'll leave a little early tomorrow and pick it up on our way," he offered.

"No. It has to be homemade."

He looked at a hopeful Sallie, who was standing as still as a statue and not blinking. Then he looked at me. While not one of his facial features moved—not his eyes, eyelids, nose, cheeks, or mouth, I could still read what he was thinking. A real couple didn't need a blink or lip-curl to understand. They needed a year of being together and being in love. He "told me" he knew we weren't done talking and trusted I could let it go for as long as operation kid snack took. I did the one blink back.

Ryan accepted my nonverbal reply and spoke once again to his daughter. "Okay. We need to pick something easy then. It's late. Come on." He secured her little hand in his and started once again out of the room.

But Sallie ceased their action. "Bethany." She reached for my hand once more.

"Uh …" He sideswiped a look at me, and I couldn't help but look away. "Bethany already made dinner. I think it must be my turn in the kitchen."

"Both of you," she pleaded. "Please. We're supposed to do it as a family."

I squinted and tilted my head ever so slightly at the little one in our presence. Sallie's snack was for the camp talent show the next evening. But, somehow, I think she was already putting on a little act right there in the game room. I had already slightly debated if the treat had to be homemade. But, supposed to do it as a family? Really?

Truth or fabrication, I couldn't let Sallie down. There had already been enough of that for one day. And if I was right, she was encouraging our joint participation because she was worried about what she had heard and what we were trying to conceal. She didn't need any more drama or friction or sadness in her life. Not only had she lost her mother, but Sallie had been old enough to witness and understand the signs when Ryan and Kari's marriage had been crumbling. Had there been scenes like ours in the game room? And even if she wasn't keen on the negative vibe between Ryan and me, I couldn't turn her down, anyway. Her including me meant she was definitely on board once again with me being a part of her life and us as a family.

With the ingredients available, we could have either made "dirt" dessert or pineapple angel food cake. Since the dirt involved refrigeration and there wasn't an easy way to serve it, that was almost immediately vetoed, much to Joel's chagrin. Joel's presence was to Sallie's chagrin. But

Ryan reminded her that she had insisted it was a family activity. He could bounce back words to his advantage, too.

The angel food cake was easy to mix up but took a while to bake. We had put it in the oven and were discussing what container to bring it in when Ryan's phone rang. I didn't even try to disguise my eye roll. It was probably a fabulous offer for another client whom he wouldn't hold his personal relationship against.

"Daddy, it's GiGi," Sallie called out, looking at her father's phone.

That's what I got for having unkind thoughts in my head. Business would have been better. Irene Hynes was the poisoned icing on the cake I called that day.

Ryan, I'm sure, felt the same but didn't let the kids know his detest of their maternal grandmother. Even after the incident at the hospital, when he spoke about Irene to the children it was in a neutral tone. They hadn't, however, seen one another, despite Irene finally trying to contact Ryan to set up a time to see the kids. Ryan had, up to that point, ignored her.

Recognizing the kids knew their grandmother was on the line, he couldn't any longer. "You want to talk with her?"

"Yeah, sure," Joel answered.

"Okay, give me my phone. I'll put it on speaker and you and Sals can both talk."

Irene's nails-on-chalkboard voice soared through the immense kitchen as soon as Ryan had connected the phone. "Ryan, well, I'm glad you answered. I—"

"Hi, GiGi!" The Thompson kids said almost simultaneously, and, therefore, shut down whatever uncouth comment their grandmonster was about to say.

"Oh, oh, hello, Sallie. Hello, Joel. What, uh, what are you two doing? How are you?"

"We're making …" Joel looked at me for a confirmation of the food name, but I wanted absolutely no part of the conversation with Irene.

Luckily, Sallie saved me in her typical I-know-more-than-you-do attitude with her younger brother. "Pineapple angel food cake."

"Yeah," Joel agreed. "I couldn't remember whose cake it was."

I put my hand up to my mouth to stifle a laugh. Thank goodness for Joel. He really was a bright light of sunshine.

As I was rinsing cookware in the sink, Ryan put the last few items away. It was weird how in sync we were, despite the fury burrowed beneath our skin. We were a good team in so many ways.

"What is the cake for?" Irene asked.

"My talent show," Sallie offered a little shyly.

It was actually very surprising that it was Sallie who was going up on the camp stage and not Joel—a true character reversal where the siblings were concerned. Joel would have been up there doing an impromptu dance for sure. But he wanted no parts of practicing a routine, which Ryan said from the start was part of being on the stage. While it bothered Joel initially, he seemed to have gotten over it and moved onto something else. Sallie, on the other hand, had signed up on a spur-of-the-moment, yeah, let's-do-this kind of whim. Since then, she had either been super excited or super nervous depending on the day. But Sallie was not a quitter. She was a girl who, if she committed, she was all in.

"Oh … oh … oh." Came Irene's screechy voice. "I had no idea about any of this. What? What is this about? When is it?"

"Tomorrow night."

"Tomorrow! What?" You would have thought Sallie had told her grandmother the house was on fire. "Where? Where is it at?"

"Summer camp," Sallie related.

"Oh … oh, my. You're doing your ballet, right? Beautiful ballet. We need to make sure to continue your lessons."

Sallie looked at Ryan as her face immediately took on one of horror. She hated the dance class that Kari and Irene had encouraged her to take during the school year. And from what I could tell, I didn't blame her. It seemed to be part dance and part finishing school. Sallie already had better manners than most adults and found her craft in art and words, not dance. But in true Sallie spirit, she had stuck it out through completion. Ryan was going to talk with Kari about not having Sallie do it again after our honeymoon. But that obviously didn't happen.

After smoothing his hand on his daughter's hair, Ryan stepped into the conversation. "Irene, Sallie is—"

"Ryan! How come I didn't know anything about this show?"

"I guess your invitation must have gotten lost in the mail." He rolled his eyes while simultaneously throwing a bag into the trash ... which I found to be an ironic symbol when speaking with his ex-mother-in-law.

"I can't make it tomorrow! We have a social event at the country club. If I would have known ... oh. Oh, Ryan, we're going to need to discuss—"

"You know what, Irene? We don't. Certainly not right now." He glanced at his two offspring, who looked a little cautious. "Joel needs a bath. And Sallie is going to help finish the dessert. Have a good night." He tilted his head toward Sallie and Joel.

"G'night, GiGi." Again, almost in unison.

And before Irene could protest, Ryan promptly hung up the phone. He then looked over at his still apprehensive daughter. "Sals, sweetie, you don't have to go back to the dance place, okay? I promise. You should be able to do what you want to do."

"Yeah, kids get that freedom," I said encouraging Sallie, but Ryan instantly knew of my double meaning.

He tilted his head in my direction in an almost daring, patriarchal way. "Bethany ..." When I stared him down, he resorted back to the kids. "All right, I wasn't kidding. Joel, let's go. We'll get you in the bath, and Sallie, help look for a container and whatever else here." He glanced at the kitchen timer. "It should be out of the oven soon."

"I will, Daddy."

"Thanks. Shower for you tomorrow."

Kissing the top of her head, he peered at me and then left with Joel, who always seemed to find a mess wherever he went. Again, Ryan was extra vigilant with his youngest around a water source and wanted to be there. At least that was the reason I went with for him separating us into completely different areas of the home. There was some validity to it. But I knew there was also another bigger reason, too.

\*\*\*

After operation angel food was done, I helped tuck Sallie into bed. For a while, she had been insistent that she was a big girl and could do it herself. But since Kari's death, she once again liked to have someone wish her sweet dreams, turn off the light, and shut the door.

"I love you, Bethany. I love you and Daddy."

I was so touched by her words and, selfishly, needed them right then. It had been a bad day, but when I put it in perspective, it was nothing compared to what the little girl and her brother were dealing with. Knowing I was a harbor for her meant the world to me. And I had to be a sturdy rock, especially when I knew her tagging Ryan and me together meant she still wasn't sure how things were between the two of us after the game room scene. And who could blame her? I wasn't either.

"I love you, too, Sallie." I smiled.

"Bethany, are you and Daddy fighting about me?"

"What?"

Oh, geez. It was bad enough she knew there was tension. But to think it was over her?

241

"No," I followed through right away. "No, honey. No. We're just not agreeing about something. Besides"—I touched her sweet face right above the covers—"how could we fight about you? Did your daddy ever tell you that you are the reason he and I actually started liking each other?"

Her eyes grew from tiny to large in less than a second. "Me?"

"Yeah. I'm sure you don't remember this because it was over a year ago now, but you got sick at school and had to come home. So, we had to switch our meeting to this house. And had we not done that, we never would have had the time to really get to know one another."

"To love each other."

"Yeah. You are like our little matchmaker."

"I had magic powers and didn't even know it."

"Pretty much," I agreed. "You know everything's okay, right?"

"Uh-huh." She sounded a little more reassured, and I secretly wished I was, too.

"Everyone's gonna love the cake, and I can't wait to hear your story tomorrow."

For the talent show, Sallie was reading a story she wrote and illustrated. And *no one* had heard or seen any of it yet. The show was going to be the book's world premiere.

It was only when I stood up and started toward Sallie's door that I saw Ryan propped against it. "Hey," was the only thing that managed to come out of my mouth.

"Hey," he repeated quietly and then leaned a little into the room. "Good night, Tink."

"Good night, Daddy."

He closed her door behind us and followed me down the hall and into the master bedroom. A good few feet apart, we stood and looked at each other for a couple minutes. Our heated conversation in the game room had been abruptly discontinued. And it was probably best that we had been given some time in between. But there was no way we could end the night like that. Good, bad, or ugly had to be better than the aborted dialogue. We had to say something ... anything ... just the two of us.

It was Ryan who spoke first. "You told Sallie everything is okay. Is it?"

My shoulders drooped. "I want it to be," I admitted my true heart. "*You* told her earlier that we weren't fighting. Do you really believe that? You don't think that was fighting?"

"No. I do," he said at the same time as he let out a sad breath of air.

"Ryan, geez, sometimes I feel like that is all we're doing." I knew it wasn't really the whole truth, but when the ache was so overwhelming and it felt like every time we dipped our toes into the water ...

"I know," he admitted, seemingly with a hint of regret. "But, Bethany, we still are those two sitting in the living room with Sallie home sick from school. I promise." He had heard more of my conversation with Sallie than I realized. "Can I tell you something and you just listen ... let me get her name out first?"

It was my turn to sigh. For sure, he was going to say something about Kari. But I trusted by the way he asked, it would be something I was going to want to, or at least should, hear.

My silence gave him permission to continue. "Kari and I never fought. Really. Truly. Until the very end of the marriage and then after the concussion. It wasn't healthy. I realize that now. We were too busy thinking everything was fine and building careers. We never fought because we started to not really talk. We had the kids and we had sex. Sorry. We did."

"It's not like I didn't know that."

But it also wasn't like I wanted to hear about it or think about it. I'm not sure why he felt it necessary to add the last fact. Unless, oh ... because he wanted to show that our connection was much deeper than sex or careers. It was why he stopped the night the television execs were over. He only wanted to *make love* with me.

And he backed up my thought. "Bethany ... us? The kids are older and in a lot of ways more demanding. And we both have careers. But we know about each other. We talk. We get things out. It's been like that since I first got to know you. I want to know what you're thinking. It's not always going to be pretty. But there's not one single time when we've argued that I felt like ... I don't know ... like I can't do this. I love you and the world we've created so much. And I'm sorry about the adult comment. It wasn't what I meant. It's just that I have so many things I have to think about and consider all the time."

"Okay." In my heart, I knew all he said was true and, maybe, because of that, I knew we could discard the earlier mudslinging and move on to what really mattered. "Can we get back to what all of this is all about, then?" I asked tentatively. "Why are you so opposed to me taking the television show offer? I need you to explain it to me, Ryan."

He resituated his stance and brought his bottom lip up a tad, as if debating what exactly to say. "All right." At least our conversation was much calmer compared to the earlier standoff. "You know how you asked me a while ago what you had to do to measure up to Kari?"

"Yeah," I answered quietly, not knowing exactly where he was going with the question. "It was another time we argued and one I am not proud of." I recalled my jealousy over his bar fight with Olsen. "I know I should have been more understanding of what—"

"You were," he interrupted. "What I'm trying to say is, part of my reaction today? It's kind of like how you felt then." My eyes automatically scrunched my confusion, and he continued. "It seems like you aren't thinking of me or putting us first ... how quickly you made up your mind about leaving for Nashville."

"Oh, Ryan, I was just excited. I should be allowed to be excited. I wasn't thinking about what taking the show would entail. But it certainly wasn't because I don't think of you or those two little ones, who I adore. You are always in my core." And that core ached so hard at the moment. "I guess because I've been taught to always look for the good. And things have, in general, worked out. So, I think they always can."

"They don't." Was that the bitterness of a divorcee who said those words or someone who had been in the entertainment industry for a while?

"Ry …" I soothed verbally. And then I had to. I had to say it. I didn't want to regret *not* saying it, and we were at least in a semi-reasonable talking mode. "I know there is a lot to consider, but I have to tell you, I think I want to do it … at least be considered or hear more. And, no," I continued, touching upon the other thing that had seemed to set him off, "not because I want the spotlight. Not at all. I want it because I want to write and inspire and be inspired. I thought you understood that. Ryan?" I said his name when he momentarily closed his eyes. And then I gave my concluding statement. "I need you to see if there is a way for this to work … at least try."

His eyes opened and he shook his head ever so slightly. "I don't know how it can. There's commitments." He let go of a significant breath of air. "But for right now … we're too … it's too … Can we put this whole thing on pause for tonight, please?"

The staring game resumed for a moment or two. And I lost … at least with our eye-lock. I couldn't handle looking into his sad or disappointed or worried eyes. I knew I was the source for their appearance and that gave me regret. But he had said that was what was good about us—talking, getting things out. I had to trust that we both said what we had needed to and to, indeed, let it sit for the night. It was going to be a give-as-good-as-I-got-but-not-leave argument.

I did step away, though … to the walk-in closet. I discarded the slacks and red top I had been wearing all day and, in their place, put on my white spaghetti-strap tank and light blue pajama bottoms—very unsexy. At least he knew, as if there was any doubt, what I was thinking.

"You're going to sleep?" he asked, nonetheless.

"I don't know. I guess."

It was early. But what else was there? He wanted to nix the topic at hand, and talking about anything else seemed so fake. How was your day, honey? Well, we already knew the answer to that. Or, the weather? Seems like more record highs in the ten-day forecast. Uh … no.

After a cautious look at me, he offered up a medium ground by glancing at the television. "Why don't we watch the next episode? We haven't been able to see—"

"Uh …" I hesitated.

"Bethany, we need a breather. I don't want to go from arguing with you to going to sleep. I wouldn't be able to first of all, and—"

"My 'uh' was because I didn't want to make you any angrier."

"What? Why?"

"I may or may not have already watched the next episode." I exaggerated grinding and showing my teeth.

"You wha …? You watched it without me?" He wasn't really mad—certainly not in comparison to the other trials and tribulations of the day—but it *was* something we did together.

"I'll watch it again, though," I offered, thinking *that* was what a compromise was. "I want to see if there were any hidden Easter eggs I missed."

He grabbed the remote and placed it in my hand. I noticed how he touched me softly as he did so and gave me those same wistful eyes from before. And then as he changed into similar sleeping attire—a light blue T-shirt and baggy black sweats—I found the episode.

Although we were in bed together, we didn't touch and

certainly didn't snuggle up against each other as we naturally always did. My eyes were on the screen, but my thoughts were elsewhere. Besides the car ride to get the kids—which quite honestly was a blur of pure fury—I hadn't really had much time to myself to think, replay, and consider all that had happened. I needed that. And Ryan was right, watching a TV show—especially one I had already seen—was a good solution. We both needed to quit reacting at the spur-of-the-moment and let it sit.

I started a mental timeline by backtracking to the moment I got his call and then moving forward. On certain recollection points, I actually looked over at him. He'd look back but not say a word. It was probably wise. Some of the day and his earlier words made more sense since we were silent and reflective. Other parts, though, were still a puzzle with missing or broken pieces.

Thinking so long and hard, on top of the emotional energy spent that afternoon and evening, must have put me to sleep because I was suddenly forced awake by, "What? Wait! What?" On Ryan's words, my body popped up from its sleep state to see him staring at the television screen.

"What?"

"Sorry." He placed his hand on mine with a side glance. "I wasn't expecting that ending."

"Oh." I felt the heat and tension that had instantly arisen in my fear start to settle. "Mmmm-hmmm." The show had stunned me, too, with its episode end.

"How are they going to wrap it up now?" He clicked off the television.

"Doesn't look good." I gave my pessimistic review. "And there's only two episodes left."

# CHAPTER TWENTY

Unfortunately, the sleep I had discovered rather quickly did not last me through the night. I woke up very early—even for my daily early-shift work—and laid in bed for a while. Ryan was asleep, but I knew he hadn't fared much better than I had. His constant middle-of-the-night shifting and throat-clearing instead of calming whistle breath had told me that. Gosh, I loved him and knew, no matter what, that eclipsed everything. But why couldn't we have it all? Didn't we deserve to have happiness?

Giving in to what would be my day, I tiptoed out of the room and down to the kitchen. Coffee was a definite must. I filled the pot with water as I did every morning and started with the scoops, adding a little extra. Even without the early wake and the emotional night before, the new day was going to warrant the power of a strong blend.

I was doing some Yoga poses while listening to the machine's spurts and gurgles when Lyric shuffled his way into the kitchen, pawing my bare feet and shins. "Hey, are you as messed up as the rest of us?" I bent down and rubbed the top of the dog's head. "Or are you just really a bloodhound and not goldendoodle? You searched out that coffee awfully fast." When Lyric licked my face and started whining, I stupidly tried to rationalize with him. "I know you think since I'm up it's time for you to go out. Look, cutie-patootie, it's way too early."

But the whining continued and I gave in, letting the dog out to the backyard. I figured if I was already up and making the coffee, I may as well let the dog out and continue my morning routine. I could go back up, get dressed, and go to work. I opened the coffee shop, anyway. Why not get there early and enjoy some extra time in the quiet solitude of the store? Maybe being away could help clarify things for me, or I could at least write some lyrics.

It didn't take me long to get ready. So not to disturb Ryan, I decided to skip the shower and take mine after work and before the talent show. My work attire never demanded anything formal. Casual and comfy were definitely more of the trend … and one which Willow frowned upon. I was also a minimalist when it came to makeup—just lipstick and mascara. Although, I would add complementary brown eyeshadows and a blush or bronzer if I was going out in the evening. Looking in the mirror that morning, though, I decided to apply a little foundation. The shadows under my sleep-deprived eyes seemed to already be forming. It made me, once again, think about how different Kari and I were. I knew she had changed a lot from the time she and Ryan first started dating. Her rapid rise to international singing fame had done that. And I couldn't help but wonder if she had once been a minimalist girl, too.

I wanted to kiss Ryan good-bye because it seemed right … no matter what issues we were sorting through. But I also didn't want to wake him. Goodness knows, he needed rest for whatever the day was going to unfold for him. So, I decided to make my way back down the stairs and leave a note near the coffee pot. He would be used to the coffee being ready, just not to me being gone.

I got detoured on my way, though. I passed Sallie's

room—door shut the way she liked it—and then Joel's room—door ajar. Again, siblings who couldn't be more different. I had taken a couple of steps down the stairs when I heard his voice.

"Bethany?"

When I turned to look, Joel was standing at the edge of his bedroom. "Hey, what's up?" I whispered to the little boy. "It's still so early. Really early. Your daddy isn't even up yet."

"Oh." He rubbed at his eyes. "I can't sleep. Can I come down with you?"

"Yeah?"

I don't know why I said it as a question. Of course if he wanted or needed to, he was welcomed. Heck, I could use a little friendly companionship, too.

"Come on." I reached out my hand and waited for him to take the couple of steps to meet me. After we jointly walked down the staircase, I made a suggestion. "Come get the coffee with me. None for you, though." I poked his little belly, and he did a sleepy giggle.

"I don't like coffee."

"You don't *need* coffee." As he sat at the table, I poured myself a hearty mug. "Can't sleep, huh?" Blowing on the beverage to cool it, I sat down immediately next to the sweet, little boy.

"I'm trying." He was near tears. "But I can't sometimes."

The poor kid. I could hear the sincerity in his words. He had done much better since making his bargain with his father. His sticker reward chart was filling. Motivation to be with Ryan was strong. I understood that myself. But seeing Joel's current distress made me wonder if it was making things better or worse. Was he behaving but actually getting even less sleep? Did he hold his fear in most nights and stop himself from calling out just to win the prize? On top of being a good kid, Joel was also competitive like his dad. He wanted to win ... no matter what. Was he still afraid of going to sleep? Or, would he simply be that kid and adult who didn't require as much sleep as the rest of us average bears?

"I know you're trying, Joel." I rubbed my hand on top of his, and he looked up at me with what appeared to be grateful eyes. "We're proud of you. And you know what? I couldn't sleep either. That's why I'm up."

"The sheep thing doesn't work," he proclaimed, surely hoping he had a teammate on his side.

I couldn't help but smile at the straight way he approached life and hoped that character trait never changed as he grew older. "No, I never thought baa, baa, blah, blah worked, either. My mind just goes back to whatever I was originally thinking about." I took a sip of the java and then used my quiet, soothing, practically middle-of-the-night voice. "Is there anything you want to talk about? Anything you're thinking about?"

He looked at me for a second, and I wondered if he would say anything. But then his bottom lip extruded over his top one and he shook his head no. Was he being brave like the superheroes he admired, or did he truly not know what he was thinking about and keeping him awake?

In case it was bravado, I tried a different approach. "Can I tell you why *I* couldn't sleep ... what I was thinking about?"

"What?" His voice rose on the single word, as if he were surprised I had sleep thoughts, too.

And because not only was I raised to always tell the truth, but because, like I told Ryan, I thought it was sometimes good for the kids to see us hurt and scared, I admitted to Joel what was bothering me. "I was thinking ... sometimes no matter how much you love something, it hurts you. I was thinking ... sometimes you really want something to be different or for something to happen that just can't, and it's really hard to accept. I was thinking ... if I can't count sheep ..." I paused for a quick smile at the very attentive little boy. "I can think of things that make me happy."

"Like hugs?" he asked.

His suggestion was perfect. It was true. Hugs really were something that made me happy.

"Yes. Hugs help a lot. And you, sir, give some of the best." I pressed my finger to his nose. "Your hugs make me happy and help me." I fondly recalled his overture in the kitchen on the Fourth of July.

He reached over and wrapped his arms around my torso the best he could. "Your hugs help me, too." The sweet honesty was such a treasure to my battered heart.

"I'm glad," I replied and then tilted my head at his. "That wasn't a yawn, was it?" When he scrunched his lips together as if to hide it, I ran my hand over the top of his head. "What do you think? Wanna try going back to bed? I'm gonna go into work, but your daddy will be up pretty soon and—"

"You're going to work already?" Ryan entered and stood across the table from us.

"Yeah." Dang, even with drama between us, seeing his sleepy-eyed self made my heart pitter-patter.

"It's only—" He looked at the kitchen clock as if he needed a witness.

"I know. Sorry if we woke you," I offered.

"I heard the dog, and then when I didn't see this one"—he nodded toward Joel—"in his room ..."

"Oh. Oh. Sorry." I shot up from my chair. Eeech! "We were chatting, and I forgot Lyric is still outside." I imagined the dog out in the dark, probably wondering if he had been abandoned—just another member of the Thompson abode confused and sad. "I'll go right now and let him in on my way out. Coffee is done," I said as I went to pass by Ryan.

"Bethany, why—" He touched my elbow as I stopped his question.

"I need a little time to myself before the store opens and the rest ... the rest of the day happens."

Silence filled the few inches of space separating our bodies. I had wanted to kiss him good-bye when he was asleep. But now that he wasn't, I didn't know … mostly because I wasn't sure if it was what *he* wanted.

When I took another step away, he placed his hand on mine, squeezed, and kissed me quickly on my cheek. "See you for dinner."

\*\*\*

The phone rang at exactly the wrong moment. The beeping refrigerator was warning that it had been left open too long and the timer on the oven was sending out its signal, too. I had to get the homemade tortilla chips out at precisely the right moment or they would burn. I finally had that mastered to the perfect culinary science. So, knowing it was Ryan's ringtone, I asked Sallie to answer my phone.

"Hi, Daddy," the seven-year-old spoke into the phone as I, having secured the oven mitts in place, opened the appliance. "Yep." She listened to the other line and on my nod, closed the door to the refrigerator. "She says she's knee-deep in guacamole. But I think she's only fingers-deep." I chuckled at her recounting the words I had used to have her answer the phone. "Yeah, I know. We learned that in school." The A-plus student seemed to beam with pride. "Yep." She was right, though—I had finished mashing the avocados and would need to soon add the other vegetables and spices to make the homemade guac. "We're having cheeseburgers and chips and guacamole."

"And ice cream!" Joel, who was at the table, belted out his favorite item, while playing on his tablet.

"Joel, you are supposed to be setting the table," I reminded him of one of his chores.

"You're not?" At first, I thought Sallie was speaking to her brother, but then I realized it was to Ryan. "You're coming to the talent show though, right?" Those words made me halt all action, look at Sallie, and pay stricter attention. "Daddy, I want you to come to the show. I need you to." She whined, and the wave of nerves she had been riding up and down since I picked her up at camp seemed to hit a dangerous crest.

"Sallie, press the button so we can all hear." I had just put the patties in the skillet and needed to be cautious with flipping them. "You know how to do that, right?"

I was about to do it myself when Ryan's voice soared through the kitchen via the speaker. "Sallie, are you still there?"

"She put it on speaker," I called out. "What's going on? You're coming to the show, aren't you?"

"Yeah, yeah," he reassured right away, and I let out a breath of relief. "But I can't make dinner."

What? Really? Did he think he was going to avoid me two nights in a row? Talk about not acting like an adult.

Conscientious of Sallie and Joel's attentive ears, what I said instead was, "What? You said you were."

"Daddy, you're gonna miss rock and rolly guacamole!"

I would have laughed at the nickname Joel and Ryan called one of their favorite food items I made. But I was too upset. I wanted him to come home. I wanted to talk, especially after having some time apart and not corresponding all day. I was ready. But, obviously, he was not.

"Yeah. I know," Ryan answered his son. "I'm really sorry to miss rock and rolly."

"Why? Why can't you—" I started to question again.

"A last-minute meeting ... can't be helped." There was a slight pause, as if he could actually see my rolling eyes or transcribe my doubting brain. "It's important. I promise. And I promise I'll be at the show. I'll just have to meet you there."

"You're not even coming home first?" Missing dinner was bad enough, but we weren't even going to have a second alone or as a family unit until after the show?

"There's no way. It's across town and—" My scoff must have been more audible than I thought because he suddenly changed what he was saying. "Are you all right with that?"

Noticing Sallie's expectant and worried look, I agreed. "Yeah. It's fine."

*Fine* but far from perfect. In fact, it was not even in the same universe as perfect. Or ideal. Heck, it barely cleared fine.

"Thanks," he said plainly, and when he got nothing else from me, he moved on to the kids. "Sals, I'll be there. Joel, save me a seat, okay?"

"I will!" the youngest Thompson gleefully yelled out.

"All right. I've gotta go. I love you guys."

The kids repeated the sentiment back to their father. I did not. Instead, I smashed the patties down extra hard onto the hot skillet and hit the end call button.

\*\*\*

Ryan slid into the empty seat next to mine just as I had done the third—or thirtieth—glance at my phone to see if he had texted and what time it was, since he was cutting it much too close to the opening curtain. He had promised he would be there, and I had always trusted his word. But, admittedly, I had started to doubt.

"Hey," he breathed out a little heavily as I put my phone on silent and placed it back in my purse. "Did I miss anything?"

Immediate sass harpooned my thoughts. My feelings. You missed my feelings. That was what I *wanted* to say. But I let it go because a) it was a public place, b) his face seemed to match his shirt's wrinkled arms as if they had been tugged back and forth all day, and c) I knew I was guilty of the missed-feelings sentiment, too. My morning in the empty coffee shop had helped me not only sort out sugar packets but also my thoughts.

"No," I said. "But it's ready to start."

I handed Ryan his program after he placed the bouquet he had been carrying on the empty seat on the other side of him. Sure, I wished they were for me. But I knew better. It wasn't necessarily because I didn't think he would do something like that as an apology, but because we had talked about him getting something for Sallie's performance.

"She'll be tickled by those." I nodded at the flower arrangement and couldn't help but get at least one jab in. "I'm glad you could squeeze that into your schedule."

He either didn't detect my sarcasm or chose to ignore it. Knowing Ryan and his incredible understanding of how I ticked, he most likely knew the truth. "And Ella didn't help send them."

I squinted at him, having wondered for the month-plus. "My magnolias?"

"It *was* my idea," he quickly confirmed, as if I was going to be mad about it. "She just was the one who coordinated with a florist in Carolina."

I wasn't sure what to say. It was a fleeting, soft moment between us—one we truly hadn't had in over twenty-four hours, and I didn't want to ruin or jinx it. But my hesitation to reply caused him to move on to more practical issues.

"Where's Joel?"

I pointed in the direction of young master Thompson, who was making his way to our seats along with his camp buddy, Isaac, and his mom. "Felicia thought it was a good idea for the boys to do a bathroom run first."

Ryan smiled, but it was in Joel's direction. "Yeah, no doubt."

"You still don't know what Sallie's story is about?" I was keeping up our pleasantries, although I *was* truly curious.

"Nope. Only, of course, that it is part of the unicorn series." He cited the many books the young author-to-be had written about unicorn's adventures in school, on the farm, on her birthday, and many more. "She's kept it tight-lipped like all the rest until release day." He put his fingers up in mock quotation marks.

"Daddy!"

Joel bounced in front of the two of us, and, once again, I couldn't help but think how excited he was just seeing his father. I saw it with Sallie, too. Sitting a few rows in front of us in the roped-off section for the performers, she had continuously turned around to look at Joel and me while we had been waiting for Ryan to arrive. Her teeth-clenching, eyebrow-squeezing glances at the empty seat for her dad had said it all.

"Hey, Joe." As he greeted his son, Ryan gave a distance thumbs-up to a relieved Sallie.

"You're in my seat," Joel informed his father as the lights flickered, telling everyone to be quiet and take their seats.

"Sorry. You can sit on the other side of me. Here, I'll move the flowers, and you can sit there."

"But I was sitting next to Bethany."

"Oh, buddy, maybe I can sit here now," Ryan tried.

"Hi, Ryan." Felicia, once again behind us with Isaac, tapped on Ryan's shoulder.

"Hi, Felicia," he returned the greeting.

"Hey, you should know there was someone talking to Joel when we were—" Isaac's mother's words got cut off as the lights went completely dark, and Ryan gave in to his son, scooching over to allow the five-year-old to sit between us.

It wasn't much after the show started when I saw Ryan pull out his phone. Pressing only a few buttons, he then looked at the screen for an extended period of time. His eyes, brows, and mouth made a series of tiny, quick movements before the smallest of exhales—none of which I could interpret. And because his seat was two away from me, I could not see the phone's screen. He looked at it a little longer and then over at me. If his previous facial expressions were hard to read, the one at me was impossible. It was almost as if he was looking right through me ... or, no, into me. Just as I furrowed my eyebrows in question, the crowd erupted in applause for the end of the two sisters magic act. And when I glanced back at Ryan, he had put his phone away.

We sat through a karate demonstration and some loose tumbling before a couple of singing performances. Had we been in a better place emotionally, I would have definitely made some wise crack to Ryan about how even elementary-aged kids were far ahead of my singing skills. I'm sure he would have laughed. He may have even given his judge Ryan score. But we certainly weren't in our carefree, joking place.

As a young pianist took the stage, Sallie got out of her seat and Ryan nudged Joel. "Your sister is next." He pointed to Sallie's name in the program, and the proud sibling, who had managed to sit relatively still throughout the show, sat up a little straighter.

After another round of applause, the voice from beyond the screen—who I internally called The Great and Powerful Oz—announced, "Next up is author and illustrator Sallie Thompson, reading her own original story."

And then Sallie was up on the older, wooden stage and in front of the microphone. As she waited for her homemade book cover to appear on the screen behind her, she looked to the three of us. Ryan gave her a beaming smile, and I wondered why he couldn't have been as supportive of me over my latest prospect. I couldn't give my selfish thought any more cred, though, because Sallie had begun reading.

"Unicorn's Rainbow Adventure by Me." Before continuing, she looked at the screen to make sure "Oz" had flipped to the next picture. "Unicorn had a happy life. She loved the color pink." On her own cue, Sallie did a little curtsey in her pink and white polka dot dress. She seemed to be a natural performer, which shouldn't have surprised me, considering her genes. "Unicorn had lots of hay and oats for breakfast. They were healthy and safe for her to eat."

Healthy and safe food? Hmmm, was that in reference to me? Did living with someone with a severe nut allergy affect her enough to put it into her story?

"She got to travel all around the world." Sallie's image of the unicorn with hay changed to one of the Earth with a heart, and I thought of Kari on her world tours. "Her favorite thing to do was walking on the rainbow and eating candy corn because it was the same shape as her swirly horn." That line got a light trickling of laughter from the crowd ... so much for healthy food. "One day a hunter captured her."

I swung my head quickly to where Ryan was sitting. Sallie's stories were never scary. They were actually always much more reality-based—besides, obviously, the main character being a unicorn. Ryan didn't meet my look, but it was because I knew he was watching and listening with the same intensity I was.

"He took her to a dark place and told her it was the end of the rainbow." As she continued, I couldn't help but wonder why we hadn't insisted on reading it first. "Unicorn didn't know there was an end. She was scared and all alone." Gone was the bright full rainbow and equally so unicorn, and in its place was a dark picture with a dripping—as if it was crying—rainbow.

Ryan's shoulders sagged but his eyelids opened even more. I am sure any early childhood expert would have little red flag emojis popping up all over their brains. Even with my limited knowledge of child pedagogy, I thought her words sounded as if she had been abducted or was a victim of some type of abuse. But we knew better. And, really, anyone knowing of Kari's passing should have been able to figure it out. Kari was gone. Sallie felt scared and alone. It was understandable, yet so sad.

She was still reading alongside a picture of a unicorn with a red X covering it. "He told her unicorns are not real."

Oh, gosh, really? Was she still thinking about princesses not being real? I thought we had proven that truth. But, unicorns? I'm not sure how to justify that one. All I knew was, I wanted to hold her. I couldn't even imagine what Ryan was thinking. On top of it, Joel was starting to ask if, indeed, unicorns weren't real. But Ryan shushed the inquisitive young man, and we listened to Sallie some more.

"But she was brave. She told the hunter that once upon a time they *were* real but now live in our hearts." And a huge red heart appeared on the screen behind Sallie.

Ryan did turn to me that time. He shook his head ever so slightly, and I brought my lips together. We both recognized that "living in hearts" was what he had told Sallie about her mother.

"She picked a red flower, and it started to sparkle magic everywhere. The hunter let her go, and they became friends. They lived happily ever after. The End."

On the obvious end of Sallie's tale, Joel started doing a literal round of applause and Ryan got out of his seat to give her a standing ovation. I did, too. Although, it took me a second or two longer to react. I was still processing. As a songwriter, I put meaning in every single lyric I wrote. Word choice was so important to me, even if the artist or listener never got all of the intended symbolism. Maybe I was reading too much into a seven-year-old's prose, but I didn't think so. I thought it was brilliantly done even, and maybe especially, the ending. The red flower? She often admired the single, thornless red rose I had preserved after Ryan's romantic proposal. And she knew my sparkling ring had originally set on it. Sallie had thought it was like a princess fairytale. Oh, if only we could get that happily ever after.

Not much long after Sallie's revealing portrait of words, was the break. Only the matter of a few minutes, it wasn't even worthy of a legitimate stretch. It was just a chance to get all of the performers set for the ensemble finale.

Joel, however, took advantage right away. "Can I get a brownie?"

"Did you have any yet?" Ryan actually looked at me and Joel did, too, both knowing I would tell the truth on the matter.

But Joel fessed up first. "Yeah."

"Dude, I'm starving," Mr. Skip Dinner admitted. "Get a big one, and we can split it. Unless Bethany wants one, too."

I shook my head. I had to be careful with homemade desserts, and ever since landing in the ER because of a brownie, I was particularly cautious with those. Besides, I wasn't hungry at all. Being at a stalemate—or whatever we wanted to call it—with Ryan was like putting a lap band around my tummy.

"Quick," he shuttled his son off in the direction of the dessert table, which was only a few feet or so away. He then turned to me. "Well, that was quite a turn in the Unicorn Chronicles."

"Hmmm. Fact or fiction?"

"Yeah. Yeah." I'm pretty sure he purposefully answered it twice.

"I'm glad it had a happy ending," I offered.

"I think she feels that, too," he seemed to say in a more relaxed, peaceful manner.

"We all need—"

"I got two." Fast-feet junior Thompson was back. "They were small." Joel once again bounded onto the seat between us with the anything-but-small brownies.

"Joel," Ryan's daddy voice was edged with warning. "If you are on a sugar rush tonight—"

"I'll think of my happy things." He did an exaggerated, long, kid wink at me.

The microphone started thumping for the beginning of the finale. And I reached over and gave Joel a little hug. Yes, I needed to trust and count on my happy things, too.

\*\*\*

I remained one step back so I could get the photo op. Ryan had let Joel give Sallie the flowers, and I am not sure which sibling was honored more. Their beaming smiles right next to each other as they looked in the direction of my camera phone made everything magical for just a moment.

"Sallie, let me get one of you holding your book, too."

Since there had been a no-filming-or-photos rule during the actual performance, afterward was our only chance to preserve a memory. And, I can honestly say, I appreciated that the camp made the stipulation. Not only do amateur photogs get in the way with their kneeling in the aisles and raised phones blocking views, we, as an audience, were more genuinely in the moment by not looking through a screen. Plus, the owners would sell the entire performance at a later date to benefit the camp.

"Daddy, why are there only three cookies in the flowers?" Joel was rummaging through Sallie's beautiful arrangement of pastel carnations.

"They each are for something special—a book for the writer, a palate for the artist, and a star for the performer."

"That's so cool, Daddy!" She claimed her flowers back from her investigative brother.

I had to give Ryan a mental thumbs-up for his thoughtfulness. And while a lot of guys would have had their secretary arrange it, I was pretty confident it had been all sensitive Ryan Thompson. He had shown that to me nearly every day we were together. It wasn't just with magnolias and keepsake charms but in simple things like foot rubs and pangs.

"But there's only three," Joel pointed out again. "Who

doesn't get one?" His eyes peered at Ryan as his face inched a little closer.

I loved that it wasn't even a question in the young boy's mind that I was in the four people versus three cookies mathematical equation. I had felt like a member of their family even before things got formal with moving in or a ring. But it was super sweet to hear it, especially when our life seemed so unbalanced. And I was pretty sure Ryan hadn't been counting actual cookies but the images they represented when buying the gift.

"That's enough. You shouldn't be taking photos of my family."

My heart felt like it skipped a beat. My breath definitely hitched. Why would Ryan say that?

I slipped my phone in my purse as he spoke again. "I don't know who you are."

As he took a step toward me, I had no idea what to expect. When he stopped right past me, though, I quickly put the pieces together. I hadn't seen the gentleman holding the professional camera. But Ryan had.

I turned to get a better view of the intrusive individual. Average height and build, his dirty blond hair matched the scruff on his face. He wore black-framed glasses and was dressed extremely casually in nondescript cargo shorts and a faded T. He definitely did not seem like he belonged in the pricy summer camp crowd.

"Miss Thompson? Uh, Sallie?" he spoke, ignoring Ryan's implied question and presence. "That was a great ... act." And to confirm my thoughts, it was quite apparent he was not comfortable speaking with children.

Having been parented properly, Sallie dutifully replied, "Thank you."

"So ... not anything with music?" he continued. "Dancing? Or a singer like your mom? Her voice was out of this world. I bet yours could be, too."

"And you are?" Ryan asked more directly.

"He's the guy who was talking to me before the show,"

Joel answered before the actual subject in question did.

"Wells." The man finally switched his camera to his other hand and stuck his right one out for Ryan to shake. "Wells Easton. I'm with *Rock On Digest*. Perhaps you've heard of us, Mr. Thompson. It's a newer division of—"

"What?" Ryan's hand, which had only loosely accepted Mr. Easton's, dropped. "Why are you—"

"We're doing a full feature on the kids of music royalty … the impact of growing up with a famous singing icon."

"What? Oh, no. No, you're not." Ryan stood a little in front of Sallie as if to block her view, and I took it upon myself to grab Joel's hand.

"It's legit. And, it's—" the magazine rep started.

"Absolutely not interested. No comment. You know, you need to ask permission for kids." Ryan's tone remained even but firm.

He was used to dealing with those situations in the business he was in and also having been with Kari. But involve his kids? Oh, I was hoping Mr. Easton would take no comment as the final answer.

Not only did he not, but, by no fault of his own, he stirred the pot … the witch's brew. "Your mother-in-law suggested I find you here. She said it was all right. Mrs. Hynes already told us some things—" On his words, I inched closer to Sallie, too, so both kids were near me.

"First of all," Ryan interrupted, "she's not my mother-in-law. And, second, it's not all right. Didn't I just say that?" His even tone wasn't so even anymore, but he did manage to keep his voice low. "And she has no right or permission to grant you access to my kids. The only person who does is me … and Bethany." He tagged on and nodded, if not looked, in my direction.

Although I didn't react outwardly, his comment did take me a little aback. Besides the emergency cards at the camp, that issue had never been brought up between the two of us. But even if it was only a powerplay for the press, it didn't matter. Getting the point across that the

Thompson children were not to be questioned, photographed, interviewed, or bothered at all was what was important.

"I think you need to leave." Ryan pointed his finger, giving the cameraman a physical direction to the auditorium doors.

"Ryan," he tried a more friendly approach. "I simply want to ask the kids or you—how about you?—some questions. Like I said, it's a piece about—"

"Look, I've had a long day. There's a lot going on," Ryan admitted, and I couldn't help but think the man standing in front of us didn't even know the half of it. "And I am not going to get into this with you. If you're not going to have the common courtesy to leave, then we will. Please delete those photos. Kids, let's go … car."

It didn't matter that Ryan and I had a disagreement the day before or that it hadn't been resolved and was still very heavy on top of us. We would stand united in public and for the children. Ryan offered his hand to Sallie, who readily took it, and I started walking with Joel, who I think was still more concerned about the cookies than his father's words or actions involving the man with the supposed press credentials.

The circulating natural air felt so refreshing and welcoming as we made our way outdoors. In a way, it was kind of nice we had to make a hasty exit. I didn't feel much like mixing and mingling with the rest of the friends and families at the performance. Even though everyone in general was accepting of me, the day camp had been Kari's gig … Kari's territory. They were her friends—for as much as she could have had any with her hectic schedule. What I really wanted was to be home and have an honest, good conversation with the man I loved.

Trying to keep his voice low, Ryan was asking more to himself than me why anyone even associated with the press was allowed into the show. I tried to rationalize with him that it wasn't a publicized event and that only the camp members and family knew about it. So, who would ever think press would know or even want to attend?

"I'd say I can't believe Irene—" Ryan started.

"Who was that guy?" Sallie, who was then walking a little ahead of us with Joel, turned in our direction.

"He's … What did he ask you, Joe? Did you say anything to him?" Ryan answered with a question of his own.

Joel almost came to a complete stop as he looked at both of us. "He was asking about Mommy."

"He—"

Before Ryan could get anything more out, Joel announced, "I didn't say anything. He is a stranger." He did a dramatic, confident one-nod. "And Isaac's mom told him he better talk with you."

"So, so smart. I got two great kids," he proudly boasted as we walked another step or two.

"Here's the car." I hit the remote to unlock the Audi. We had arrived before Ryan—his late arrival making for him to have a worse parking space. "Go ahead and get in." I signaled to the kids.

"That's all right, they can go in mine."

"It's fine." I opened the back door for Sallie and Joel.

"No, I know you need a break. You haven't had any time to yourself." Did he recite my words from that morning in mockery or simply to be considerate? "I'll take them," he reiterated in a tone that squashed any further discussion.

Sallie's roaming eyes from her father to me and back again, confirmed the conclusion. She didn't need to bear witness to even the slightest conflict between Ryan and me again. Especially after hearing her unicorn story, I knew she needed to believe in happiness winning out.

Spotting Wells exiting the building's doors and knowing Ryan didn't want to give the reporter even one more chance at a question or photograph, I said, "See you at home."

"Yeah," he grunted. "Let's go." He put a hand on each of the kids' backs, and they scurried at a faster pace into the depths of the packed parking lot.

# CHAPTER TWENTY-ONE

Sure, there were times when I wished I had a moment to myself. But driving back to the house alone was not one of those. It gave me too much time to think and question all of Ryan's words and actions that evening. From skipping dinner, to the late arrival, to the distracted phone gazing ... to his insistence on leaving with the kids. What did it all mean? What part did I play in it? And how did it match up with what I wanted to say to him?

Since I got home first and needed to keep my mind as decluttered as possible, I decided to text my family the photos of Sallie and Joel from post-show. I was surprised to get a bunch of emojis and a congrats message right back since it was later at night on their side of the country. But it was Ella, and she usually stayed up late. Hearing the garage door open, I thanked my sister via text and went into the kitchen with Lyric to fill his water bowl.

Ryan and the kids didn't enter the actual house immediately, though. It was quite a few minutes before I heard the garage door shut once again and then the door to the breezeway open. Why hadn't they gotten out of the car right away? I wasn't concerned about carbon monoxide. I was worried about another possible Ryan-delay tactic. They were already returning home later than I had expected.

"I still wanna go to your office." I heard Joel say.

"You will." Ryan's voice filled the kitchen as the three of them entered.

"There's the superstar." I put on the biggest smile I could for Sallie, considering the uneasiness that laid underneath my heart. "Sorry I didn't get a chance to really tell you, but you did great, Sals. It was such an amazing story. How do you feel?"

She looked up a little shyly at me, and Ryan smoothed his hand along the back of her head. "I didn't know there would be so many people."

"Yeah," I acknowledged the show's large crowd. "Were you nervous?"

"A lot." Her eyes opened a bit more.

"Well, you didn't show it."

"Like you," the little girl replied to me as Joel started kissing/wrestling with the dog on the kitchen floor.

"Me?"

She nodded. "On Daddy's show ... in front of all those people."

"Yeah." When I looked at Ryan, leaning against the center island, he actually gave me a smile. "But I was definitely nervous, too. You know what got me through?"

"Huh?" Her one word was filled with the anticipation that I was going to give her a golden ticket to feigning off stage fright.

I spoke the honest truth about my unexpected performance on *Singer Spotlight*'s part-one finale a year before. "Just focusing on your dad. I only saw him. I forgot everyone else was watching. He made it okay."

I peered over at the man himself. Ryan's dead-on look at me was mesmerizing, as if he was back there a year before on that soundstage, too. Could he—we—make it okay again?

"Yeah. I think I want to still be a teacher when I grow

up … and maybe write … but not read it to anybody!" She trained my thoughts back to her.

"First of all, Sallie, you have plenty of time to decide. And, second, you will be successful in anything you do. Having a great teacher means everything." I didn't have to, but I wanted to. I surveyed my eyes past a still-attentive Ryan on my way to looking at his son. "Joel? Still want to be a lifeguard?"

"I am going to be the next Avenger and protect everyone!" He sprung his arms out and started to pretend-fly around the room.

"Oh, brother." Ryan rolled his eyes and shook his head in fake exasperation. "Super-Joel and Sallie, take the dog out, please. And then I want you to go right after and put on your pj's. Bethany and I need to talk."

"Daddy, are you going to tell her—"

"The dog, please," Ryan interrupted Joel. "Unless you want to clean up the pee he is surely going to do on the floor after so much water and wrestling."

"Ewww! No." Joel's nose scrunched. "I'll take care of him forever." He really was extra cautious with Lyric since the LEGO incident. And after learning of his anxiety about anyone being sick, I understood why.

Sallie suddenly bombarded my legs in a powerful embrace. I hugged her back and gave a sliver of a smile as she walked off with Joel and Lyric. There was suddenly a pit in my stomach. Something was up. I could feel it. Sure, things were still tense between Ryan and me. That I had thought about. That I knew we could talk through. But it was more. Standing alone with him in the kitchen … his straightforward, emotionless face made me fearful.

"Ryan?" I practically whispered with every ounce of ache, frustration, confusion, and love going into his name.

"You really want it?" he asked, practically bracing himself against the counter.

"Want?" I suddenly realized how incredibly silent the house was without the dog or children in our immediate presence.

"The Nashville gig."

"I told you I did. But I'm being selfish. And I'm sorry I didn't stop to understand what you were trying to say about being apart and how it changes … well, how it changes everything."

The early morning cafe opening had done me a lot of good. I had really settled my brain down and thought things through a little more rationally rather than emotionally. I realized his fears were justified, even if they had little to do with me. The scars Kari had left on him by becoming a different person and being away on tour so much changed him forever. He wouldn't be able to simply dismiss that it might not happen again. And I wouldn't want him to. It would change the man he was and the one I desperately loved.

"Well, I want out." He said it so matter-of-fact, it was kind of scary.

No … it was downright frightening. He wanted out? He wanted out of us? Because I wanted an opportunity to advance my career? I had apologized. I said I understood. And he wanted out? What?

In case I didn't comprehend, he added, "And I want the kids out."

"What are you talking about?" I managed to ask while the pit in my stomach turned to nausea. "I I—"

I didn't get to tell him I loved him because his next word was pure devastation. "Leave."

"Leave?" I repeated.

I was replaying in my head the night of our very first date. Back then he had said that same word to me. He had practically pushed me out the door when he had found the syringe in my purse. Of course, he hadn't known it was for my allergy. But what wasn't he getting now? And how could I make him understand? I was too stunned to react. Every single emotion was bombarding inside my brain, trying to compete to see which one was the one that was going to kill me. I couldn't leave anywhere because I couldn't move.

"I talked with the producers of the Nashville show today like you asked." He hadn't moved either, and he had just said something that seemed almost like a change of subject.

"You what?" I managed. "Ryan, what are you talking about? I'm so upset right now. I don't care about Nashville. I care that you want out."

Dang it. Threatening tears were burning behind my eyes. I didn't understand any of what he was saying. And, at the same account, I didn't know that I wanted to.

"Bethany, listen to what—"

I was starting to hear my own breathing because it was becoming erratic. "What? I … I'm trying, but—"

"They came up with a compromise. You could totally hate this. They love it. I have to say it is kind of interesting."

"Ryan!" I screamed, and I didn't care who heard. "What are you talking about?"

"I talked with the producers of the Nashville show," he repeated his previous statement. But maybe he needed to since it was taking everything in me to comprehend. "They proposed that they put both of us on the show. What do you think?"

"Huh?"

"They're still looking for one more person to be on a team for the business side."

I was trying desperately to follow his line of conversation. "You?"

"Yeah. Since it's the same production company as *Spotlight*, they offered to get me released from there and be on the new show. Sonny was actually instrumental in all of this … your initial offer and bringing me over. I guess dessert and drinks here the other night really made an impression. So, the *Spotlight* people were who I was meeting with at dinner time."

"Oh." Things were starting to ... "Oh."

"It was easier in person. And then we got the Nashville folks on the line to see if we could iron it out completely."

"You're talking about us both leaving. Both of us leaving California? We would both do the show in Nashville?"

"Yeah," he was back to his matter-of-fact voice. "They're pitching us as the spouse team or spouse versus spouse."

"Spouse ..."

"We'll be married by then."

I swear I was ready to vomit. The jacked-up emotional ride I was going through was enough to make me do it. But, thankfully, I hadn't had much in my stomach.

Instead, I spit out words. "I thought ... I thought ..."

"What?" For the first time, I think he truly understood how upset I was. He reached his arm out to my shoulder.

"I thought you wanted me to leave. I thought you were kicking me out. I thought ... Oh, gosh. You scared me so bad. I'm not even sure what we are talking about right now."

"Lenay ..."

"Ry?" I rubbed my eyes, surely displacing mascara everywhere.

"Ye—"

"Can you hold me, please?"

"Yeah. Yeah." And he masterfully enveloped me in his arms.

My body was on fire. I knew it was from the heat of my blood pressure and anxiety. And laying against his taut torso only made me warmer, but I didn't care.

He pulled me arm's length away and tilted his head toward mine. "Okay? You okay? Can we maybe be on the same page now? No one is leaving anyone. At least I hope not."

"We're just going to be the next Blake and Gwen."

"Ha! Ha!" He legitimately laughed, which was so

welcoming to hear. "I'm no Cowboy."

"I'm no blonde."

"No, you're not." The smile rose on his face as he touched my long, brunette hair. "But interesting, right?"

"Yeah. Definitely." Definitely since I knew what was actually happening *and* we could be together. "Why didn't you tell me any of this? Why didn't you call and let me know what was going on? I was so mad at you for skipping dinner. I thought you were avoiding me."

"I know." One side of his mouth curled up in regret as he softly touched my face. "I didn't want to say anything until I knew it really had feet ... that it was a strong possibility. There were a lot of pieces to fit together. I didn't want to risk putting it out there and then for it to be another no."

Oh. "Oh. Okay. I guess I understand that." I understood *him*.

"And I wanted to wait and have it be me who was telling you ... not your manager." His sweet sentiment only lasted a second, though, because it made me think.

"But you *are* a manager. How will you be able to film in Nashville and still—"

"You know when I'm doing *Spotlight*, everyone else at the office is basically doing the other work. They know what they're doing. I want to—I need to—spend more time with you and the kids. Since I won't be able to be hands-on in the city, though, I'd relinquish most of it to them more officially."

"Ryan, no," I denied, knowing my fiancé. "That is you. You love your business. You built your business. It is what—"

"I love the kids and I love you." He spoke with precision and confidence. "And then, yes, I love my business. It was what I dreamed of and thrived for. And I'll still have it. It will just be like a mini break while we get settled and married and begin the show. And I'm sure I'll do some remote stuff. Then I can start a branch in

Nashville. It really is Music City. It's a better place for you to grow and learn professionally. Plus, there's not as much entertainment industry and cameras everywhere." He seemed to sigh in relief on that fact.

"So, you're talking about moving to Nashville permanently?"

"Yeah, if that's what you want. I didn't say yay or nay to the show deal. But it *is* worked out. I got the final confirmation right as Sallie's show was starting tonight. I said I needed to talk with you first."

"What I didn't do with you," I lamented, not able to meet his eyes.

"Hey." He gently lifted my chin with two of his fingers so we were once again eye-to-eye. "I have baggage, and I should have first and foremost told you how phenomenally proud I am of you."

We both needed to let each other's transgressions go. We should have done so the night before. But it had all still been too fresh and emotional.

"The kids," I changed the subject instead. "What about them with all of this?"

He pressed his lips firmly together, almost as if he was trying to repress his emotions.

"Obviously, I was concerned about how this change would affect them. So, one of the first things I did was talked with their counselor. We discussed holding on to key things like the photos, and jewelry, and stuffed animals to preserve the memories but also getting away from the sad ones. I think it will be good, especially after the garbage that went down at the talent show. They don't need to be here and some of the … If Maks wants to see them, he can visit. And maybe we'll need some trips to LA. But they'll have me and you consistently."

His inclusion of me made me do a temporary detour of the Nashville subject. "Ryan, what you said to the reporter about me having the rights or whatever with the kids … I know you were grandstanding …"

"Not. At. All," he punctuated with determination. "You're not just marrying me. You're essentially marrying all three of us. I want to make that official. I know we haven't talked about it. But before Kari died it really wasn't a consideration, I guess. Well, you can think about it. Sheez, I know there's a lot to think about."

"What? I don't understand." Add it to my list of overwhelming discussion topics.

"How do you feel about adopting them?" He made it crystal clear, and my bottom lip gaped from the top. "Really becoming their …"

He stumbled on the word I was sure was going to be "mom." Even though Sallie had used it for me outside of my presence and I basically acted as one for the two of them, Kari was, and forever would be, their mother. And she should be. I would never want to take that away.

"Their parent." He settled with, and, in all actuality, since our blowup regarding that word, it was even more meaningful. "You'd have every right as me," Ryan said and then emphasized, "There'd be no difference. Sort of like—"

"Like Garrett." I felt even more sentimental.

"Well …" He touched my hand, surely sensing I needed an emotional break. "I was going to say the Audi."

"The Audi?" My voice went up an octave on the mention of his car that I drove.

"Yeah, it's been in both of our names the whole time." He smirked that damn sexy smile of his and then resorted to his real answer. "Yes, like your brother."

"I can't believe you with the car." I rolled my eyes and let it pass. "But, Ry, the kids? Of course I would be honored. They should have a say in it, though."

"See, just thinking that way …" He shook his head and bit his upper lip, fighting off his emotions. "You always do that—me going to Iowa, the summer reading group—you think of them. That is why they love you … and your hugs." He smiled warmly, surely recalling my scene with

Joel that morning. "So, are you good with it … all of it? The move? Both of us on the show?"

"I always wanted to live in Nashville but kind of landed here."

"Thank goodness you did."

The sweet look in his eyes and his upward curved mouth told me he felt exactly the same way I did. How different and lonely my life would have been had I not ended up in California. Neither of us would have ever known such love.

"Yeah," I agreed softly. "So, absolutely, I would move. But, what about you? Is this *really* what you want? I love you, Ryan." I actually got to say those words and proved their meaning by putting him first. "But I don't want you to make this huge decision because of me or because we were arguing."

"Listen here, Lenay. As much as I would do anything for you—and I would." Every smile of his seemed more and more relaxed. "This is about *all* of us. And I'm not taking it lightly. I devoted the whole day thinking everything through." There was detailed-oriented Ryan. He always claimed I had the structured, firstborn, Type-A personality, but he had his act most definitely together. "I told you I talked with Joel and Sallie's counselor. She is going to set us up with a colleague and some resources in Nashville. And just now, I talked with the kids. I stopped at the park on the way back and told them what might be happening. Of course, they had questions, but they're ready for a new adventure."

"That's why you were a little late … and in the garage." I put it together.

"Joel couldn't stop talking about it, and I wanted to be the one to tell you. Because, honestly, I am equally as excited … more every minute. It wasn't something I ever thought about but, weirdly, is exactly what I want."

"I know that feeling." I reflected once again on our life goals conversation more than a year before. "Like sitting on a sofa with a divorcee and two kids."

His warm smile told me he knew exactly what I was referring to. He squeezed my hand before throwing me a little tease. "So, Joel, Sallie, and I are moving, and we would really like you to come with us. Are you on board?" As if on cue, his words were bracketed by the sound of Sallie, Joel, and Lyric's feet running up the steps. "And, if so, same team or game on, wifey?"

"First of all, let me say this. I wasn't going without you." I defined each word so my truth was cemented in his brain and heart. "I knew that this morning and … really? I knew it all along. I told you, I would not bail. I meant that."

Ryan and I were not Willow and Til. We wanted the same things out of life—both in the present and in the future. We had discussed that very early on in our relationship, and it hadn't changed. Ryan had said it wouldn't work, otherwise. And he was one hundred percent right.

"And you know the reason for that?" I continued, citing one of his fears. "It's because the only thing that could possibly change me is not being with you. I would hate it, and I would hate me, and—"

"Can I admit something to you?"

"Yeah, of course."

"Yes, I've seen it happen. I've seen people change." He didn't need to say her name—we both knew. "But I realized it was me, too. I had become a different person. Being with you has helped me find my way back. I love you so very much, Lenay."

I felt the wave of burning tears trying to make their way to the shore of my brown eyes again, but at least that time it was due to relief and love … most of all love. "I love you, too." I wiped at a tear—it was his. "And I most definitely want us to be on the same team." Ryan and I made the perfect team in so many ways, and writing music was the initial one. I couldn't imagine trying to compete against him. I wouldn't want to. I wanted to be that couple again in the living room, learning from and making each other better.

He smiled and then made me do the same. "My thoughts exactly. Just as long as that team doesn't involve baseball." He poked his pointer finger into my side.

"Hmmm …" I sassed back. "Then I might have some negotiation points."

"Oh, boy." He shook his head. "Of course you do. Do I have to put on my manager hat, Miss Negotiator Extraordinaire?"

"I hope not."

"Okay." His soft sigh was, I'm sure, because the day had been emotionally exhausting but also out of jest since he could trust me, my easygoing tone, and what I would "demand." "Lay them on me."

"One …"

"How many are there?" he interrupted.

"I'm not sure." I scrunched my nose up. "Is there a limit?"

"I do charge overtime."

"No, you don't. Fine. Fine. I'll make sure to pay you for your services." With that comment, I gave a wink. "One," I started again and leaned over to peck a sweet kiss on his lips. "I get a say in picking the new house."

"Easy. Done. Absolutely. I want you to know … all those factors in making this decision? One was getting our own completely fresh start—where the memories and the imprints—"

I know he chose that word deliberately because of our talk about Kari and counter space. And I appreciated it. Even though the house was spectacular, I had been living with Kari's ghost … even before she died, and that wasn't healthy for anyone involved.

"Everything is just ours," he continued. "That means a lot to me, and I know it does to you, too. Plus, your singing architect input will be much appreciated." Ryan mixed sentiment with humor while recalling my fleeting career aspiration when I was much younger.

"Thank you." I met his lips with mine again. "Two. You let me make you some fresh guac since I may have been a little upset earlier and threw your dinner away."

"Rock and rolly!"

I had to stop laughing at his reaction before continuing. "And finally—three." I kissed him again and said, "We never stop fighting"—I paused for the slightest of seconds to emphasize my sincere look into his eyes—"for each other."

It was his turn to kiss me, and it was long and sweet and so needed. "After asking you to marry me, this sounds like the best deal I've ever brokered."

"For real," I recited in the comfort of his arms.

"I guess we're heading to Nashville."

I knew he didn't mean the form of the word "head" in reference to our coin, but it made me think of it. So, I confirmed. "Yep, heads it is. Tails must have been California."

# SNEAK PEEK AT *WHISKEY GIRL*
Ella's story
Coming 2022

I ran my hand along the smooth, cool, silver metal. It was the ideal size to fit inside my pocket. When we purchased the dress, neither my sister nor I had chosen it with that in mind. And my mother most certainly had not. But, oh, it worked out so perfectly.

The boisterous gathering faded as I left the crisp air of the outdoor venue and officially entered the hotel. I knew my destination. I hadn't officially scouted it out beforehand, but it had been part of the overall checklist.

I brought up the bottom of my floor-length dress so it would be easier for me to slide onto the only empty bar stool. The place was packed. But the noise level was tolerable, especially since the hockey game—which seemed to have brought in the majority of the patrons—had just finished. The final score on the television screens and the numerous team-jersey-wearing guests told me that.

Outside, some couples were dancing and others were sipping champagne or wine. I felt like neither. I wanted something fitting of the feelings I was trying to bury— feelings I knew weren't necessarily warranted but fertilized because of simple jealousy. I felt like having something worthy of the silver treasure I had tucked in my pocket earlier in the day.

"Any chance you can fill this up?" I presented the flask to the bartender, who had dutifully made his way over.

"Sure. What's it gonna be? What's your pleasure?"

"To not be here." When I admitted the truth, I could feel more than see the guy to my immediate left turn in my direction. "But, since that isn't really an option, I guess I'll have whiskey."

The bartender swept his arm out and behind to showcase the variety of choices at my disposal. I liked a good drink, but being a connoisseur of brands and proofs and whatever, I was not. While I knew a good ole standby was Jack, my eyes crossed over another brand, which I knew was perfect for my current, personal theme.

"Black Velvet," I settled on.

I passed the container over as I glanced at my dress. It wasn't velvet, but it was black and formal for the occasion. I loved the simple style—a square neckline with an open back and no frilly embellishments except for the sides of the legs which were black lace, sparkled every so often with white pearls.

While I waited for the golden colored beverage to be poured, I thought about how I had only used the flask during my senior year in high school. It had been the cool thing to do—sneak into events and add a little extra something-something to an otherwise legal beverage. In college, underage or not, nothing was hidden. But, somehow, now at age twenty-three, I resorted back to those teen years. A lot of it was because I had only accidently come across the silver beauty when looking through old stuff in the room my sister and I had shared growing up. But another part was because the flask screamed secret and naughty, and I kind of liked that.

"Is that to go?" The bartender broke into my thoughts. "Or are you starting a tab?"

"Put it on the groom's," I proclaimed.

"The wedding guests are supposed to h—"

The other thing the dress pocket held was my ID, which I promptly placed on the bar. "Sister of the bride. I was the one who actually organized a lot of this gig." I knew how the bar system was set up for the wedding guests. With a small guest list and wine and champagne already offered outside, we knew few wedding goers would find their way inside. "Is the last name proof enough?"

"Yep. And the attire. Bridesmaid?"

"The one and only."

"Enjoy, Ella. I'll put it on Mr. Thompson's tab." He slid my card back and walked toward the other end of the bar.

"You're her sister."

I turned more definitively to my left and the man who had spoken those words. He was wearing dark pants and a white button down, which made it obvious he wasn't one of the casual hockey fans. But I hadn't seen him at the wedding or the reception. And even though I had been preoccupied with attending to all the little details no one else seemed to care about but drove me crazy, I surely would have noticed that man. I mean, he was drop dead gorgeous…in that loose tie and relaxed, slightly wavy but not overly long hair kind-of-way. Almost like one of those *Games of Thrones* Stark brothers but with a dirty blond hue instead of dark brown.

"Bethany's sister?" *GOT* look-alike man inquired again.

I managed to answer. "Depending on the day … yes."

Oh, geez. I didn't know him. I probably shouldn't have said that … at least not with the snarky inflection I had. He could have been one of Bethany's friends, and I didn't need it to get back to her or our family. I was pretty much already considered the black sheep of the Opala clan and, if not, why add any drama to the day. Especially because, in reality, I loved my older sister—despite some of our two-sides-of-the-same-coin differences. Sometimes, though, it was hard seeing her get all the breaks I couldn't seem to—a phenomenal and growing career, financial stability, and a romance that love songs were literally written about.

Luckily, my fellow bar mate chuckled. "Hmmm."

Feeling a little more secure with my initial response, I

ventured with, "So, you're a part of this wedding hoopla? Who …? I don't remember seeing you."

"Yeah, I missed the actual ceremony with my flight being delayed. Just came in for the reception but didn't stay long. Thought I could handle it. It's nice they included me, though."

I took my first swig from the flask … mostly as a way to put the pieces together that the obvious out-of-towner had presented me with. He was invited but couldn't handle it? Everyone besides my family was from out of town. Ryan's family stretched across the United States, and both he and Bethany had friends in California. I couldn't connect any definitive dots. And the alcohol was not helping the process. I was beginning to realize champagne on an empty stomach topped off by a swig of Black Velvet was making me a bit tipsy.

"I'm sorry. Who are you?" I just came out and directly asked.

"Maks. Maks Hynes." He took a swig from his glass, half filled with a slightly lighter liquid.

"Hynes."

Yeah, that name sort of sounded familiar. But, why? I purposefully tried not to scrunch my face in confusion.

"Hynes," I repeated. "Maks." And then it hit me … sort of like the alcohol was starting to.

# *See how Bethany and Ryan's story began ...*

**HEADS**
**CAROLINA**

GREA WARNER

How did a sheltered girl from Carolina end up in a national scandal involving one of Hollywood's most powerful music couples?

When want-a-be singer Bethany Opala tries out for a TV talent show, she is rejected. But then comes an amazing offer ... a songwriter's dream. Bethany has the opportunity to learn and develop her skills with top music manager, Ryan Thompson.

With a mutual passion for music and words, Bethany and Ryan's writing partnership develops into something more ... something love songs are written about. And while it isn't wrong, it isn't right, at least in the public eye.

Surrounded by secrecy and half-truths, Bethany doesn't know how much she should put up with. Especially, when one more rejection could scar her for good. Will her decision to leave not only Ryan, but the music business and California, come down to the toss of a coin?

## *Excerpt:*

When I lifted my eyes away from the six-year-old, I found her father propped against the staircase banister as if he had been casually standing there watching our entire interaction. He probably had been. But was it because he was a protective father making absolutely sure who was at the door, despite the guard at the gate announcing my arrival? Or, was he doing it to keep his distance from me?

Our eyes only met for the slimmest of seconds before we both took refuge in looking back at Sallie. Yes, it was a good thing we had a buffer. Just spotting his intense deep blue eyes on me was enough to make my body tighten.

"Daddy, can Bethany watch with us?"

"Let her in," Ryan said a little more succinctly that time.

As Sallie stepped aside, I more properly entered the residence and shut the door behind me. I normally would have instantly shrugged off my shoes and started walking further into the interior of the home. But my sandals remained fastened as did my stance.

Ryan, who I noticed was barefoot, answered his daughter's question. "Bethany isn't here to watch princess movies, Tink." Her lower lip stretched out in the cutest little pout as Ryan continued, "You better go make sure your brother doesn't change the show. He's the slyest four-year-old I know."

With her eyes seemingly growing wide at Ryan's suggestion, she belted, "He wouldn't dare!"

My belly bounced at the little girl's dramatic exit. Ryan actually laughed out loud and shook his head. And then … there we were. Alone.

"So … uh, about recording …"

Despite all the conversation starters I had internally scripted on the ride over, that was what came out. It was not even close to being as melodic or smooth as I had hoped. In fact, it was like a stuttering, old vinyl. Although,

I suppose anything was better than the silent tension that had invaded the foyer in the matter of seconds.

"Can we deal with the elephant in the room first?"

"There's nothing—" I tried to just move past the fictional, ugly, gray mammal who wasn't only occupying the room but also my brain.

But Ryan denied me. "Bethany, we have to talk about the fact that we kissed."

*Available at all book retailers.*

# Fall in love with the Country Roads series:

*A young woman content with her solitary life.*
*A rising country music star.*
*They were friends once ... until their lives took them down separate roads.*

Now, years later, when a child volunteers his uncle to sing for a fundraiser, LARA FAULKNER realizes it is none other than her college pal, FINN MURPHY. As the two get a chance to reconnect, Lara reveals to a compassionate Finn details of her shocking past and the traumatic decision she had to make.

Through trust and love, the bond between Finn and Lara deepens as the country singer manages to get an emotionally scarred Lara to let down her self-proclaimed walls. But will secrets, lies, and tragedy cause a bumpy detour on their road to complete happiness?

Grab the whole series!

Available in Ebook and Print at all major book
retailers.

# ABOUT THE AUTHOR

Grea Warner wants you to cry. She wants your heart to break a little, too. Why? Because that means you feel her characters as if you were one of them. With a background in daytime dramas and a realistic approach to life, Grea writes novels that blur the line of Women's Fiction and Romance. If you're a fan of binge-watching a TV series or have a passion for the arts like Grea, then you'll love her fictional serials. Follow this best-selling, award-winning author on Facebook, Instagram, Twitter, Goodreads, and BookBub.

⌨Website: http://greawarner.com/
⌨Publisher                                    interview:
http://www.inkspellpublishing.com/grea-w...

✦Socials:
    Twitter: @grea_warner
    Instagram: greawarner
    Facebook: https://www.facebook.com/Grea-Warner
    YouTube                trailer                link:
https://www.youtube.com/watch?v=yrz9DjROoIM
    GoodReads:
https://www.goodreads.com/author/show/17230140.Gre

a Warner

**BookBub:** https://www.bookbub.com/authors/grea-warner